D0105209

# ACCLAIM FOR COLLEEN COBLE

"Incredible storytelling and intricately drawn characters. You won't want to miss *Twilight at Blueberry Barrens*!"

—BRENDA NOVAK, *NEW YORK TIMES* AND
*USA TODAY* BESTSELLING AUTHOR

"Coble has a gift for making a setting come to life. After reading *Twilight at Blueberry Barrens,* I feel like I've lived in Maine all my life. This plot kept me guessing until the end, and her characters seem like my friends. I don't want to let them go!

—TERRI BLACKSTOCK, *USA TODAY* BESTSELLING AUTHOR OF *IF I RUN*

"I'm a long-time fan of Colleen Coble, and *Twilight at Blueberry Barrens* is the perfect example of why. Coble delivers riveting suspense, delicious romance, and carefully crafted characters, all with the deft hand of a veteran writer. If you love romantic suspense, pick this one up. You won't be disappointed!"

—DENISE HUNTER, AUTHOR OF *THE GOODBYE BRIDE*

"Colleen Coble, the queen of Christian romantic mysteries, is back with her best book yet. Filled with familiar characters, plot twists, and a confusion of antagonists, I couldn't keep the pages of this novel set in Maine turning fast enough. I reconnected with characters I love while taking a journey filled with murder, suspense, and the prospect of love. This truly is her best book to date, and perfect for readers who adore a page-turner laced with romance."

—CARA PUTMAN, AWARD-WINNING AUTHOR OF *SHADOWED BY GRACE*
AND *WHERE TREETOPS GLISTEN* ON *TWILIGHT AT BLUEBERRY BARRENS*

"Gripping! Colleen Coble has again written a page-turning romantic suspense with *Twilight at Blueberry Barrens*! Not only did she keep me up nights racing through the pages to see what would happen next, I genuinely cared for her characters. Colleen sets the bar high for romantic suspense!"

—CARRIE STUART PARKS, AUTHOR OF *A CRY FROM*
*THE DUST* AND *WHEN DEATH DRAWS NEAR*

"Colleen Coble thrills readers again with her newest novel, an addictive suspense trenched in family, betrayal, and . . . murder."

—DiAnn Mills, author of *Deadly Encounter*
on *Twilight at Blueberry Barrens*

"Coble's latest, *Twilight at Blueberry Barrens*, is one of her best yet! With characters you want to know in person, a perfect setting, and a plot that had me holding my breath, laughing, and crying, this story will stay with the reader long after the book is closed. My highest recommendation."

—Robin Caroll, bestselling novelist

"Colleen's *Twilight at Blueberry Barrens* is filled with a bevy of twists and surprises, a wonderful romance, and the warmth of family love. I couldn't have asked for more. This author has always been a five-star novelist, but I think it's time to up the ante with this book. It's on my keeping shelf!"

—Hannah Alexander, author of The Hallowed Halls Series

"Second chances, old flames, and startling new revelations combine to form a story filled with faith, trial, forgiveness, and redemption. Crack the cover and step in, but beware—Mermaid Point is harboring secrets that will keep you guessing."

—Lisa Wingate, national bestselling author of
*The Sea Keeper's Daughters*, on *Mermaid Moon*

"I burned through *The Inn at Ocean's Edge* in one sitting. An intricate plot by a master storyteller. Colleen Coble has done it again with this gripping opening to a new series. I can't wait to spend more time at Sunset Cove."

—Heather Burch, bestselling author of *One Lavender Ribbon*

"Coble doesn't disappoint with her custom blend of suspense and romance."

—*Publishers Weekly* on *The Inn at Ocean's Edge*

"Veteran author Coble has penned another winner. Filled with mystery and romance that are unpredictable until the last page, this novel will grip readers long past when they should put their books down. Recommended to readers of contemporary mysteries."

—*CBA Retailers + Resources* review of *The Inn at Ocean's Edge*

"Coble truly shines when she's penning a mystery, and this tale will really keep the reader guessing . . . Mystery lovers will definitely want to put this book on their purchase list."

—ROMANTIC TIMES REVIEW OF THE INN AT OCEAN'S EDGE

"Master storyteller Colleen Coble has done it again. *The Inn at Ocean's Edge* is an intricately woven, well-crafted story of romance, suspense, family secrets, and a decades-old mystery. Needless to say, it had me hooked from page one. I simply couldn't stop turning the pages. This one's going on my keeper shelf."

—LYNETTE EASON, AWARD-WINNING, BESTSELLING AUTHOR OF THE HIDDEN IDENTITY SERIES

"Evocative and gripping, *The Inn at Ocean's Edge* will keep you flipping pages long into the night."

—DANI PETTREY, BESTSELLING AUTHOR OF THE ALASKAN COURAGE SERIES

"Coble's atmospheric and suspenseful series launch should appeal to fans of Tracie Peterson and other authors of Christian romantic suspense."

—LIBRARY JOURNAL REVIEW OF TIDEWATER INN

"Romantically tense, but with just the right touch of danger, this cowboy love story is surprisingly clever—and pleasingly sweet."

—USATODAY.COM REVIEW OF BLUE MOON PROMISE

"Colleen Coble will keep you glued to each page as she shows you the beauty of God's most primitive land and the dangers it hides."

—WWW.ROMANCEJUNKIES.COM

"[An] outstanding, completely engaging tale that will have you on the edge of your seat . . . A must-have for all fans of romantic suspense!"

—THEROMANCEREADERSCONNECTION.COM REVIEW OF ANATHEMA

"Colleen Coble lays an intricate trail in *Without a Trace* and draws the reader on like a hound with a scent."

—ROMANTIC TIMES, 4½ STARS

"Coble's historical series just keeps getting better with each entry."

—LIBRARY JOURNAL STARRED REVIEW OF THE LIGHTKEEPER'S BALL

"Don't ever mistake [Coble's] for the fluffy romances with a little bit of suspense. She writes solid suspense, and she ties it all together beautifully with a wonderful message."

—LifeinReviewBlog.com review of *Lonestar Angel*

"This book has everything I enjoy: mystery, romance, and suspense. The characters are likable, understandable, and I can relate to them."

—TheFriendlyBookNook.com

"[M]ystery, danger, and intrigue as well as romance, love, and subtle inspiration. *The Lightkeeper's Daughter* is a 'keeper.'"

—OnceUponaRomance.com

"Colleen is a master storyteller."

—Karen Kingsbury, bestselling author of *Unlocked* and *Learning*

# TWILIGHT AT
# BLUEBERRY BARRENS

# Also by Colleen Coble

# TWILIGHT AT BLUEBERRY BARRENS

## COLLEEN COBLE

THOMAS NELSON
*Since 1798*

Published in Nashville, Tennessee, by Thomas Nelson. Thomas Nelson is a registered trademark of HarperCollins Christian Publishing, Inc.

Brief quotation from *The Princess Bride* by William Goldman. Copyright © 1973, 1998, 2003.

Thomas Nelson titles may be purchased in bulk for educational, business, fund-raising, or sales promotional use. For information, please e-mail SpecialMarkets@ThomasNelson.com.

Publisher's Note: This novel is a work of fiction. Names, characters, places, and incidents are either products of the author's imagination or used fictitiously. All characters are fictional, and any similarity to people living or dead is purely coincidental.

ISBN: 978-0-7180-9069-2 (Library Edition)

**Library of Congress Cataloging-in-Publication Data**

Names: Coble, Colleen, author.
Title: Twilight at blueberry barrens / Colleen Coble.
Description: Nashville: Thomas Nelson, [2016] | Series: A Sunset Cove novel ; 3
Identifiers: LCCN 2016014088 | ISBN 9781401690304 (softcover)
Subjects: LCSH: Man-woman relationships—Fiction. | GSAFD: Romantic suspense
fiction. | Mystery fiction.
Classification: LCC PS3553.O2285 T95 2016 | DDC 813/.54—dc23 LC record available at https://lccn.loc.gov/2016014088

*Printed in the United States of America*

16 17 18 19 20 RRD 6 5 4 3 2 1

*For my beloved Amanda Bostic.*
*Thanks for unfurling my suspense wings!*

# ONE

Melissa's breath came hard, and the pressure in her ears built as she sprinted up the slope toward the top of the cliffs. The glow in the east told her she would have to hurry if she wanted to see the sunrise from Mermaid Rock. Small pebbles skittered away from the soles of her sneakers, and the sound set her on edge.

She glanced over her shoulder. While she'd seen no one on the trail, the hair on the back of her neck stood at attention, and she kept expecting to find a bear's gaze boring into her in the darkness. In spite of her careful perusal of the surrounding area, she saw nothing but piles of pink granite gleaming in the faint glow of the coming sunrise.

When she finally reached the summit, the view swept away her unease. The sun peeked over the water and bathed everything in a pink halo that heightened the color of the cliffs. She sat on a rock and inhaled the salty air. It was a perfect morning, but she would soon have to go back and face what she'd come to Maine to do.

Heath wouldn't be happy, but she couldn't continue this

way when she didn't want to be with him anymore. When had their giddy love changed? When Heath had been in law school, they kissed over takeout as they cuddled on crates at a table constructed from a box crate.

Now that they had everything, they really had nothing.

And what was she going to do about the girls? They adored their father. Taking them away from him would be a terrible idea, but she couldn't leave them behind. Even if that decision had been made, she wasn't sure she could go through with it.

Pain began to pulse behind her eye, and she rubbed her forehead. This was so hard. She didn't want to think about their fight, the way his voice shook with fury, but the memory swamped her.

"What's this?" Heath tossed a sheaf of papers onto the table at the coffee shop.

The aroma of espresso suddenly turned Melissa's stomach when she saw his expression. "What's what?"

The children's activity director at the hotel, Lisa Greenhill, sat at the next table over and lifted her head at his raised voice. Melissa hunched her shoulders and turned away from the curious stares. Her heart pounded as she peered up at her husband.

His eyes were narrowed in what looked like hatred, and his nostrils flared. His normally smiling lips were pressed together in a straight line. Her gaze leaped to the papers, and she bit back a gasp. He knew. "I can explain."

His lip curled. "Explain how you've been meeting him behind my back. And that scum, of all people."

She straightened and met his gaze. "He's not what you think."

"No, he's worse." He clenched and unclenched his fists. "I could kill you for this, Melissa. I don't know how I can live with this."

For an instant she cringed. Would he hit her? She'd never feared Heath before today. He was the gentlest of men and had been a good husband. She couldn't help it that she'd fallen out of love with him. The words of explanation died on her lips. If the shoe were on the other foot, she'd feel just like he did.

She tipped her chin up. "I'm sorry, Heath. It j-just happened. I didn't mean for it to."

"Don't even think about taking the girls." Steel laced his words. "No judge in the land would give you custody."

She thought of the airline tickets she'd already bought for them. They'd get over losing her more easily than they would losing Heath. But could she leave without her babies? It went against everything she believed in. She'd look like a terrible mother, and maybe she was. She'd always thought a woman who would leave her children for a man was the lowest of the low. But she had to think of what was best for the girls. Maybe she should stay and ignore her own happiness, but the thought of it brought tears rushing to her eyes.

"I'm sorry, Heath."

"Sorry isn't good enough. You'll regret this, Melissa. I'll make sure of it." He spun around and stalked away.

A sound brought her out of her reverie, and she started to turn. Before she made a full rotation, hard hands gripped her throat from behind. Her eyes widened, and she tore at the fingers.

She tried to speak or scream, but nothing came out. Spots danced in her eyes, and her vision began to darken. Air, she needed air. She tried to pry away the vise crushing her neck, but she . . . just . . . couldn't. Then the ground rose to meet her.

Kate Mason trained her binoculars on the cliff face high above her. She'd left her yellow Volkswagen parked on the dirt road up top, and she and her sister hiked in to this remote beach on Folly Shoals, just off the Schoodic Peninsula in Downeast Maine, to see the brightly colored beaks in the craggy rocks. "They're here just like Dixie said!"

It had taken half an hour to hike down here, and she hadn't been sure it was worth it. Even the ranger they'd run into had laughed at the notion of puffins nesting here, but there they were with their bright parrot-like coloring and awkward movements. She'd heard the rumor about these birds, but she'd been afraid to hope it was true. Atlantic puffins had never been known to nest on Folly Shoals. As far as she knew, there were only five nesting sites in Maine.

Her sister, Claire Dellamare, snatched at the binoculars. "I want to see."

Kate handed them over and shivered as the early morning fog rolled in. Even though it was late June, the wind was cold off the sea, and her thin jacket did little to hold back its bite.

Claire adjusted the binoculars and gasped. "You'll have to notify Kevin." Their cousin was the local game warden, and he'd want to monitor this site.

"I'll call him." Her pulse jumping, Kate studied the puffin nest way above their heads. A bird with a fish in its beak landed in the burrow.

Kate and her twin looked much alike with their dark-blonde hair and big blue eyes, but while Claire had the sharp business mind it had taken to run an aviation business, Kate was just getting past the chemo fog from the aplastic-anemia treatment that had saved her life. Correction—Claire had saved her life by showing up in time to be a donor for the stem-cell transplant Kate had desperately needed.

Claire handed back the binoculars. "I heard they mate for life."

"Which is the only reason you're interested in them. You like anything to do with romance these days." Kate smiled at the color washing over Claire's cheeks. "You'd move your wedding up if you could."

"I would. My mother wouldn't hear of it though, and everything is booked now. Luke and I will just have to wait it out. It's only a few more weeks. You're still going to sing, right? You need to quit hiding that amazing voice of yours. You're as good as Adele."

Kate's cheeks warmed. "Not hardly. But yes, I'm not backing out on you." She lifted the binoculars to her eyes again and trained them up the jagged cliff of pink and gray to the ledge jutting out over the rocky shore about forty feet up. She greedily stared at the nesting burrows. Such an exciting sight was rare.

Something other than birds filled her field of vision, and it took a moment for her to register what she was seeing. Frowning, she adjusted the binoculars. It could not be what it seemed.

The figure sharpened into focus, and she made out long blonde hair fanning out on the rocks at the base of the burrows. Wait, was that another person beside the woman? She moved her field of sight and saw short dark hair and muscular arms.

She leaped into action. "Two people are hurt. I think they might have fallen off the cliff, maybe while looking at the puffins. We have to get up there!"

Claire caught at her arm. "We don't have climbing equipment."

Kate pulled free and headed for the water. She had to try

to get to the base of the cliffs and climb up. She kicked off her shoes and waded into the pounding waves. The frigid water took her breath away, and a huge wave tossed her back onto the sand. Gasping, she turned for another try, but Claire grabbed her arm again.

Claire held her in a tight grip. "You can't! The waves are treacherous here. We need help. I'll call the Coast Guard. Kevin too." She dug out her phone and placed the call.

Kate paced the wet sand. There had to be something she could do. She peered back up at the rock face. A movement drew her attention, and she saw a plume of dirt from the back end of a pickup truck. Mud caked every inch of its body, and she couldn't make out the color or model as it drove along the high road. It likely had nothing to do with the accident, but at least the guy could have stopped to help.

Claire ended the call. "Luke's Coast Guard cutter is less than five minutes away."

Was it too late already? Kate looked at the figures at the puffin burrows. They weren't moving. She eyed the rugged and weathered sea cliff that soared straight up into the air. Claire was right—there was no way they'd be able to climb up.

Two hours later the Coast Guard told her the couple was dead. Kate couldn't have saved them even if she'd tried.

# TWO

The small clapboard cottage where Kate grew up sat squarely in the middle of their blueberry barrens just off Highway 1, about fifteen miles northeast of Summer Harbor. The placement of its windows and shutters made the house, painted two shades of blue, seem to smile a welcome that she badly needed after the morning's events. She got out of her yellow Volkswagen and shut the door.

Her best friend, Shelley McDonald, came down off the porch as Kate pulled into the driveway. Her long red hair gleamed in the sunlight. Her pale skin never tanned, so she usually covered her bare legs with jeans. "I brought lunch, homemade lobster bisque. It's in the kitchen. And chocolate for dessert. You need a little TLC."

Kate hugged her. "I'm still a little shaky. And to top it all off, I had a flat tire on the way home." She followed her friend up the porch steps to the house. The aroma of bisque wafting out the screen door made her mouth water. She and Claire had spent hours going over what they'd seen and heard at the cliffside, and lunch should have been eaten two hours ago.

She led the way to the kitchen and washed her hands, filthy from changing the tire, then got down two Fiesta bowls in bright orange, Christmas gifts from Claire last December. "The news is all over Downeast Maine, huh?"

Shelley took the bowls from Kate. "You have no idea. I stopped in to buy the bisque at Ruth & Wimpy's, and everyone stopped me to ask about it. I couldn't tell them much, not even the names. Does the sheriff know what happened?"

"They're investigating. He thinks it might have been a murder/suicide. The husband might have killed his wife, tossed her over, then jumped himself." Kate shuddered, remembering the bodies. She pushed the thought away and focused on Shelley. "About ready to go?" Kate hated to ask. Her friend's looming move didn't make her happy, but Shelley seemed thrilled. She had taken a teaching position in Rock Harbor, Michigan, half a continent away.

Shelley nodded. "Tomorrow's the big day. Pray for me. I'm dreading that drive across country by myself. At least I'm not pulling a trailer full of furniture. Everything is packed up, and the movers come in the morning. I'll leave right after they do. I'm going to take my time and stop when I feel like it. I want to see Niagara Falls on the way, and I might stop off in Ohio Amish country and have a big plate of homemade noodles and pie."

"It's all about food with you." The hot bisque, rich with lobster and butter, hit Kate's taste buds. "Oh man, this is so good. I could eat it every meal."

"Me too." Shelley surveyed her on the other side of the table. "How's Claire holding up? She's got a lot going on with the wedding approaching."

"She's okay. Luke arrived on scene right away." She rubbed her forehead. "Let's talk about something else, okay? The reason we were even there was because there's a new puffin nesting site!"

"No way!"

"I saw it with my own eyes. I'm going to let Kevin know." Kate lifted the spoon to her mouth and froze at the purplish mark on her arm. She set her spoon back in the bowl and examined the skin. "I've got a bruise. A big one."

Shelley studied her extended arm. "Looks like a thumbprint. Did anyone manhandle you today?"

Kate started to deny it, then remembered her plunge into the water to try to reach the cliffs. "Claire hauled me out of the sea and wouldn't let me go back in. The riptide was bad. Think I should see the doctor?"

"Your color looks good. Are you feeling okay? Any weakness, heart palpitations, nosebleeds?"

"No, nothing. I feel great." But staring at the bruise made her feel a little light-headed.

"Then put it out of your mind. You're cured, Kate. That aplastic anemia is never coming back."

Kate reached for her huge blue-and-white bag and pulled out a small amber bottle of lemon oil. She dripped a couple of drops of it into her water. "Can't hurt."

"No, it can't hurt." Shelley sat back in her chair. "You have to quit worrying though. You seem to be stuck in yesterday. I want to see you move on and make a new life. Are you going to stay in Folly Shoals forever? You don't even like working the blueberry barrens. You only quit school and came back because your mother insisted. You don't have to do that anymore."

"With her in jail, there's no one else to take care of the fields." She knew her duty even if she didn't love it.

"And would that be so bad? The neighbors can harvest any of the berries they want. The rest can rot. It's not your concern."

Shelley shook her head. "I see you wincing. The entire world doesn't rest on your shoulders. It's your turn to find out what you really want out of life. What makes you happy and fulfilled. God gave you specific gifts, and you're not using them at all."

"I'm running the children's department at church. That's using my gifts."

Shelley rolled her eyes, then smiled. "I'll give you that. I see your joy in working with kids. But you love color and texture. You've got an artist's heart for creativity, and you never get to use it. You're great with people, but you rarely see more than Claire and me except on Sunday. You're stuck in a loop here. Maybe you're the one who should be looking for a new job somewhere else." Shelley's eyes widened, and a grin spread across her face. "I know! Come with me to Rock Harbor. The place I rented has three bedrooms. You can live in one and look for a job. It would be a fresh start."

Kate shook her head. "Claire is here. I've just found her again and I can't leave her." But Shelley's words resonated more than she wanted them to. Was she really stuck in this place, unable to move forward with her life?

Drake Newham rolled over in his big bed and looked at the clock. Two in the morning. In the distance he could hear the hum of cars and trucks on I-93. Traffic in Boston was a constant, even in the middle of the night. The moonlight filtered through the curtains and illuminated the faces of his two nieces who'd crawled into bed with him an hour ago. It was nearly an every-night occurrence since his half brother and sister-in-law had died a month ago, and his chest felt heavy from trying to conceal his grief.

He still couldn't wrap his head around the fact that his older brother was dead. Heath had so much to live for—a thriving law practice and a beautiful family that was the envy of everyone, including Drake.

He tucked the covers around his nieces, then swung his legs out of bed. He'd taken to sleeping in sweats since he was up with the girls so much. They'd get through this somehow, though right now it looked as hard as climbing Mount Everest.

Over the past couple of weeks he'd reached for the phone to call his brother until the stab in his gut reminded him he'd never hear Heath's voice again. How was it even possible to bear this much pain? Drake couldn't imagine how the girls felt. They cried a lot and clung to him even as he'd clung to them as all he had left of his brother.

He peered out the window. For the past week he'd had the uncanny sensation of being watched, and yesterday he'd taken a quick turn down an alley to escape a black pickup he'd been certain was tailing him. Unsure of what had awakened him, he slid his feet into slippers and padded down the steps to the kitchen. A snack of peanut butter and crackers sounded enticing. Maybe he'd pull up his computer and see if he could find out anything new about Heath's death.

The sheriff in Maine was certain Heath had killed Melissa, then himself. Drake didn't buy it. Such behavior was so unlike Heath, who was outgoing, upbeat, and the eternal optimist. Nothing Melissa could do would ever drive him to do something like that. He loved his kids way too much to leave them orphaned. And they'd been so happy. Melissa was the type of wife Drake would have picked for himself—faithful, loving, a good mother.

Then what had happened? An old client out for revenge? Someone who'd gone to prison because of Heath? If that were the case, the list of suspects would be long and complex. Heath had practiced law as a defense attorney for ten years, and it would take time to go through every single case.

The moonlight gleamed off the stainless-steel appliances in his huge kitchen. He'd cooked more in here in the past month than he had in the entire two years previously. His life had changed dramatically since the girls had come to live with him. He would do anything he could to make them smile again.

His slippers crunched on something, and he looked down. Glass glimmered back at him, and a warm breeze touched the back of his neck. He whirled toward the window and saw the curtains flutter. Someone from the outside had broken the window, and the glass had fallen on the floor. Was the intruder still inside?

He grabbed a butcher knife from the block on the granite countertop and ran for the stairs to check on the girls. His phone was upstairs too. His breath sounded harsh in his ears as he took the stairs two at a time and stepped into his bedroom.

The girls were still sleeping, so he grabbed his phone and dialed 911. With the police on their way, he left the call connected, then pulled out the flashlight from the bedside table and shone it around the room and into the walk-in closet.

No one appeared to be hiding in the bedroom. He wanted to investigate the rest of the house, but he didn't dare leave the girls alone, so he locked the door and forced himself to wait by the window. Once he saw the flashing light of the police car pull into the driveway, he unlocked the door and eased back out, then shut it behind him.

He stood at the top of the stairs and shone the light up and down the hall. The thought of going downstairs without the girls felt unsafe, so he retraced his steps. He laid down the knife and scooped up one little girl in each arm. Five-year-old Phoebe never budged, but eight-year-old Emma's eyes fluttered before she settled back against his chest. Huffing from their weight, he descended the stairs as fast as he dared to the house's entrance.

As he reached the living room, a fist pounded on the door. "Police!"

He laid the girls on the sofa, then went to answer the door. Two police officers charged inside.

The woman looked around. "You reported an intruder, Mr. Newham?" In her thirties, she was about five-five but muscular.

He nodded. "My kitchen window was busted out. I haven't probed through the house because I didn't want to leave the girls alone."

"Smart decision," the male officer said. About forty, he was slightly overweight with thick graying hair. "That way?" He pointed past the living room.

"Yes." Drake glanced at the girls who were still sleeping, then followed the officers as they began to walk through the house.

After they looked in the kitchen, they swept through the dining room, living room, laundry room, then stopped outside his office door. It stood ajar. "I keep this door locked." He reached to the wall and flipped on the hallway light. The illumination revealed the doorjamb was splintered.

He swallowed, then peered past the officers as they pushed

open the door and flipped on the light. Papers, pens, file folders, and upended file drawers lay strewn on the floor. It would take forever to pick through everything and determine what had been taken. What had the intruder been after? His blueprints were spread out on top of the desk.

He bent over and examined the drawings. "These were in a drawer, but at least they're still here."

The female officer turned to look at him. "What are they?"

"Drawings of a new drone. I've already got several million dollars' worth of orders for it." Drake's start-up of ten years ago had taken off in a big way in the past couple of years thanks to his innovative designs. "Could the intruder have taken pictures of the plans?"

"It's possible." She eyed the damaged door. "Is there anywhere you can take the girls and stay for a few days while we investigate this? You definitely shouldn't stay here unless you get some good security."

"I have an alarm system, but it didn't trigger when he broke the window."

"Probably disarmed."

Which meant a professional. Drake's thoughts veered again to his dead brother and sister-in-law. "I think I'll take the girls on a vacation and get out of here." Downeast Maine might hold the answers he craved. But just in case, he shot off a text to his attorney to check out any competitors who might be sniffing around.

# THREE

The crimson leaves of the blueberry barrens merged into the gorgeous gold and magenta of a Maine sunset. The rich color looked bountiful, but Kate fought the sting of tears as she looked at the fields. The red leaves held few marketable blueberries. She'd counted on the area's bees to pollinate her fields, but her gamble hadn't paid off.

Claire shaded her blue eyes with one hand. "Let's check the other field. It can't be as bad as this one."

"It's worse. I checked there first. I should have rented honey-bee hives. It's my own fault." Kate held up her hand as her sister started to speak again. "And no, I won't take any money from you. I've been thinking about getting a job anyway. Maybe it's time I looked for a life apart from the barrens. Shelley mentioned it when she left a couple of weeks ago."

Shelley's words about leaving this area came back to haunt her, too, but Kate pushed them away. Nothing could induce her to leave Downeast Maine. It was home and always would be. If she'd been sharper and more aware of things right after her stem-cell transplant eighteen months ago, maybe she would have made a different choice about the bees. But it was no use crying over it now. She had to figure out a way to survive until next year.

A frown formed between Claire's eyes. "But you love growing blueberries. It's been your life. We'll figure this out together."

"I've just tried to make the best of it. It's not my first choice of a career, and it's not all I can do either. There are other jobs out there, ones I might really like. I'll give it some thought."

Claire pressed her lips together and looked away. Kate knew what she was thinking. There weren't many jobs in this depressed area other than fishing, lobstering, and serving tables—all careers Kate wasn't qualified for. She'd tried serving tables once, and she was fired after a day for dropping three trays and being brusque to customers who were too fresh.

God always provided a way out of her difficulties. He wasn't going to fail her now. And the thought of leaving these blueberry barrens behind felt a little like a fresh start—something she desperately needed. But that didn't mean she'd have to leave Claire to find a new profession.

Claire tucked a blonde lock that had escaped her updo back into place. "You could let me pay you to take over planning my wedding. I'm about to pull out my hair."

"You're quite competent to plan your own wedding, and you know perfectly well that everything has been done. I don't want your money." Kate turned to stare back over the fields.

The two had been separated for most of their growing-up years. Claire had been raised with the best of everything in Boston while Kate had stayed here on the blueberry barrens. She'd never thought to leave this place of rocky shores, but maybe she would have to.

The thought brought a lump to her throat. She would do anything she could to stay near Claire, even if it meant waiting tables. Her sister was the most important thing in her life.

Kate gazed at the empty cottage across the road from the one she occupied. It had potential with its steep gabled roof and dormers. "What if I fixed up the cottage and rented it out? Is that a stupid idea?" The thought filled her with energy. If there was one thing she loved, it was decorating and home-improvement projects.

Claire's eyes widened. "That's a great idea! You don't have a mortgage, so it would at least provide you with a little money to live on. I could give you the money to fix it up."

"Only if it's a loan. I can pay you back after harvest next year. It won't take much, maybe two thousand or so. I can do a lot of the work myself." Her thoughts raced through what needed to be done: fresh paint, new hardware on the cabinets, fresh bedding, and some decent used furniture. "There are never enough rentals for tourists this time of year with the blueberry festivals coming."

"Luke and I will help." Claire shaded her eyes with her hand and looked toward the road as her fiancé's new black truck rumbled to a stop. "He's right on time." She waved as Luke Rocco climbed out of a big Dodge four-by-four. "I'll see you later. Lunch tomorrow at the hotel?"

"You bet." Kate hugged her and waved at Luke, a dark-haired, handsome man in his early thirties.

He draped his arm around Claire and gave her a lingering kiss before escorting her to the passenger side of his truck. A wistful pang struck Kate. She was unlikely to ever have a man look at her the way Luke looked at Claire. Kate could never have a child, and what man would want a wife as barren as these fields?

She squared her shoulders and lifted her chin. That didn't mean she couldn't have a full life though. She was alive, and two years ago she'd thought she was facing the end. She'd found her twin sister, a sister she'd only dimly remembered as a "secret" friend during her childhood. Kate had nothing to complain about.

The sun fell fast, plunging the landscape into darkness. The lights of her house beckoned, and foliage snapped under her sneakers as she picked up her pace. A cup of coffee and a square of dark chocolate would raise her spirits. She'd put on a CD and belt out her favorite songs along with Adele while she fixed dinner. After dinner she'd play an old movie and cuddle up with Jackson, her new twelve-week-old furball.

She whistled for her golden retriever and smiled when he shot around the side of the house toward her. She knelt to rub his fuzzy pelt. "Good boy. Did you miss me? I bet you're hungry."

He yapped at her and raced for the back door. She started to follow, then paused at the front of the yard to pick up an empty Coke bottle someone had tossed out. Flatlanders, most likely. She went to the side of the house and squinted in the dark until she made out the vague shape of the trash can. Hadn't she left on the porch light?

She tossed the bottle in the trash, then saw a hoe she'd left leaning against the house. She grabbed it and carried it toward the gardening shed. There was always something to do around here.

A strangled scream rang out from down the vacant road. Kate turned to investigate but saw nothing but an owl flap its wings as it soared into the sky. Maybe it had been a luckless rabbit caught by the bird. Why was she so jumpy this evening?

She examined her mood and realized she'd been on edge for weeks. It was little things she'd noticed, like an unlocked door when she'd been sure she'd locked it and sounds outside the window. Chemo brain was not for the weak. Shaking her head, she turned toward the back door.

A figure ran around the edge of the house and tried to dart around her to get away. Kate acted on instinct and brought the hoe up like a baseball bat. She swung the sharp edge at his head. He rolled away, but the hoe still connected with his left bicep. Jackson's ears came up, and he barked.

The man let out a howl and managed to jump to his feet as she swung the hoe at him again. The blade hit him in the back as he disappeared into the looming darkness.

Kate's legs were like pudding as she ran for the back door. Once inside, she locked the door and leaned against it with her hands shaking. This intruder hadn't been her imagination. She pulled out her cell phone and called 911.

Claire stood with Luke in Kate's kitchen. The clock in the living room chimed eleven times as the teakettle began to shriek. In spite of the late hour, she was wide awake from worry. She pulled the kettle from the heat, then turned to Luke and lowered her voice. "I don't want her staying here by herself. Who knows why that guy was hanging around here."

Luke was the best man she'd ever met. Loyal, caring, and strong. She still couldn't believe she was going to be lucky enough to marry him. Living here near her sister was a dream come true. This was the spot she'd longed for all her life even though she hadn't realized it.

His thick black hair was damp and uncombed since he'd

come here straight out of the shower after she called. His warm brown eyes met hers. "We're here for her, honey. You think she'd move in with you if you insisted?"

"She's so independent." Claire heaved a sigh and poured steaming water into the teapot. "I suppose she's had to be without any real support. Back me up when I ask her, okay?"

He put his hand on her shoulder and leaned in to brush his lips across hers. "I always back you up."

His touch never failed to speed up her pulse. She cupped his cheek. "I know you do. Let's go interrupt the party. I'm sure she's told Danny over and over what happened. She probably needs the break by now. Grab those, would you?" She indicated the plate of brownies by the sink. She'd found them in a container on the counter, and they looked freshly baked.

Danny and his deputy looked up when she and Luke entered. Jonas Kissner knew Kate well from school and would be sympathetic, as would the sheriff, who treated Kate like a daughter. They both must have been off duty because they were in jeans and T-shirts. They'd probably been called from a relaxing evening at their homes.

Claire set the tray she carried on the coffee table. "I thought a little break would be good. Kate has been through a lot the last few weeks. You're probably about done questioning her, right?"

"We are." Jonas reached for the teapot and poured out a cup, then sat back with it in his hand. His burnished-red hair gleamed in the lights. "It's after eleven. We checked all through the house, and everything seems to be untouched. There were footprints in the mud out back. I think maybe it was probably just a flatlander who got lost and cut through your yard on his way back to his truck, and you scared the tar out of him, Kate."

"I hope you're right." But Claire's heart sank when she saw how calm Kate was. If she thought there was no danger, she wouldn't budge from this house, and Claire wasn't at all sure the deputy was right. She offered him the tray of brownies, and he took two.

"You found the brownies," Kate said. "They're made from okra, eggs, and sugar-free chocolate chips. Healthier, you know."

The men exchanged dismayed glances, and Jonas took a cautious bite. His pale-green eyes widened. "Pretty good for being healthy."

Kate had been on a health kick ever since she'd begun recovering from the aplastic anemia that had nearly killed her, and while most people rolled their eyes and humored her, Claire wanted her to do anything that gave her comfort and courage. It had to be hard never to know if that disease might rear its wretched head again.

Claire handed her sister a cup of chamomile tea. "I think you should move in with me for a while."

Kate's blue eyes crinkled in a smile as she took the tea. "You're getting married soon, and I'd just have to move back out again. I'm not living with newlyweds. Besides, you heard Jonas. It was likely a lost tourist. Once I really thought about it, I realized he wasn't really attacking me, just trying to get past me." She looked at Danny. "I'm sorry I bothered you two. I'm a little skittish since finding the two on the cliff, and I overreacted."

"Better safe than sorry." Sheriff Colton's red handlebar mustache quivered as he nibbled the edge of a brownie. He smiled and took a bigger bite. "But I think it's fine to stay home, Kate. Be vigilant of course. But I don't think the guy was trying to get in your house. There are no muddy footprints by the door, and the prints we found came from the woods. If a flatlander comes by the station to say he was attacked by a crazy woman with a hoe, I'll just point out he was trespassing and any woman would defend herself."

Claire pressed her lips together and met Luke's sympathetic gaze. He shrugged and grinned. He liked Kate, but what man would want his new sister-in-law living with them right after they got married? Not even Luke, the symbol of male perfection in Claire's eyes. But she couldn't quell her uneasiness. This road held no other residents with the other cottage empty, and some maniac could break in without a soul nearby to hear her scream.

She suppressed a shudder and took a sip of her tea. "Kate is thinking about renting out the cottage down the road."

"Is it worth renting out?" Danny mumbled past his mouthful of brownie.

"It's a good, solid cottage," Kate said. "It just needs a little TLC. I could probably rent it for a decent amount to a tourist."

"At least you wouldn't be alone out here," Luke said. "If you got scared, you could run to the neighbor's. Or call. It would put your sister's mind at rest. Mine too."

"Good idea." Jonas rose and grabbed his hat. "I'd better be heading home so you can all get some rest. Sorry you had such a scare, Kate."

She rose to walk him to the door, and Claire followed with Luke and the sheriff. Kate opened the door. "Thanks for coming so fast. I promise not to cry wolf again. Next time I'll think it through."

"You didn't cry wolf. We want to know if there's a problem." Jonas smiled down at her. "And anytime I get to see my old friend is a good day."

"Call us if you need us." Danny put his Boston Celtics baseball cap on his head and went out the door behind Jonas.

Kate stepped onto the porch behind Claire and Luke. "I feel pretty foolish about now. I'm sorry I kept you up so late."

Claire hugged her until the stiffness left her sister's shoulders. "Don't you dare apologize. You're supposed to call me for anything. Get some rest, since it's clear I can't coax you into coming home with me."

But walking to her car, Claire still felt a deep sense of unease at leaving her in the dark night. She turned with her hand on Luke's truck. "I'm going to send out a security guy tomorrow. If you're going to live out here, you will have a security system. Don't even try to argue me out of it."

Standing in the wash of the light spilling through the doorway, Kate looked small and vulnerable. "I won't try to talk you out of it. See you tomorrow."

Claire climbed into Luke's truck, and he shut the door behind her, then got behind the wheel. "She'll be okay, honey. I asked Danny to send a patrol out this way on occasion, and he said he would."

She reached over and patted his hand. "You're a good man, Luke Rocco. I'm glad you're mine."

# FOUR

Drake stopped in Ogunquit for ice cream for the girls. They'd all needed a break, and he needed a chance to get out of the car and away from their squabbling. No amount of placating seemed to settle them down, and he didn't want to come off as the big bad uncle when they needed love and understanding right now. Though he'd kept an eye on the rearview mirror, he hadn't spotted any sign they were being followed.

They sat at a table overlooking the water. The wind whipped the waves into whitecaps, and the girls squealed as ducks waddled closer for a bit of bread. He grinned as they tossed the birds a bit of their cones. It felt like just another summer day, a bit of normalcy in a world gone crazy. He tossed away his napkin and empty cup, then called Rod Sisson, Heath's partner in the law office.

Rod answered on the first ring. "Drake, I was about to call you. Listen, I've found a great private investigator to dig into what happened. I'll text you the number."

"That's good, really good. I'm on my way to Folly Shoals myself."

There was a pause, and Rod's voice grew louder. "That's the best news I've heard since the sheriff called. Someone has to take charge. I've gotten nowhere with the sheriff. He's still clinging to that cockamamie idea of it being a murder/suicide."

Rod had been Drake's strong right arm through all this. Everyone else had urged him to let it go and let the authorities up in Maine handle it, but Rod had been doing everything in his power to find out what happened too.

Drake's phone dinged with a text message. "I got your text now. I'll give the guy a call. Thanks for finding someone." He watched the girls walk to the edge of the water and take off their sandals. They waded into the lapping waves a few inches. He moved closer to them but stayed far enough away so they couldn't overhear him.

"Good. Sloan is a great guy. I've known him a long time. He told me it's crazy how often the law gets focused on a rabbit trail and misses the real clues. I think he'll be a great asset. Are you doing okay with the girls?"

"They're a handful." Drake grinned when a bigger wave made the girls squeal. "I'm trying to pitch them a break because of all they've gone through. I'm not sure what I'm going to do with them when we get to Folly Shoals. I need to be able to investigate on my own."

"You should have left them with Brylee and me. They would have fit right in with my three."

"And you would have been dealing with five girls all under the age of ten." Drake laughed and shook his head. "I couldn't do that to you. Besides, they really need to be with me."

"Yeah, yeah, I get it. You could hire a nanny."

"A nanny." The idea took hold. "I'd thought to have my aunt Dixie help out, but she's getting up there in years, and two girls this young would wear her out fast. But she's lived there for ages, and she's the postmistress. She'll know everyone and then some. I'm sure she'll have a good recommendation for me. I'll only need someone for six weeks."

"Glad I could offer something helpful. It feels wrong to be sitting down the hall from Heath's office and know that he's never coming back. And that there's not a thing I can do to change it." Rod's voice broke, and he cleared his throat. "I want to hang that murderer from the highest tower."

"Me too. And I'll find out who did this. Nothing is going to get in my way. The trail is getting cold, and I want to light a fire under the sheriff and insist he consider some other theories."

"Let me know if there's anything you need, anything at all. I'll pay for the private investigator. The business can afford it, and Heath would have done the same for me."

"You don't have to do that. I can afford it too."

"You have to let me help." Rod's voice broke again. "Heath was the best friend I ever had. It's the least I can do."

"All right. Thanks, Rod. I'll contact the guy and I'll be in touch." Drake ended the call and immediately dialed the texted number.

"Sloan Investigations." The man sounded young.

"This is Drake Newham. Rod Sisson recommended I contact you."

"Oh yes, Rod's a good friend. We went to college together."

The man's self-satisfied tone struck Drake as odd. Did the guy think he automatically had the job because of his connection to Rod? "Can you tell me about your experience in investigation?"

"Um, well, I'm really just getting started. I worked as a dispatcher for the police for a while, but I got tired of the hours." He named a small town in South Carolina.

Drake frowned and watched the girls as they licked their ice cream cones. "I really need someone with a lot of experience. This could be dangerous. We could be going up against a major criminal."

"I'm sure I can handle it." Sloan's voice took on a defensive tone. "This could be a big break for me."

"I'll have to think about it." Drake ended the call and motioned for the girls. Time to track down a killer. He didn't need the help of a self-serving rookie. This was too important.

It was only the third time he'd used the housekeeping key card, stolen over two years ago from his mother when she worked here. He wiped sweaty palms on his jeans and stared at the door. He'd seen her walking on the beach, and when he found she was staying at the hotel, he'd been unable to resist the temptation. He had plenty of time too. This time of year the seedy hotel had low occupancy, and the staff was down to bare bones for another week.

He glanced down the hall and saw no one. His hands were steady as he quickly unlocked the door and turned the handle. Holding his breath, he eased open the door, then smiled. She hadn't flipped the security lock. Hanging on to the door, he let it slide back into place with only a slight click.

The sound of a shower running beckoned him across the plush carpet and past the unmade bed. A bracelet lay curled on the bedside table, and he took it before following the sound of running water.

Her jeans and T-shirt were in a puddle on the floor outside the open bathroom door, and he stood with his feet on either side of them to peer through it. His reflection in the steamy mirror was fuzzy. He brought up his cell phone and snapped off four quick pictures of her in the shower. Her head was back and her eyes were closed as she rinsed her blonde hair. The fogged glass door irritated him with the way it obscured his view.

Back at his house, he'd be able to enhance the pictures and enjoy them in private. He eased a few inches more into the room, and his sneaker squeaked on the tile floor. She gasped and opened her eyes. He leaped back and ran as she let out a shriek.

His chest tightened as he raced for the door. She was screaming like his grandmother's teakettle as he let himself out and sprinted down the hall for the elevator. She couldn't have seen his face—not with the steamed-up glass—could she?

As the elevator door shut behind him, he realized he was grinning from ear to ear. The rush of voyeurism always left him higher than a line of cocaine. And it was just as addicting. No matter how many times he swore he wouldn't do it again, he couldn't help himself.

He thrust the key card back into his pocket until next time. Next time maybe he'd get up the nerve to go back to his favorite girl's. He loved everything about her—her courage and her astounding beauty. She belonged with him.

# FIVE

Drake had never been to Downeast Maine, and the bickering between his nieces in the back of his Land Rover was enough to sap every bit of his enjoyment of the rocky coastline to his right.

He passed a blueberry field and turned away from the water to take a better look. He'd always heard of the Maine blueberries, but he hadn't expected the leaves to look red. He needed to get a picture.

At least he'd made it out of Boston without a tail. He'd had the distinct feeling someone had been watching him for days, and he'd been careful as they packed up and left town. Now wasn't the best time to leave someone else in charge of Newham Drones, but it couldn't be helped. He had a great plant manager in place and good employees.

A call from his plant manager rang through the dash of his vehicle, and he punched on the audio. "You don't have to check on me every hour, Lakesha. The girls and I are all still alive."

He didn't want anyone to know the real reason behind his decamping from his business—not even someone as trustworthy as Lakesha Lacy. In her fifties, she viewed herself as his surrogate mother. She'd be frantic if she knew someone had broken into his home, so he'd just told her he was taking the girls on an extended vacation and hadn't even told her where he was headed. It was too dangerous.

"Glad to hear it. This isn't a great time to be gone though. You had a visitor this morning. A representative from the Fish and Wildlife Service was here. They're interested in that new drone!" Her voice rose with excitement. "They have a few modifications they'd like, but it's nothing you couldn't do."

He straightened and his pulse kicked up a notch. "I thought it was a long shot when you suggested sending them a prototype. This is great news!"

"But you need to turn right around and come back, Drake. You're the only one who can make those modifications. This is your baby."

Everything in him wanted to do just what she said. A contract this big on this new drone was something most manufacturers only dreamed of. In a few years he'd be firmly established. He glanced in the rearview mirror. All his work would pay off with the ultimate security for him and his employees.

"Where are you, Drake? I don't get all the secrecy. You won't even tell me where you're staying."

He looked at his nieces. They had to feel secure while he tried to get to the bottom of what happened to their parents. He owed it to them. He couldn't go back, not now. "I don't know yet. I'm looking for a cottage to rent for the next six weeks, and I'll let you know when I figure it out." A shriek from his five-year-old niece punctuated his words. "Listen, I have to go. You can handle it, Lakesha." He ended the call before she could protest.

He probably should have tried to book something rather than just picking up and coming here without any planning, but he'd been afraid Lakesha would talk him out of doing what he had to do.

He pulled the Land Rover onto the side of the road, then turned to focus on his nieces. His heart twisted every time he looked at them. Five-year-old Phoebe was the spitting image of Heath with dark hair and big blue eyes, while eight-year-old Emma had her mother's blonde hair and hazel eyes. It was still hard for him to believe they were his responsibility now.

He was doing a lousy job too. All his efforts to make up for their loss were getting him nowhere. They'd grown more fractious and hard to deal with every day of the past month since he'd gotten the call that Heath and Melissa had fallen off a cliff in Folly Shoals. He had a feeling their deaths were tied to the break-in at his house. And he wasn't sure the girls weren't in danger either. This was for the best for all of them.

He saw a cottage with a steep-pitched roof and flowers in front of the porch that made him think of a storybook painting. Looking closer, he saw the lifted shingles on the roof and the peeling paint on the shutters, but at least it was empty. And its backyard should have a distant view of the ocean.

A woman carrying a paintbrush emerged from the faded front door. About thirty, she was attractive enough that he noticed the streaked blonde in her short hair and the way her curves filled her jeans and T-shirt.

He took the SUV out of park and drove to the edge of the driveway and lowered his window. "Good morning. I wonder if you know of any places for rent in the area? I'm looking for a rental for the rest of the summer."

Her big blue eyes looked him over. "How soon do you need it?"

"As soon as possible. Any chance this place is available?"

"It will be. I have some painting and repairs to complete on it." She shaded her narrowed eyes with her free hand, and her mouth pinched. "Are you from around here?"

"No. Could I see it?" He shut off the engine before she answered.

She took a step back. "I don't think so." The wary light in her eyes faded when Phoebe and Emma threw open the back doors and emerged from the SUV. "Your kids?"

"My nieces." He didn't feel like explaining the whole situation to a suspicious stranger.

Emma put her hands on her hips and stared at the cottage. "It looks like a Hansel and Gretel house."

Phoebe shuddered and sidled behind her sister. "Is there a bad witch inside?"

The woman smiled. "No witches. I used to love to come here to visit my uncle. It's got lots of great places to hide."

Phoebe stepped out from behind Emma and ran toward the house. "I want to see!"

"Phoebe, come back here," he called. To his surprise she stopped and retreated. He held out his hand to the woman. "Drake Newham."

She hesitated, then took his hand. Her fingers were warm but firm. "Kate Mason." She released his hand after a quick shake.

Hadn't he heard the name somewhere? "About the house. Can we see it?"

She nodded. "It's got two bedrooms and two bathrooms. Come on inside."

He followed her up three steps to a front porch that held a worn swing and rocker. The red paint on the front door had faded to a dull reddish-orange, and the door creaked as she opened it. He stepped inside and blinked as his eyes adjusted to the lower light. The lingering odor of paint hung in the room, and his nose detected the scent of some kind of cleaning solution as well.

His gaze took in the light pouring through the tall windows. "Good space. I like the high ceilings."

Kate showed him through the rest of the house. Both bedrooms were large and airy, though they needed painting. The oak floors needed refinishing, but they'd do for the summer. They ended up back in the living room with Emma and Phoebe both still in the guest room staking out their areas.

"I think the girls have already decided. I'll take it."

Her full lips curved. "It's six thousand for the rest of the summer."

"That's fine." He almost smiled at her shock at his quick acceptance of her exorbitant price. She'd expected him to dicker, but he'd seen the decrepit Volkswagen sitting in the drive across the road. "When can we move in?"

"I should have it ready in a week or less. There's a nice hotel on Folly Shoals if you want to stay at the Hotel Tourmaline for now."

"I'll do that." He handed her his card. "Call me when it's ready. And if you know of a good nanny, I'm looking to hire one for the summer as well."

He herded the girls back to the SUV. He had the rest of the summer to get to know more about her. Maybe she could help him search for answers. From her broad New England accent, she'd lived here all her life.

Kate watched Drake's fancy gray Land Rover disappear in a cloud of dust down the dirt road. "Six thousand dollars." Saying it aloud should have helped her accept the reality of renting the cottage, but it still seemed surreal. She was bound to wake up any moment and discover it had been a lovely dream. With that money she might be able to replace her wheezing refrigerator. Even better, she could afford a nice wedding gift for Claire. She hadn't been too sure about him until the girls scampered out of the backseat. After the man appeared in her yard the other night, she'd been on high alert for the slightest hint of danger.

Claire's little white convertible pulled up in front of the cottage, and her sister climbed out. Her hair was in a careless ponytail, a look Kate found childishly adorable after seeing Claire so often with her hair in a prim updo, and she wore white shorts and a pink top.

Claire's gaze roamed over her. "You've got a silly smile. What's up?"

"I rented the cottage!"

"Already?" Claire tightened her ponytail and dug out a stick of lip gloss.

Kate settled on the settee on the porch and patted the cushion beside her. "Sit down and I'll tell you all about it."

Claire's eyes widened, and she paused in her lip gloss application as Kate launched into how the man had stopped out of the blue and asked to see the cottage. "The rest of the summer?"

"I asked for double what I thought I could get, and he said yes. Six thousand dollars for six weeks!"

A frown crouched between Claire's eyes, and she put the lip gloss back in her purse. "You don't think he's some kind of criminal, do you?"

Kate felt a little prick in her bubble of happiness. She hadn't thought of why the man might be so agreeable. Was it possible he wasn't what he seemed? He was very attractive, but she wasn't one to look at just physical appearance, and she hadn't sensed any kind of danger swirling around him once she saw the girls.

She shook her head. "I don't think so. He had his two nieces with him, and he was driving a Land Rover. I figured he was a flatlander looking to get away from the city's heat."

Claire's expression cleared. "I'm sure you're right, but I think I'll have Kevin run a check on him just to be safe. You're so isolated out here."

Kevin O'Connor was the area's game warden and Claire and Kate's second cousin. Because his mother and Kate's mother had a falling out years ago, he and Kate had only gotten to be friends in high school when he was dating her friend Mallory. He'd be able to complete a quiet query that wouldn't rile anyone.

"You're just overreacting because of that flatlander. He won't come back here." It was better to assure Claire rather than tell her how she'd checked the locks and the new security system three times before going to bed the past two nights. And she hadn't slept well, jerking awake with every sound outside. "But it wouldn't hurt to check him out. He didn't wear a wedding ring."

Claire's lips curved. "You looked?"

"Well, yeah. He was about six-three with dark curly hair. Nice manner. A Captain America type. He seemed to be a professional of some kind. He sure had his hands full with the kids though. They're going to run him ragged this summer, I think."

"Why'd he have them instead of their parents?"

"He didn't say. Maybe they're out of the country or something. I could tell he wasn't used to dealing with kids though. He wanted to hire a nanny, too, but I don't know of anyone looking for a job like that."

Claire crossed her ankles and leaned back on the settee. "You could do it."

"Me?" The thought hadn't crossed her mind. She studied her nails, which were in terrible shape from the painting. It would take some serious work to get them looking halfway decent.

"You're good with kids."

"And I'll never have my own anyway, is that what you're thinking?" The hot words burst out of her throat, and her eyes burned.

Claire took one of her hands. "That's not what I meant at all, Kate. You *are* good with kids. I've seen the way they flock around you at church." She squeezed Kate's fingers. "None of us knows what the future holds. Luke and I want children, too, but there's no guarantee we'll have them. But I want you to know that if it's possible, I'll be an egg donor if you want."

The offer lodged in Kate's stomach, and the impact spread up to her chest as Claire's words sank in. *Egg donor.* She hadn't even dared to hope for such a thing. And it was expensive, but she knew Claire's offer included the cost to accomplish such an unbelievable gift.

Her eyes filled with tears, and her throat tightened as she clutched her twin's hand. "I-I don't know what to say." She tried to laugh but it came out like a choked sob. "It's not like I have a husband waiting in the wings, but thank you."

Claire gave a final squeeze to Kate's fingers, then released her hand. "You'd do the same for me. But in the meantime, gather those kids you love close, let go of your fear, and embrace what you enjoy. The renters will be across the road, so it would be easy to care for them."

"And I could use the money. I suspect the pay would be really good. It would be better than trying to wait tables."

"It's probably a better job than anything else you'd find right now."

Sticky fingers, crafts, swimming, and rafting combined to make an enticing kaleidoscope of a summer. Kate examined her hesitation and sighed. "The kids will be leaving at the end of the summer. I'm not sure I can handle the abandonment."

"We're adults now. No one can ever split us up again. You can't live your life terrified of losing someone, Kate. There's no joy in that."

Maybe not, but there was safety. Maybe she was ready to risk it.

# Six

The view of the hotel from the water as Drake approached Folly Shoals by ferry didn't do it justice now that he stood in front of the huge glass doors. With its gray stone walls and mullioned windows, the Hotel Tourmaline surveyed its Downeast Maine location of wind-tossed waves and rocky crags like the masthead of a great ship.

He turned his SUV over to the valet and stepped onto the pink granite floors inside the lobby. The lavish hotel rivaled anyplace he'd stayed in London or New York. The domed ceiling soared high above his head, and skylights let in the Maine sunshine.

His aunt hailed him from the bank of comfortable sofas and chairs clustered around a fireplace that ascended to the roof. "You should have called me sooner, honey." Dixie Carver was his mother's only sibling, and after his parents retired to Costa Rica, he'd seen her more than he'd seen his mother. The girls shrank behind him at Dixie's loud voice.

She threw her arms wide and clutched him to her ample chest. "You don't have to stay here. I could squeeze you all in with me."

He'd been to her one-bedroom house many times, and it wasn't an option. "Thanks, Aunt Dixie, but we'll be fine here. And I've rented a cottage, so you'll see a lot of us this summer."

A carefully penciled-in brow over her hazel eyes rose, and she adjusted her small round glasses. "What aren't you telling me, young man? A man with your kind of busy career doesn't bury himself in the north woods without a good reason." Her gaze softened as she stared at her nieces. "Though the good Lord knows you've got your hands so full it would take two helpers to carry all the burdens."

He rescued a glass bowl full of enamel balls on the beautiful table from Phoebe. "Phoebe, this is your great-aunt Dixie. Emma, come say hello to your aunt too."

Emma shuffled her backpack off her shoulder. "Aren't you too old to be wearing overalls?"

A laugh from Dixie turned into a snort. "I always say a woman should speak her mind, little girl. You're well on your way to running your own company." She gravely shook hands with the two girls. "I'm sorry about your mommy and daddy."

Whoa, most people ignored the girls' loss. Drake took note of the way both his nieces sidled closer to their great-aunt.

Emma's eyes filled with tears. "Did you know our daddy?"

"Honey, he spent every summer with me. He and your uncle here used to go fishing off my dock every day. They'd bring home the biggest fish you ever saw. Your daddy was a good man."

A lump formed in Drake's throat. He remembered those summers spent at Dixie's. She'd moved here from Georgia when he was ten, and he'd been over every inch of her barn and property. He and Heath had slept in the attic under the eaves and listened to the owls in the trees outside the window. They'd roped everything from cats to squirrels in the yard and had learned to swim in the cold water of Sunset Cove.

It wasn't right to be here without his brother.

Phoebe slipped her hand into Dixie's. "I miss him. And Mommy. Could you show me how to fish?"

"I'd be as tickled as a monkey with a new banana. You have your uncle Drake bring you over. I've still got your daddy's fishing rod in the barn." Her eyes were wet when she looked up at Drake. "You bring these young'uns by to see me, young man."

"I will." Most days he was uncertain how to cope with the girls. They cried often for their parents, and he didn't know the words to comfort them, so he usually tried to change the subject and distract them. He saw now that they needed to be heard, to be able to talk about their parents.

It was going to be hard to dredge up those memories and face the ache of missing his brother, but he had to do it.

A pert young woman dressed like Steve Irwin in khaki shorts and shirt approached with a smile. "I'm Lisa Greenhill, the children's activity director. We're about to go on safari and look for wild animals in the area. Would your children like to go along?"

Phoebe pulled away from Dixie. "Can we go, Uncle Drake? I want to find a penguin!"

It was the first thing she'd shown interest in since her parents died. He looked at his aunt.

"Lisa will take good care of them. I've known her from church since she was a sprout."

He grinned and nodded. "I'm not sure you'll find a penguin, but you can go. Leave your backpacks with me."

Both girls dropped their packs at his feet and went off with the activity director. He watched them go with a strange sense of déjà vu. A summer of exploration and new beginnings, just like he and Heath had. *Please, God, let it be so.* The children needed a way to start over after such a horrendous loss.

He looked back at his aunt. "You said all the right things, all the things I can't seem to figure out how to say."

"You just have to listen, Drake." She tapped his chest. "Listen with your heart. They've lost their whole world." She crossed her arms over her chest. "Now I want to know exactly what you know. What really happened to Heath and Melissa?"

He glanced around the hotel lobby teeming with people checking in and out. "Let's go up to our suite, and I'll tell you everything."

The engagement ring sparkled on Claire's left hand, and she still wasn't used to the heavy weight of it. She picked her way over the large rocks along the shore toward Sunset Bay where Luke's boat was due to dock in about an hour. A tern uttered a sharp *kee-arr* overhead, and she paused when she saw a pair of puffins in the sea cliff above her.

She'd have to tell Kate. Today would be a great day to be up in her plane, but its engine was being worked on, and she'd be unable to fly for another week or so.

She shaded her eyes and looked down the curve of water to the bay. A Coast Guard cutter could be seen in the distance, so Luke would be here soon. Picking up her pace, she edged so close to the water that the splash from a cold wave hit her sandal, but the terrain was less rocky here. She reached a large, flat rock that protruded into the ocean. She clambered over it, then stopped when she saw what appeared to be a pile of black-and-red rags covered in seaweed and caught in a tide pool.

She gasped. A face was hidden in a tangle of hair.

Claire's pulse kicked as she leaped the last few feet and reached the woman's side. She knelt and touched the woman's shoulder, but before Claire could speak, the sensation of cold, stiff flesh penetrated her consciousness. She stifled a scream and scrabbled back, landing on her rear end in the surf. The cold water instantly soaked through to her skin.

Claire couldn't look away, and her chest compressed until she couldn't draw a breath. In an instant she was remembering finding Jenny Bennett's dead body in that cave. Her hand flew to her throat, and she tried to pull in air. The choking sensation intensified, and she did thirty seconds of belly breathing as her counselor had told her, and the tightness in her lungs began to ebb.

She stumbled to her feet and dug her cell phone out of her pocket. It was a little damp but the screen lit up, so she called 911 and told the dispatcher about the body she'd found.

"I'll stay here until the sheriff arrives." Her voice shook. "Please hurry. Sh-should I pull the body farther onto the beach so the tide doesn't take her out? I think she's moved a few inches."

"Game Warden O'Connor is near your location. He'll likely arrive first, but I'll get the sheriff on his way too," the woman said. "I think it's best if you don't touch the body. Do you want me to stay on the line with you?"

Claire saw Luke's boat offshore and waved. "No, that's fine. My fiancé is nearly here, and he'll wait with me for Kevin's arrival."

"It shouldn't be long," the dispatcher assured her.

Claire ended the call and went to stand near the woman's body. Poor thing. She looked to be in her early twenties with her whole life ahead of her. Seaweed mixed with her long blonde hair, and her jeans and a lacy top lay carefully draped to cover her nude body.

The scene looked staged to her. What if a killer was stalking their area? She swallowed hard and took a step back. She and Kate had watched too many *Criminal Minds* episodes.

She lifted her head at the crunch of shoes on rocks, then turned and saw Luke heading her way. Tears sprang to her eyes, and she launched herself against his chest. His arms came around her, and he held her close enough that she could hear his heartbeat under her ear.

"What's wrong, Claire?" He kissed the top of her hair. "You're trembling."

"A-a woman. Over there. She's dead." She lifted her head and gulped. "I called the dispatcher, and Kevin will be here any minute. I-I was just remembering finding Jenny's decomposing body in that cave."

Admitting her feelings made the trembling intensify. She prided herself on being strong and resourceful, but there was something so hateful about a crime like this that made any woman quake in her shoes.

She pushed herself away from Luke and curled her hands into fists. "I want some kind of weapon. Bear spray, a gun, something."

His brown eyes held pity as he looked from the woman back to Claire. "Let's not overreact, sweetheart. The sheriff may find this woman's killer right off. But I'll make sure you have some bear spray on you. And I'll stay close until we know what's going on."

At least he realized what had happened to this woman. A small-craft motor echoed over the waves, then grew louder until she could see the warden-service insignia on the side. Kevin docked and strode across the rocks to meet them.

His gaze went straight to the dead woman, and he winced. "You okay, Claire?"

How did she answer that? Finding this kind of crime in her seemingly safe little town was like finding a poisonous spider in a banana. She might never feel safe again. No woman would until this killer was found.

When she didn't answer, he stooped to touch the woman's neck. "Rigor mortis has set in."

She shuddered when she remembered the stiff, cold flesh. "I noticed."

He stood and looked around. It was going to be difficult to find footprints since this area was covered with rocks. Claire stood in the shelter of Luke's embrace as Kevin swept the area for clues. In the distance came the wail of an ambulance, but it was too late for this poor woman. Much too late.

# SEVEN

T he hotel suite, lavishly decorated in pinks and golds, looked out on the blue waters of Sunset Cove. Drake strolled the suite with his aunt on his heels. Two bedrooms, one on each side of the large living area, had their own bathrooms. The girls would like their massive jetted tub and the gleaming stainless-steel fixtures.

Aunt Dixie grunted as they returned to the living room with its overstuffed leather furniture. "You made of money, boy? One night here would cost me a week's income."

He grinned. "I'm doing all right. People like my drones." His smile faded and he stared at his aunt. "What do people here say about Heath's and Melissa's deaths?"

Her gaze narrowed, and she adjusted the pencil holding her salt-and-pepper hair in its bun. "That Heath killed her, then killed himself."

He pressed his lips together and looked out the huge window to the water. "I don't believe it."

She sank onto the sofa. "You know something. I can see it. What have you found out?"

"Heath's office was handling the defense of Chen Wang, a Chinese crime lord the FBI has been after for over ten years. Heath

COLLEEN COBLE

received threats from the organization that if Wang went to jail for murder, Heath and his family would be dead the next day."

"But the trial hasn't happened yet, right?"

He shook his head. "It's not for another three months. But I think it's related somehow."

"But why would Wang kill the man who was defending him?"

"Maybe he thought Heath was mishandling the trial, and he'd punish him, then get a new attorney. Or maybe it's not Wang at all. Maybe a rival drug lord ordered it. If Wang went to jail, he'd be out of the way." Drake ran his hand through his hair. "I'm just trying to look at all the angles."

He went to sit on the sofa opposite his aunt. "Someone broke into my house and rifled through my office. Whoever got in knew how to turn off the alarm. So I threw the girls' things in a suitcase, turned my business over to the plant manager, and came here to investigate on my own."

A frown settled between Dixie's eyes. "Good heavens, boy, what makes you think you're any safer here? At least in the city, a police car is minutes away."

On the surface his decision didn't make much sense, but he knew in his gut that his brother's death would go unsolved if he didn't investigate it himself. The sheriff believed it was a murder/suicide, and Drake had no real proof other than instinct. Instinct had served him well all his life, and he wasn't going to discount it now.

Dixie eyed his face when he didn't answer. "I see your mind is made up. You be extra careful with those children there. Bring them to me when you go on your wild-goose chase."

"You're still working at the post office. I'm looking to hire a nanny. I'll make sure they are safe before I go sleuthing. Know of a good nanny in the area?"

She huffed and pressed her thin lips together. "I'll think on it, but this makes me spleeny, Drake. Some high schooler won't be able to handle those girls. They need someone with depth and discipline."

"So find me one. They need to be kept busy and happy while I investigate. I don't want some starched librarian who raps them on their heads with a ruler if they don't mind."

She shook her finger at him. "Discipline didn't hurt you any."

She had that right. Their parents were loving, but he and Heath had toed the line. Still, his heart ached at the pain his nieces were experiencing. They just needed to have a good time this summer and try to move on. "I wasn't planning on getting a high schooler but someone with maturity. Let me know if you think of anyone."

His cell phone rang, and he looked at the screen. It was a local number he didn't recognize. "Drake Newham."

"Hello, Mr. Newham, this is Kate Mason."

"I didn't expect to hear from you quite so soon. The cottage isn't ready now, is it?"

She gave a nervous cough. "Well, no, but I'd like to talk to you about the nanny position. I'm interested in it myself."

He blinked and raised his brow. She'd seemed nice enough and had paid attention to the girls, but he didn't know much about her. "I see. Do you have experience with kids?"

"I'm the Sunday school director at our church. I can give you my pastor's name and number if you'd like to speak with him. I'm good with kids and always have been."

Her confidence made him smile. Sometimes the best employees were the ones who had the most belief in their own abilities. "Sure, text me his contact information."

"I'll do that as soon as we hang up. I've lived here my whole life, so just ask around. People know me."

"How about you meet me here at the hotel for dinner with the kids tonight, and we can discuss it more? I'd like to see you interact with the girls before I make up my mind."

"That's fine. What time?"

"Say five? The girls are used to eating early."

"I'll be there. The Oyster Bistro? The Sea Room is fancier, and the girls wouldn't like the food as well as at the Bistro."

"If that's where you want to go."

"It's to the right of the elevator as you get to the first floor. See you at five."

He ended the call and glanced at his aunt. "You know Kate Mason?"

She adjusted the pencil in her hair holding up her bun. "Of course. A good girl who's been through a lot. She had some kind of blood disease and had to have some treatment after chemo. But she's fine now. She wants to care for the girls?"

He nodded as his cell phone gave a message alert. "I'll talk to her pastor and see what he says."

"She goes to my church too. You can't do much better than Kate."

So maybe his search was over. He liked what he'd seen from her so far.

Kate slicked a bit of lip gloss on her lips and surveyed herself in the mirror. Thanks to hair spray and pins, she'd managed to get her short curls into an updo like Claire's, and she thought it made her look smarter and more sophisticated. But was that the right look for a nanny? She tugged at the hem of her denim skirt, then slipped silver hoops in her ears. It would have to do.

With her car keys in hand, she was heading for the door when her cell phone rang. She frowned when she saw Sheriff Colton's name on the screen and answered it.

"Sorry to bother you, Kate." His voice was terse, unlike his normal jovial demeanor.

"What's wrong, Danny?" She stopped by the door when he released a heavy sigh.

"Don't quite know how to say it except to spit it out like a watermelon seed. Your uncle Paul escaped from prison last night."

She gasped and leaned against the doorjamb. "Escaped? You mean they don't know where he is?"

"That's right. He knows these woods like I know every surface of my gun, so I'm betting he'll be headed this way. Let me know if he contacts you."

"I can't imagine he would though. Not after what he did."

He'd murdered Luke's mother to keep her from telling how she'd seen him burying Kate's half sister's body. Everyone in this area knew what he'd done, and someone would turn him in. Coming here would be stupid. Or would it? He could live off the land and hide out for years up here and never be spotted.

"I'm about to call Claire. She needs to be especially vigilant. While Paul was in prison, he talked about making her pay if he got out."

Claire had unraveled the secrets of that day so long ago, and

Paul hated Claire, even if she was his own niece. Should Kate even pursue this job with Drake? Claire might need her around more.

"She's had enough on her plate today. I hate to add to it," the sheriff said.

"What do you mean?" Kate hadn't spoken to her twin since this morning. Claire had called and left a message a couple of hours ago, but Kate hadn't had time to call her back. She'd planned to do that on the drive to the hotel.

"She discovered a young woman dead on the beach. Choked and raped, at least that's the preliminary call by the coroner before the autopsy."

"Oh no!" Kate's fingers went to her own neck. "Who was it?"

"A tourist."

"I'll call Claire right away."

"Give me fifteen minutes to tell her about Paul."

"Okay." It was a good thing the wedding was coming up in a couple of weeks. Luke would take good care of her.

Kate glanced at the time as she put her phone away. If she delayed any longer, she would be late for dinner with Drake, though she was in no mood for this position now when every part of her wanted to be with Claire.

She drove down Highway 1 to Summer Harbor, singing with the radio to calm herself. By the time she parked her Volkswagen in the lot and got to the ferry, fifteen minutes had passed. She found a seat at the front and called her sister.

Claire answered on the first ring. "Kate, did you hear about Paul?" Her voice was choked and upset.

"Yes, Danny called me. Is Luke there with you?"

"Yes, yes, I'm fine. But I'm worried about you out there on that dead-end road alone. You know he's going to come straight back there. You're his only real family with our mom in jail too. Where else could he go for help? I think you should come stay with me."

"I don't think he'll show up." Her confident pronouncement sounded false in her ears. "Besides, the new renter will be right across the road. And I think I'll be busy with his nieces." She told Claire about the job interview. "I heard about the woman you found. Danny didn't say who it was."

"Her name was Whitney Peece." Claire's voice quivered. "She was staying at the hotel for the weekend as part of a bridal party getaway. She went missing last night after going outside a bar in Folly Shoals to get some air. Her friends thought she'd gone back to her room at the hotel because she wasn't feeling well, and she wasn't reported missing until this morning when she didn't come down for breakfast. She was only t-twenty-one." Claire broke off on a shuddering sob. "It was pretty horrible."

"Our safe little town isn't so safe anymore."

"Danny said there have been some instances of Peeping Toms too. I think he's worried. Kevin was first at the scene, and he wants Danny to issue a warning to women not to go out alone at night."

"I'm going to start carrying my handgun, just in case. And I'll keep my bear spray with me."

"Luke got me some, and I have it in my purse. I should get a license like you, but guns have always scared me."

The ferry was nearly at the dock, and Kate had just enough time to get up the hillside steps to the hotel. "Gotta go. Wish me luck on the job interview."

"I'll pray it's as good as it sounds. Call me on the way home."

"I will." Kate ended the call and got in line to disembark.

She still wasn't sure how she wanted it to go tonight. The extra money would be helpful, but there were so many problems cropping up right now, she wasn't sure she had the focus to deal with children.

# EIGHT

Kate swiped damp palms on her skirt under the table as she faced Drake. Lordy, but he was handsome. His dark curly hair just begged to have a woman run her fingers through it, and he had that solid muscular build she'd always found attractive. No studious, wiry type for her. She was drawn to strong good looks, and Drake had them in spades with his bulky arms and square jaw. Peeking at his left hand, she saw no faint tan line where a ring might have been either. But that didn't mean he didn't have a fiancée in the wings somewhere.

She blew out a breath and squared her shoulders. If she wanted this job, she had to corral her emotions and quit mooning over him. It was so unlike her, and she couldn't blame her straying thoughts on chemo brain. She eyed the two girls who were both engrossed in iPads.

Before she stopped to think, she reached over and plucked both tablets out of their hands. "It's bad manners to use those at the table, girls. Before you know it, you'll be adults, and you need to have at least some idea of how to carry on a conversation."

Phoebe's eyes widened and her lower lip protruded. She looked up at her uncle with beseeching blue eyes. "I want to play *Angry Birds.*"

"And I want my book back." Emma reached across the table.

Kate moved the iPads out of the way. "What grade are you in, Emma? Tell me about the book you're reading. I'm still a book nerd myself."

Emma's frown eased, but she kept her gaze fixed on her tablet. "*A Wrinkle in Time.*"

"Oh, that's my all-time favorite book! I've read it at least ten times. How far have you gotten?"

Emma picked up a linen napkin and began to pleat it. "They just got to the planet Camazotz. Meg's father is trapped there." Her hazel eyes searched Kate's face. "It made me wonder if my mom and dad are there, too, instead of in heaven."

Kate inhaled and shot her gaze to Drake. Their parents were dead? His dark-brown eyes were moist and filled with pain. She swallowed down the lump in her throat and searched for a way to answer the little girl. How well she remembered the feeling of abandonment caused by her own father's neglect. Emma's father was dead, but that didn't change the little girl's sense of betrayal. Mommies and daddies weren't supposed to leave their children for any reason. Could she even say Emma's parents were in heaven? Kate had no idea of their spiritual state, and she didn't want to misstep.

Drake pulled his niece into a one-armed embrace. "Emma, honey, we talked about heaven, remember? You'll see your mom and dad again someday."

Tears pooled in Emma's eyes, and she jerked away from her uncle. "I want to see them *now.*"

Kate mouthed *I'm sorry.*

Drake's jaw hardened and he shrugged. "So, you must be a strict disciplinarian."

His tone told her what he thought of that type of behavior, but she tipped her chin up and met the skepticism in his gaze. "Kids need both love and structure. Give one without the other and they have no guidelines to go by. When they are grown and out in the world, it's like turning a five-year-old loose in a car on a four-lane highway without ever having handled a steering wheel."

Something shifted in his eyes and he sat up straighter. "I hadn't thought of it that way." He stared down at Emma's bent head, then across the table to Phoebe, who was beside Kate. "My aunt thinks highly of you."

"Who's your aunt?"

"Dixie Carver. She runs the post office."

"I adore her! Everyone here knows and loves her. I didn't realize you had family here. Why aren't you staying with her instead of looking for a place to rent?" Wait, why had she said that? Maybe he'd change his mind, and she really wanted him to take her cottage.

"Her house isn't big enough, and I was afraid the girls would wear her out."

Kate saw his point. Dixie worked a full-time job and she wasn't young anymore.

He took a sip of his coffee. "I called your pastor. He had nothing but great things to say about you. What didn't he tell me about you? What are some of your bad habits?"

She blinked and grinned. "I have a quick tongue, and I generally speak before I censor myself. You'll never have to wonder what I really think about anything. I have no patience for whining, and if a kid tells me she's bored, it's a good way to be given a cleaning job. I'm a bit of a health nut, and I'm apt to dose you with essential oils if I notice a sniffle."

"My aunt said you had been sick. Are you sure you're up to watching two energetic girls?"

Her chest squeezed. There was always gossip in a small town, but she was beginning to think people might continue to talk about her illness forever. "I'm fine now. Most of the time a stem-cell transplant is an actual cure for aplastic anemia. If I can keep up with fifty kids in junior church, I can keep up with two little girls."

His gaze lingered on her face. "You look the picture of health. How are you in the mornings? Grumpy or cheerful?"

"Disgustingly cheerful."

"I'll make sure I down two cups of coffee before you show up then. I don't like to talk until I've got some caffeine in me."

She chuckled and picked up her fork. "Does that mean I'm hired?"

"I'm going to think about it overnight. I'll call you in the morning."

"I'll be waiting by the phone. I like the girls, and I'd love to spend the rest of the summer with them." Judging by the way her pulse skipped when her gaze met his, she wasn't sure how wise it was to be around their uncle every day. The last thing she wanted was to risk her heart on someone who would pick up and leave at the end of the summer.

Claire patted the ground around the rosebush she'd just planted and stood. "This will give us some nice color in a few weeks, and it's probably all we can do today. It's getting too dark to see."

The beautiful old house in the woods seemed to preen in the

sunset with its newfound glory. The renovation was complete with new siding, roof, and windows as well as a complete gut and remodel inside. This time next week their wedding guests would gather here for a garden wedding before going to the Hotel Tourmaline for the reception.

Luke's jeans were muddy, and he had a dirt smear on his cheek. "By the time we see buds, I'll be living here too. Finally." His slow smile built to a grin as he wiped away a smudge on her chin. "And I'm never letting you go."

She leaned into his embrace and rested her head on his chest. The reassuring thump of his heartbeat under her ear eased the tension out of her. This was where she belonged. How blessed she was to have found Luke. One more week and they'd be married.

His hand stroked the length of her hair, then settled at her waist. "It can't come too soon for me. By this time next year we could have a baby."

She lifted her head and searched his expression. "You're sure you want to try for a baby this fast? I thought you might just be a little jealous of our time." She wanted to give him an option to back out of having a baby right off the bat, though she desperately wanted one herself.

"I've always wanted a big family. You do, too, right?"

She nodded. "And I'm thirty-one. If we want more than one child, we need to get started." She stilled and looked away. Poor Kate would never be able to have a baby. How would she feel when Claire got pregnant? Would it make things strange between them? She'd spent too much time in her life away from Kate to want anything to come between them now.

Luke turned as tires crunched on gravel. "Kate's here." His hands dropped away from Claire as they turned to greet her.

The little yellow Bug had mud on its tires and fenders. The recent rain had left the drive like a bog. Claire advanced to hug her sister, but her welcoming smile froze when she saw Kate's frown. "What's wrong?"

Kate slammed the car door and strode toward her. She wore a cute denim skirt that showed off her legs and a formfitting blue sweater. Her short, curly hairstyle suited her heart-shaped face, so like Claire's. "I think I blew the interview. You know how I hate for kids to be disrespectful?"

Claire nodded. "I do too."

"The girls were playing with their iPads at the dinner table, and I took them away without thinking."

"You didn't! They aren't in your charge yet." Claire took her twin's arm and guided her up the brick walk to the rocking chairs on the newly built porch. "What did Drake say?" She shot a warning glance at Luke, and he nodded before picking up the yard tools to put them away in the shed behind the house.

"Not much, but I could tell he didn't like it." Kate sank onto the chair and doubled over with a moan. "And I was so close. He said he wanted to think about it overnight, but I bet he doesn't call in the morning."

Claire flipped on the porch light, then sat beside her in the other rocker. "Maybe it's not as bad as you think. How did the girls react?"

Kate sat up and exhaled. "Like you'd expect. They whined about it. At least he didn't make me give the tablets back. We ate dinner, and he hardly asked me any questions other than what were my worst traits that the pastor wouldn't tell him." She let out a chuckle. "I told him I don't like whining and I speak my mind. I bet that sealed my fate." A grin spread over her face.

"Guess I proved what I was saying. And I'm crossing into whining territory myself, so I deserve to be given a job I hate, like planting roses."

Kate's smile faded. "And the worst faux pas was that I got Emma to talking about her book and she wondered if her parents were in Camazotz and not in heaven. I just thought Drake was a good uncle taking them while they were on a trip or something. I obviously upset them."

It didn't sound good, but Kate was such a crusader. She wanted to help everyone she saw, and she often rushed in without thinking through the consequences. But now wasn't the time to harangue her. "I could go see him. Maybe try to smooth it over. Or we could get the pastor to call him."

Kate shook her head. "It won't do any good. Let's talk about something else other than my lacking social skills. The house looks great. Everything ready for next weekend?"

"Everything." Claire ticked the items off on her fingers. "My RSVPs are back, the reception is planned and ready, the house is done, the hotel reservations for guests are made, and my dress has been tailored to fit. Luke won't tell me where we're going on our honeymoon, but he told me to pack a bathing suit and not much else. I'm hoping for Hawaii."

Amusement lit Kate's eyes. "I'm not telling."

"You know? You little traitor. Come on, tell me where we're going."

"Only if you take me with you."

"Not a chance." Claire smiled at her sister. "Isn't this the best thing ever? I mean, you and me together after all these years, and it's like we were never apart. I can talk to you about anything."

The smile on Kate's face stumbled and fell. "It's the glue

that keeps me together." Her gaze searched Claire's. "Will you still have time for me after you're married?" She bit her lip and looked away as scarlet swept up her face.

Claire took her sister's hand. "Nothing will change, Kate. You'll just have a brother as well as a sister. Luke loves you. He'd never come between us. You have to know that."

"Why does everything have to change? Everyone I love is in jail except for you. I know that sounds needy, but I'm scared you'll leave me too. What if Luke gets transferred to somewhere else and you have to move?"

A brief spasm of panic tightened Claire's chest. There was no guarantee Luke would stay at this post, and she'd go wherever he went. She forced a smile and squeezed Kate's fingers. "Nothing can come between us ever again. Please trust my promise. I won't let you go again. Never."

Before Kate could answer, something zipped by Claire's cheek, and her hair fluttered in its wake. Something thunked the wall behind her, and she turned around to see a crossbow bolt sticking into the brand-new clapboard siding.

Something trickled down her cheek, and she touched it, then looked at her fingertips. "I'm bleeding," she whispered.

"Into the house!" Kate grabbed her arm and hoisted her out of the chair and through the door. "Luke, there's an intruder!"

# NINE

In the sleek new kitchen Kate dabbed a wet paper towel on Claire's cheek. "Thank the Lord it's superficial. I don't even think it will leave a scar. Hold that against the cut."

While Claire pressed the towel against her cheek, Kate peered out the window into the dusk-shrouded backyard. Luke, gun out and at the ready, crept around the edge of the house. In his other hand he held his cell phone to his ear, and she exhaled. He must be calling for help.

She looked out over the new back deck, elegantly furnished in blue and white. As Claire had said, everything was ready for the wedding, but would it even be safe to hold it out in the open? Kate had a sinking feeling she might know who had shot that arrow.

Claire tossed the paper towel into the cabinet trash can. "It's stopped bleeding. You think it was an accident?" Her face was a little pale, and the mark on her cheek looked like a faint scratch now.

Kate turned and raised a brow. "Only an idiot would aim a bolt toward a house."

"Maybe it was a kid with his first crossbow, and he lost control."

It made for a nice explanation, but still staring at the line of trees behind the house, Kate shook her head. "I think it was Uncle Paul."

Claire's eyes widened, and she took a step back. "Why would you say that?"

"His favorite weapon is a crossbow. It's how he has taken down every deer and moose he's brought home to the freezer." Kate shivered and hugged herself. "The thing is, if he wanted to hit you, he would have. So what's his game? Is he just trying to terrify you to get back at you for him being sent to prison?"

"Maybe he stumbled and missed. Or was startled." Claire grabbed the cherry-red teakettle and filled it with water, then put it on the induction cooktop. "I need some tea. Want some?"

"Sure. I'll try to get my breathing back in order." The back of her neck still prickled, and Kate rubbed it.

The back door opened, and Luke stepped inside, bringing the fresh scent of the outdoors with him. "Whoever it was, he's gone now." His gaze went to Claire, and he winced when she turned enough to show the mark on her cheek. "Let me see." He stepped closer and moved her into the wash of light from the ceiling globe. "I don't think it needs stitches." He brushed a kiss on top of her head. "Does it hurt?"

She shook her head. "I'm fine. Did you call the sheriff?"

He nodded. "Kevin is closer though, and he's on his way." He glanced at Kate. "I saw where the guy was standing. The grass is matted down across the road in a stand of ash trees. It looks like he hiked in. I didn't hear any motor vehicles."

"She thinks it was Paul." The teakettle shrieked, and Claire moved to lift it from the heat.

Luke stared at Kate and took a notepad from his pocket. "You think Paul got out and came here for revenge?"

"I don't know what his plan is, but remember Daryl in *The Walking Dead*? That's my Uncle Paul. He's deadly with that crossbow, and he knows these woods better than most people know their bedrooms."

"But you don't know it's Paul," Luke said. She stared back at him and said nothing until he shrugged. "Okay, I get it. You know him better than I do, and you're sure. But Kevin will be here shortly and we have no proof."

"He hung out at this old house a lot when he was hunting. You found that mattress on the floor in the downstairs bedroom, remember? He probably didn't know you'd taken it over since he's been in prison. It might have ticked him off when he saw Claire on the porch and realized the house was hers." Kate accepted the hot mug of tea Claire handed her. "I don't know what he was thinking. I need to find him. He'll talk to me."

At least she thought he would. They'd always been close. He'd been the only real father figure she had, and he'd taken her fishing and hunting more times than she could count. He'd comforted her when her mother was too harsh and remote, which was most of the time. She was certain of his love even though his actions had shaken her faith in all she thought she knew about family.

Surely there was some good left in her uncle. He could have killed Claire today, and he didn't.

Claire pulled out a chair at the chunky farm table. "How can you track him down?"

"I know his haunts. And maybe he'll call me or come by the cottage."

"Won't he be afraid the law has your place staked out?" Luke asked.

Kate pulled out a chair beside Claire and sat. The thought of seeing Paul hauled off to jail again tightened her throat. And what if someone shot him right in front of her? He was still her uncle, part of her. She didn't want him hurt. "I'll have to see if I can find him."

But where? Wait, he'd had a new girlfriend. What was her name? It didn't come to her right now, but it would. Maybe he'd gone there.

The distant roar of the waves expending themselves on the rocky shore added to Drake's turmoil as he watched the girls throw bread to the gulls. The birds fought viciously for their crumbs and pecked at any other gull that dared to try to snag a piece of their treasure. The girls laughed at the birds, then tossed them more bread to fight over.

"Kind of like people, aren't they?" The wind tugged at Dixie's hair bun and had put a hint of pink in her weathered cheeks. She was barefoot on the cold sand, and her legs beneath the rolled-up denim overalls looked cold and chapped.

He frowned down at his aunt. "I'm not tracking with you."

"Everyone's natural inclination is to get all they can and can all they get. They never think about other people until they're taught about compassion and caring."

"You think I should hire Kate Mason, don't you? But she grabbed those iPads right out of the girls' hands. I thought that was a little bold. They've been through a lot." He'd tossed and turned a lot last night and awakened with the decision to find someone sweeter and gentler.

She shrugged and tugged her camo jacket a little tighter around her shoulders. "That's life. And if we give them a pass for every bump in the road, they'll turn out just like so many self-absorbed teenagers you see every day. You want that for them?"

"I don't call losing both parents a 'bump in the road.'" Not many kids had to face that kind of heartbreak. He wanted to see Phoebe sleep without a lamp on again. He'd give up every cent in his hefty bank account to hear Emma laugh again.

His throat tightened, and he looked out to sea where a large yacht scooted past the rocks. Heath had loved sailing. They'd spent many happy hours on their family boat when they were growing up.

Sometimes the pain of his brother's loss was too much to bear. He had to find out what happened or he'd never have peace.

His aunt touched his arm. "I'm not saying it wasn't a tragic, horrible event, Drake. But if you're not careful, you'll ruin those girls. Do you think Heath would have wanted that?"

He shook his head. "He was always strict with them and insisted on good manners. He started taking them to soup kitchens as soon as they were born, and every Christmas they took loads of presents to homeless people in Boston."

"Then don't mess up now, kiddo. Take a firmer hand with them. It doesn't mean you don't love them. In fact, it means you love them enough to train them for living a productive life."

He studied her rugged face. She'd always been a no-nonsense sort of woman, and she made a lot of sense now. "Maybe you're right. I'm just not sure about Kate."

She wagged a finger at him. "That girl's had a tornado of events in her life, and she's emerged still kicking. You want a strong mother figure for them, someone whose strength the girls can emulate."

He held up a hand. "Whoa, mother figure? No nanny will take Melissa's place."

"Of course not. I should have said role model. That suit you better?"

"It's just for six weeks. I hardly think Kate or anyone else would have that big of an impact in such a short time."

"You'd be surprised." Her voice was soft, and she turned to look out at the water.

He counted back to how many days in total he'd been around his aunt and realized it wasn't a whole lot more than that. He and Heath had come here for a week every summer starting when they were ten and until they were eighteen, and then a weekend here and there after they'd grown up. Maybe a total of sixty-six or seventy days. It wasn't much more than the forty-five or so days a nanny would be with the girls. The impact Dixie had on him had been profound.

He studied the topknot on her head and the sag of her shoulders. She'd been widowed when she was twenty-five and never had children, but that was about all he knew. "Why didn't you ever remarry?"

When she turned around to face him, a tiny smile lifted her lips. "I'm a slow bloomer, but I'm working on it. Walker Rocco didn't work out, but there are still fish in the sea."

"You're seeing someone *now*?"

"Drake Newham, I might be old, but I'm not dead." Her

penciled-in brows were drawn together, and she folded her arms across her ample bosom.

He knew from her steely tone that his aunt wasn't about to give him any more personal information. "All right, I'll hire her. But if it ends up poorly, it's all your fault."

Her grin up at him held a triumphal gleam. "I think my shoulders can bear the burden."

"I love you, Aunt Dixie." Slinging his arm around her, he motioned for the girls with his free arm. "Dinnertime."

Seeing Kate's pretty face every day wouldn't be a trial, but he wasn't sure it was enough to compensate for her take-no-prisoners approach with his nieces.

# TEN

T he bar was mostly empty at only four in the afternoon. It was a little too early for the after-work and dinner crowds, but that was how Kate had planned it. The Wild Pelican was on a narrow side street that boasted peekaboo glimpses of the water from its windows. Kate had finally remembered the name of her uncle's girlfriend, and they had come to this bar where she worked to question her. From what Kate had heard, this was the same bar Whitney Peece had partied in just before she disappeared.

"Are you sure this is a good idea?" Claire whispered as Kate led the way to the polished wood bar at the back of the barn-wood-encased room. "Danny might be upset if he finds out you didn't tell him about this woman."

"He's got more important things to worry about, like finding Whitney's killer."

Kate gazed at a woman in her forties behind the bar. Her shoulder-length blonde hair held purple highlights. Her blatant sexuality would be a draw for every unmarried man in Folly Shoals. Kate had seen her once or twice at Uncle Paul's trial, but they'd never spoken.

Becky Oates put down a whiskey bottle and turned to face them. Kate stepped forward with a smile. "Hi, Becky, I'm—"

"I know who you are." Her husky voice held disinterest. "What will you have?"

"Just sparkling water with lime for both of us. Listen, you probably know Uncle Paul escaped from jail."

"Heard that rumor." Becky filled two glasses with sparkling water and dropped in two slices of lime, then slid them in front of Kate and Claire. "It's not my concern. If you're here looking for Paul, you can head right back out."

Kate masked her disappointment and took a sip of water. "He hasn't gotten in touch with you at all? I really want to talk to him."

"You want to send him back to prison." Becky's gaze flitted to Claire, and her lip curled. "Your sister here sent him away for life. I don't have anything to say to either of you."

"He tried to kill me." Claire's voice echoed off the bar mirror.

"Yeah, so you told the judge. And like I said, I haven't seen him."

Kate knew she was hiding something by the way she kept turning her back to them and the way her gaze never landed for long. "But he's called, hasn't he?"

Becky shrugged. "I've talked to him a time or two in prison."

"But not in the last few days?"

Becky held her gaze, then looked away. "No."

She was lying. "I think he'll probably call. When he does, could you tell him I need to speak to him as soon as possible?"

"I'm not your messenger." Becky went to polish a row of shot glasses on the back cabinet.

Claire nudged Kate. "Let's go." She laid five dollars on the bar top.

"What about Whitney Peece? Were you working the night she disappeared?"

The woman's blue eyes turned even colder. "When did you get a deputy badge? I already talked to Sheriff Colton about what I saw. Or didn't see would be more accurate. Now if you're finished interrogating me, you can leave."

Two men entered the bar and Kate sighed, then nodded. If Becky had been cold before, she was downright glacial now. Kate dug out a pen and jotted down her cell number on a napkin. "Here's my phone number. Please call me if you hear from him."

Becky stared at her with expressionless eyes. She picked up the napkin and dropped it into the trash, then moved past them to talk to the men at the other end of the bar.

Kate shrugged and followed her sister out into the sunshine. "That was a waste of time."

"You never know. Paul could be watching her, or she may tell him we came in and harassed her. That might convince him to give you a call. At least we tried."

Kate forced a smile. "And we're right here by the ice cream shop. That's reason enough to get some maple nut ice cream and forget all about the way she acted."

When they exited the bar, Kate saw Kevin in his warden-service truck and waved. About six-two, with chiseled features and reddish-brown hair, he attracted female attention wherever he went, but he never noticed once he'd married Mallory, who was sitting in the passenger seat. He pulled to the curb and got out, then opened the door for his wife. "I was just about to call you. I got the information you asked for about Drake Newham."

Marriage agreed with both of them. Kate hugged Mallory.

"You're going to have a baby!" She'd graduated with Mallory but hadn't seen her until she moved back to Folly Shoals when her father was murdered. Her teenage romance with Kevin had quickly rekindled.

Mallory had cut off her long, dark hair, and the short style suited her. She touched her rounded belly. "I'm barely showing. Most people haven't noticed. We're due around Thanksgiving."

"Congratulations!" She glanced at Kevin. "Come get ice cream with us and you can tell me what you found out."

They fell into step beside Claire and Kate. Kevin took a piece of paper out of his pocket. "You probably already figured out your guy isn't hurting for money. He didn't grow up with a silver spoon in his mouth though. He came by his money the hard way and has a successful hobby-drone business. His drone designs are pretty unique, and Newham Drones is booming. He's on the board of several charities, and he's a deacon at his church. When his dad retired as a union ironworker, Drake told his parents he'd buy them a house wherever they wanted to retire, and they went to Costa Rica. He might regret that now because he doesn't see them much."

Kate stopped outside the ice cream parlor. "He sounds like quite the paragon. No vices or faults you could find?"

"Well, he's a bit of a daredevil and likes flyboarding, if you call that a fault."

Kate blinked, remembering when she'd seen men flying over the water on the jet-propelled hoverboards. "That's pretty extreme and more than a little dangerous for a man who has two little girls to raise."

"Some guys need a little thrill from time to time." Kevin grinned and draped his arm around his wife.

"It's not something I want to watch." Kate shivered, then stepped through the door he opened for them. Everything she'd learned about Drake intrigued her more and more.

Kate dragged her attention from the view outside the window and held her breath as Sheriff Colton lumbered into his office. He was so tall that he ducked coming through the doorway. His basketball days with the Celtics were far behind him, but he still exuded competence. She exchanged glances with Claire. Danny wouldn't be happy they'd talked to Becky, but they'd both decided he should be informed.

He settled into his chair, then pulled his computer closer and plopped a pair of reading glasses on his nose. "Paul was spotted up near Machias this morning. So we know he's in the area. I thought maybe he was headed for Canada, but it's hard to say. You didn't see him out there today, right?"

"No. But someone was using a crossbow, and that's his weapon of choice." They'd been through all this last night when Danny and Jonas showed up in response to Luke's call.

The sheriff leaned back in his chair, and it squeaked in protest. "Lots of hunters use a bow. There was nothing definitive about the bolts either. Easton Carbon Raiders."

"That's what Uncle Paul uses."

"So do I and a dozen other hunters I could name off the top of my head." He tossed his reading glasses onto the desk. "I tend to think it might have been an accident. Claire was lucky."

Everything in Kate rebelled at the thought. "We saw Becky

Oates yesterday too. I wanted to see if she'd heard from Uncle Paul. She says she hasn't."

Danny's face reddened. "Tarnation, Kate, you know better than that." He shook his huge, sausage-like finger at her. "You stay out of this from now on. Every time I turn around you're sticking your nose into things and assuming you know more than me."

He leaned forward in his chair. "I don't want anything to happen to you. This is my job, not yours, though I'm beginning to think I need to retire with all these deaths happening on my watch. Maybe I'm getting too old for this job."

Kate's throat tightened. "You're right, Danny. I'm sorry. I thought maybe she'd talk to me since I'm Paul's niece, but she was downright hateful."

He sank back into his chair with a huff, then eyed her face. "We already have a viable suspect in Whitney Peece's homicide. A witness saw her old boyfriend outside the bar, and we picked him up. He hasn't confessed to raping and murdering her, but he has a history of violent behavior. We'll keep investigating."

"What a relief." She and every other woman in town had been tense since Whitney's body had been found.

She straightened as a familiar set of shoulders walked by outside. Hands in the pockets of his khaki shorts, Drake strolled by with a little girl on each side of him. She rose and headed for the door. "Thanks, Danny. I'll let you know if I hear from Uncle Paul." She rushed down the beige hallway and stepped outside into the bright sunshine. "Drake!"

He turned at the sound of his name and squinted in the late-afternoon sun shining into his eyes. "I was about to call you."

Her stomach clenched at his tone. She didn't get the job.

She hadn't admitted to herself how much she was depending on it until she realized it wasn't being offered. She could always wait tables for the summer, and at least he was renting the house, which would help her bank account.

She lifted a smile his direction, and a dazzling grin bounced back to her. Good grief, she was acting like a high school girl around a football jock. His strong, tanned legs stretched out from his shorts, and his biceps flexed when he pulled his hands from his pockets. It was all she could do to drag her stare away from his muscles and focus on the girls.

She squatted in front of Phoebe as Claire came out of the sheriff's office to join her. "What have you been doing today?"

"We saw whales! Uncle Drake took us out on a boat. One jumped out of the water."

"One of my favorite things to do." She glanced at Emma and saw her sidling closer to her uncle. "Did you see any calves?"

Emma nodded. "Two. They stayed close to their moms. Then we watched Uncle Drake go flyboarding. He was up in the sky!"

She held back a wince at the mental image. He needed to grow up and remember his responsibilities to the girls. They both seemed friendly enough, probably because they knew Drake wasn't going to hire her.

She rose. "Good to see you guys. I'd better let you get on with your day."

He frowned. "I think we'd better discuss your salary and hours. You have time?"

She blinked and realized her mouth was hanging open. "Um, sure."

A sparkle of amusement lurked in his dark eyes. "You thought I wasn't hiring you." He turned and pointed to a park on the other side of the building. "You girls can play while I talk with Miss Kate."

Kate glanced past his shoulder at Claire, who waved and mouthed that she'd see her later.

Phoebe set off toward the playground. "Ooh, a teeter-totter."

He waited until Emma followed her, then led Kate to a park bench. "Have a seat."

She expelled a hard and fast breath as she settled on the edge of the wooden slats. "I did think you weren't going to hire me. I was a little bold with the girls. I'm sorry about that." The apology sounded grudging to her ears, and she added a quick smile.

"Aunt Dixie set me straight. She said I was undoing all the good discipline the girls had gotten from their parents. I'm not totally convinced she's right, but we'll give it a try. Just remember they've lost both their parents."

"Of course." Maybe she had been too harsh. She'd taken their iPads without thinking. "They're very sweet, and I think we'll get along just fine. What do you have in mind?"

He looked out to where the girls were laughing as they bounced up and down on the teeter-totter. "There's something you should know before you agree to take the job." His head swiveled back toward her. "I believe their parents were murdered. I'll need you to keep the girls safe while I do some digging."

"Until last night I didn't realize they were dead." She exhaled and leaned against the back of the bench. "You've never said how you happened to have the girls. I just thought they were out of the country."

"Law enforcement believes my brother murdered his wife, then killed himself, but I don't believe it. My brother was a defense attorney. He had some threats related to a high-profile case before they died, but he was never one to back down."

Drake gave a vigorous shake of his head. "My brother loved his family. He would never do something so heinous. And my house was broken into after they died. I've been tailed. It could be about one of my drone designs, but it might be more than that. My attorney is checking out any companies who might have wanted to steal my designs, but my gut tells me everything is tied to Heath's death."

It all sounded a little far-fetched to Kate. And why come here to investigate anyway? Surely there were people to watch the kids in Boston. But maybe he'd wanted peace and quiet to look things up.

He frowned. "I can see the doubt in your eyes, but you'll need to trust me on this and take extra care with the girls in case the danger isn't over. Can you do that?"

She nodded. "I have good instincts and I'll watch them well. What are my hours?"

"You might need to be flexible with the schedule. Sometimes I might need to check on something at night, but you're right across the road. I'll pay you well."

He named a sum for the six weeks that made Kate catch her breath. It was more than she usually made in a year from the blueberries. "I'll take it."

Keeping her head when she was around this guy would take some effort, so she didn't feel a bit bad about accepting that amount of money.

# ELEVEN

Drake dropped into the chair opposite Sheriff Colton's desk. "Thanks for seeing me, Sheriff." Colton's small office held the stench of desperation. How many suspects had sat in here under the sheriff's stern gaze? Drake felt a rising sense of impatience to get this over with and get back to the girls, who were with Dixie this morning. Kate would start on Monday when the cottage was ready.

Colton was a big man, easily six feet seven inches. He wore his height well. "I'm not sure what I can do to help you, Mr. Newham. I'm wicked sorry about your loss though."

"Thanks." Drake pulled out his iPhone and pulled up a blank note screen. "Can we talk about that day? I'd like to understand the events as they unfolded."

The sheriff glanced at the big watch on his wrist. "I only have about ten minutes before my next meeting."

"So you still believe Heath killed Melissa, threw her off the top of the cliff, then jumped himself?"

The chair squeaked as the big man shifted. "Ayuh, I do. One of the employees out at the Tourmaline heard them arguing the night before. The employee reported that Mr. Emerson said, 'I could kill you for this, Melissa. I don't know how I can live with this.'"

Drake reined in his initial flinch. He couldn't see Heath ever saying something like that. "Lots of people argue and say things they wish they hadn't, Sheriff. It's hardly grounds for suspecting my brother of something so heinous."

Sheriff Colton folded his huge hands in front of him. "I understand how you don't want to think your brother could do this, Mr. Newham, but it happens. Law enforcement sees this kind of thing every day across the country. Passions get stirred and someone does something stupid."

Drake shook his head. "Heath loved Melissa. And he'd never willingly leave his girls orphaned. Someone else killed them both and threw them over the cliff. Have you looked into that at all, or are you just content to take the easy road?"

The sheriff's face reddened. "Ayuh, I always look at the full picture. Family usually doesn't want to face facts."

Drake took a deep, calming breath. He'd get nowhere by antagonizing the sheriff. "Can we go over how you got the call and what you saw when you arrived?"

His softened tone deflated the sheriff's belligerent stance, and he nodded. "Be glad to." He perched some reading glasses on the end of his nose and pulled out his notebook. "My office got a call at 8:11 a.m. telling us that two bodies were lying by the puffin burrows out on the cliff by Mermaid Rock. The Coast Guard was called first since they were close by. I headed there with one of my deputies immediately."

Drake jotted down a note to talk to the Coast Guard. "Is there a Coast Guard crew member I can speak with about this?"

"Luke Rocco." The sheriff reached for the desk phone and punched in a number. "Yeah, Luke, you in town at the café by any chance?" He glanced at Drake and nodded. "Appreciate it if you could come by for a minute. Thanks." He dropped the phone back onto the stand. "He'll be right here. He and his fiancée are next door paying for breakfast."

And the sheriff was leaving shortly. Drake read the relief on his face. "In the meantime, could you tell me what you found when you arrived?"

"The Coast Guard had secured the scene and checked to make sure they were dead. The bodies were still on the rocks when we got there. Both showed signs of soft-tissue damage from the rocks."

Drake's control began to slip at the mental image, and he pulled his emotions back. "Then what happened?"

"We called in more help and searched the scene up top. We found your brother's car parked down the hillside a bit, as though he wanted to catch her unawares. The area at the top of the cliff was scuffed, and the grass was matted down as if there had been a struggle."

"Which is why you called it a murder/suicide?"

The sheriff rose as footsteps came down the hall. "No, we didn't call it until we got the autopsies back."

"What was in the autopsy?"

"Enough. I'll send you a copy." The sheriff opened the door, and a dark-haired man about thirty ushered in a pretty blonde woman. She wore a denim skirt and ruffled white top that showed off her slim figure. The guy wore a Coast Guard uniform. She looked familiar, and he tried to think of where he'd met her. "Thanks for coming. Luke, Claire, this is Drake Newham. His brother and sister-in-law were the Emersons, that couple who went over the cliff. Drake, this is Luke Rocco and Claire Dellamare."

The woman's eyes widened at his name. She'd probably heard the rumors. He shook their hands. "Sorry to bother you, but I'm investigating my brother's death." He looked at Luke. "You were first on the scene?"

Luke glanced at Claire, then back to Drake. "Actually, Claire and her sister found the bodies."

Claire's eyes got even wider. "You're Heath Emerson's brother? Your last name is different."

"Yes, he's my older half brother. His father died when Heath was two. Then my father married our mother when Heath was four."

Her gaze softened. "I'm sorry for your loss. There isn't much we can tell you though. My sister, Kate, saw the bodies on the ledge, and she ran toward the water. We didn't see anything or hear any arguments. Does Kate know you're Mr. Emerson's brother?"

"Kate?"

"Kate Mason." Claire smiled. "You hired her yesterday for your nanny position. Your girls will love her."

*Kate.* Drake held up his hand. "Wait a second. Your sister is Kate Mason?" When she nodded, he exhaled. "Why didn't she tell me who she was when I interviewed her?"

Claire straightened and tipped up her chin. Her blue eyes were steely. "She didn't know who you were. All she knows is that the girls are orphaned. And besides, how does that impact her qualifications to care for the children?"

"Of course it impacts them. The girls will be upset if they hear she found Heath's and Melissa's bodies." He shook his head, then tossed his business card onto the sheriff's desk. "E-mail me the autopsies. I need to talk to Kate."

The strong smell of paint permeated the room in spite of the breeze wafting through the open windows. Kate put down the paint roller and smiled. The pale-gray color was exactly what she'd had in mind, and it contrasted beautifully with the designer white trim she'd painted a couple of days ago. Drake and the girls could move in as soon as the living room furniture was delivered.

Her sweet sister had insisted on going with her to a discount furniture place yesterday in Ellsworth, and Claire purchased a new sofa and chairs for her. Kate intended to repay every dime as soon as Drake paid her.

The distressed pine table and chairs in the kitchen had been salvaged from a garage sale, and Kate had done the paint treatment on it herself. New bedding added a nice touch in the bedrooms. While it might not meet Drake's usual standards in Boston, the cottage would make a lovely summer home.

Tires crunched on the gravel outside, and she looked through the window to see Drake unfold his long legs from under the steering wheel of his Land Rover. He was alone, and his stride was purposeful as he approached the front door.

She answered his knock with a smile. "The cottage should be ready in a couple more days. Want to see?"

His scowl faltered for a moment, then came surging back. "We need to talk."

She stepped back and studied his tight jaw and hooded eyes. "What's wrong?" Was it something she'd done or said? Did he hate the cottage now? If he didn't rent it, she'd be unable to pay back Claire. "Come in."

He strode past her, pausing briefly to look around. "Nice color."

"Thanks. I like it." She gestured to the kitchen doorway. "I can put on some coffee if you like. I've got bottled water too."

"I just had coffee with breakfast." He folded his arms across his chest and stared at her. "Were you ever going to tell me you found my brother's body? Talk about feeling like a fool this morning. I rented your cottage and hired you as a nanny, and you didn't even bother to tell me something that important."

She blinked and tried to make sense of what he'd just said. "Your brother's body? I don't understand." She didn't know another Newham, did she?

"You and your sister found Melissa and Heath. Don't try to tell me you forgot. People don't forget that kind of horrific event. You should have told me instead of making me find out coincidentally from your sister."

She felt the blood drain from her head. "Heath and Melissa Emerson are the girls' parents?"

"I'm sure my name was mentioned in the newspaper as the only surviving relative." But a hint of doubt had crept into his voice. "And you heard me talk yesterday about how they'd both died."

She shook her head. "You didn't mention their names, just that law enforcement suspected your brother had killed his wife, then himself. I thought they'd died in Boston from the way you talked. I saw the Emersons had two daughters, of course, and that broke my heart. I'd been praying for them, but I'm terrible with names. I'm sorry."

She reached a hand toward him, expecting him to step back, but he didn't. She held on to his arm, and he stared down at her as if trying to read her intentions. Her inclination was to look away from his intense stare, but she forced herself to hold his gaze until he finally nodded.

"You have to admit it looked a little suspicious. I felt as though you'd deliberately pulled the wool over my eyes, that you were one of those gawkers who like to prey on other people's grief."

She pulled her hand away before she couldn't restrain herself from slapping him or something equally violent. How dare he say something like that? He didn't even know her. "You stopped here out of the blue looking for a place to rent. I hadn't even decided to rent it yet."

"I remember that. That's why I thought maybe you decided to rent it the second you realized who I was."

"Well, I didn't!" She began to shake, and it was hard to keep from storming outside to get away from him.

His hazel eyes shifted and went soft. "Look, I can see I over-reacted. I'm sorry. It felt deliberate, but I know now it wasn't. I need to ask you about the day they died though."

"I don't want to talk to you. Not now and maybe not ever. Most people don't jump to conclusions the way you just did." She went to the paint pan and grabbed the brush. If she didn't get it cleaned up, it would harden and she'd have to buy a new one.

He followed her into the kitchen. "I said I was sorry. It was an honest mistake. Anyone would have made the same assumption."

"I doubt it." She turned on the warm water and scrubbed the brush. "You didn't even tell me how they died, remember?"

"I was too upset to remember that." He moved closer, crowding into her personal space. "Please, I need to know what you saw."

She tossed the paintbrush to the bottom of the sink and whirled to face him. "It's not something I like to think about. It was horrible, a horrible day. I told the sheriff everything I saw. Claire and I were watching puffins. I saw Melissa first. It was her hair by the puffin burrows that caught my attention."

He nodded. "I need you to help me prove they were murdered."

Poking into those deaths wasn't something she wanted to do, but the pathos in his eyes tugged at her heart. She turned away to finish cleaning the brush so she didn't have to answer.

He'd waited until he saw her car disappear in the distance. Rising from his hiding place in the trees, he took his time walking across the backyard. Gnats and black flies approached, then buzzed away, repelled by his Off! As always, his heart beat erratically as he approached the back door. The tools on his belt were professional ones he'd learned to use long ago, and he quickly had the lock open.

Stepping inside her house, he sniffed the enticing smell of her vanilla scent. She must have just sprayed it on. Since there was no need for stealth, he took his time circling the living room. Studying every picture of her he could find, he smiled back at the one of her with her sister. She looked so happy. If only she would look at him like that. And maybe she would, once he revealed himself to her. Once she knew how he loved her. He'd just have to get rid of that man. It added a bit of humor for him that he'd been using a drone purchased from Newham's company to spy on him.

He sat in her recliner by the fireplace where she'd been last night when he peeked in the window. Surely that was the imprint of her body in the chair, and it welcomed him. He closed his eyes and leaned his head back. There was enough room they could snuggle here together someday and watch their children play on the floor. A smile curved his lips as he contemplated the future. Surely his very desire for it would bring it about.

He rose and meandered to the kitchen where he picked up the water glass by the sink. He filled it, then fitted his mouth where a faint trace of her lipstick remained. He could almost imagine kissing her.

He opened the refrigerator and rummaged inside. There was a pizza box on the second shelf, and he pulled it out to examine the contents. One of the three pieces had a bite taken out of it, the exact shape of her perfect teeth. He found a paper plate in the cupboard and plopped the pizza on it. Once the microwave dinged, he closed his eyes as he ate the partial piece of pizza. Surely she would be able to feel his devotion.

Once he was finished he took another drink of water, then crumpled up the paper plate and tossed it in the trash. He knew the way to her bedroom from the last time, when he'd nearly been caught, so he headed for the hallway. His heart hammered as he pushed open her bedroom door. For a moment her smiling form beckoned him from the bed but disappeared when he blinked. Someday she would be there though, welcoming him with open arms.

He moved to the dresser and pulled open the top drawer. The faint aroma of a vanilla sachet wafted up to his nose, and he closed his eyes to inhale the scent. Love for her nearly split his chest wide open. She would know soon.

He opened his eyes and carefully lifted out her underwear and nightgowns, thrown haphazardly into the drawer. They deserved better treatment, so he folded each one and nestled them back into the drawer. He moved on to the next drawer that contained her T-shirts. Frowning, he shook his head at the disarray. He would teach her better soon. He folded and sorted them by color before replacing them in the drawer.

He rummaged in her jewelry box and extracted a pair of blue earrings, then put them in his pocket. When he glanced at the bedside clock, he realized he'd been in the house for two hours. She might come back anytime, so he sighed and made his way to the back door. Soon he'd never have to leave.

# TWELVE

The heavy cloud cover turned the moonless night into inky blackness. Kate maneuvered her Volkswagen along the bumpy dirt road toward her house. When she pulled into the drive, she grimaced at the dark house. She thought she'd flipped on the porch light. The yard light had a dead bulb she meant to have changed as soon as she had the money. She didn't have a ladder long enough to reach it to change it herself. The light from the car pierced a few feet into the darkness as she got out.

As soon as she slammed the door, she couldn't see more than a few inches in front of her face. With her hands held in front of her, she touched the side of the house and shuffled along to the front steps, then grabbed the handrail and mounted the steps to the small porch. Her eyes were adjusting to the pitch black now, and she started to put her key in the lock, but the door creaked. It was standing open a few inches. She really needed to ask Luke to adjust the latch. It hadn't shut right in several weeks.

She pushed open the door and started to enter, but the scent of male cologne wafted toward her. Her eyes widened and she stopped, her fingers clutching the key chain.

A man was inside. Or had been.

She backed up a few feet. "Uncle Paul?" Her voice echoed in

the entry and bounced back at her. She advanced a step closer to
the door. "Is that you?" But if her uncle was inside, wouldn't he
have turned on the light? Maybe he'd been there earlier and left.

Her groping hand touched the doorjamb, then she reached
in and flipped on the dooryard and porch lights. The instant
illumination made her blink, but she let her gaze sweep past the
tiny entry to the living room beyond.

It was empty of everything but her furniture.

She stood in the doorway and listened, but it was hard to
hear anything past the thumping of her heartbeat in her ears.
*Idiot! I should be calling for help.*

Her purse fell to the floor as she tried to dig for her cell
phone, and the contents spilled across the oak floor. Her phone
came to a stop under the foyer table, and she dove for it.

Her chest heaved, and her heart pounded as she punched
in 911 and told the dispatcher she thought someone had been
in her house. The woman told her to lock herself in her car and
someone would be there shortly, but Kate retreated only as far as
the porch.

The woman kept talking, but Kate slipped the phone into
the pocket of her jacket. The dispatcher's strident voice inflamed
Kate's nervous energy even more. She peered into the house
again. The cologne smelled elusively familiar. Did Uncle Paul
even wear aftershave or anything with a scent? She couldn't
remember, but surely he was the one who had been in her house.
Maybe he was still there, laughing at how skittish she was. He
was always telling her to grow a backbone and not be pushed
around, but no amount of inner urging made her take a step
toward the house again.

"Uncle Paul?" The answering echo made the house sound

empty. Whoever had been there was probably gone. And if it had been her uncle, he would have heard her call for help.

A faint siren pealed in the darkness behind her, and she turned to see a game warden SUV coming her way. Dizzy with relief, she whirled and ran down the steps to meet her cousin as he stepped out of his vehicle.

Kevin peered past her to the house, and his hand went to the butt of his gun. "Kate, you okay?"

"I'm fine. My door was ajar when I got home, and I smelled male cologne. I thought maybe Uncle Paul had broken in."

"Did you go inside?"

"I stepped into the dooryard and called to him. He didn't answer. The house feels empty, but I didn't want to go in by myself."

"Wise decision." He brushed past her and advanced to the porch. "Wait here."

Kate ignored his order and followed on his heels. He glanced back and frowned but didn't say anything when she tipped up her chin.

He drew his gun when he reached the door. "Game warden! Come out with your hands up." When no one answered, he stepped into the entry and began to walk through the house.

Kate followed him to the kitchen and watched him inspect the pantry. It was empty. She felt a breeze on her face and turned to look at the back door. It was slightly ajar too. "He left that way." She stepped to the door and threw the lock. "I need to get a dead bolt."

"Looks like it." He sniffed the air. "I smell pizza."

She caught the scent herself, but everything seemed to be in place. She went to the fridge and opened it. The pizza box from last night was still on the shelf, but the partial piece of pizza she'd put back was missing.

She tossed the box to the counter. No way would she eat those leftovers now. "A partial piece is missing. I don't know why he didn't eat a full piece if he was hungry."

"Where's your bedroom?"

"Down the hall." She led the way to the biggest bedroom in the small house, then stood aside while Kevin checked it out. The other bedroom was tiny with barely enough room for the double bed and nightstand it held.

"No one hiding here. Let me check the bathroom." He stepped across the hall and pulled back the shower curtain to reveal only the empty bathtub and surround. His shoulders relaxed and he holstered his gun. "He seems to have gone. I think you're right and it was Paul. You need to consider him dangerous, Kate."

"Uncle Paul wouldn't hurt me. I hope he comes back so I can talk to him. He needs to turn himself in before he gets shot."

He shook his head and frowned. "You never really knew him. I know he was a great uncle to you, but he had a lot of darkness he concealed. I caught him poaching more times than I can count, and he was always mean about it. Be on your guard."

"I will. Sorry to call you out tonight. Mallory will kill me. Is she doing okay?"

He grinned. "Now that the morning sickness is over, she's busy getting a nursery ready. We just found out we're having a boy. The girls will be thrilled when they hear about it. Haylie's at swim camp, and Sadie is having a blast at a special camp for the blind."

"That's wonderful!" They already had two girls, one of Kevin's and one of Mallory's. They both deserved to be happy. Kate led him to the door and locked it behind him before walking through the house again. The darkness pressed in on her, and her unease returned. If only she could call Claire to come stay with her.

After checking the door locks one more time, she shut off the lights and went to her bedroom. When she pulled open the dresser drawer to retrieve a nightgown, her breath caught in her throat and her hand froze over the drawer.

Instead of the jumble of colors and patterns, every item was neatly folded in organized piles. She put her hand to her throat and her pulse jumped beneath her fingers. Uncle Paul wouldn't have done this. He was as messy as a rat in a new nest.

She shuddered and whirled to draw her curtains. Who had been in here? She grabbed her phone and called her sister to tell her she was coming over. The sheriff could figure this out.

# THIRTEEN

Claire pressed her hand against the butterflies dancing in her stomach as she stared at herself in the mirror. The wedding gown was a mermaid style and accentuated her curves. She didn't even recognize herself. She turned to face her sister. "No other incidents at the house?"

Kate was wearing a deep aquamarine-blue gown in the same style. Her blue eyes looked enormous with her hair swept up. "Nothing, but I jump at every sound. The sheriff didn't find any clues, and I'm back to wondering if it was Uncle Paul. Rearranging the clothes in my drawers sounds weird, but he's been in prison. Maybe he was looking for something and straightened them without thinking. I wonder if Becky told him I wanted to see him. Maybe he hung around for a while, then got tired of waiting. It would make sense with some of the pizza being gone."

Claire's grandmother stirred from the armchair and beckoned to her. "Come here, my dear girl. I have something for you."

Claire went to take her grandmother's hand. "I'm not sure I can bend in this dress, Grandma."

Her grandmother's health had waned this past year. Age had deepened the lines around her eyes, and the constant pain she was in from arthritis made her dark eyes look sunken. Claire felt a momentary stab of panic. The thought of ever losing her grandmother was a knife to the heart.

"I can get up." Her grandmother gripped the arms of the chair and struggled to her feet. "Turn around."

Claire obeyed and her grandmother's cool fingers touched her neck as she fastened a necklace around it. Claire touched the beads. "Your pearl necklace!"

"It was a gift from your grandpa on our wedding day, and we both thought you should have it today. May you enjoy as many happy years of married life as we have."

Claire turned and bent down to embrace her grandmother's short frame. "Thank you, Grandma. I'll treasure it."

"I know you will." Her grandmother reached behind her and practically fell back into the chair.

Claire faced the mirror. The pearls finished the dress. In the distance she heard the thrum of music in the yard. This was really and truly happening. She was about to marry the man she loved and start a new life with him. The enormous blessing of it all tightened her throat.

She turned at a tap on the door. Her mother stepped inside. Her pale-blue suit was a perfect foil for her short blonde hair, and she looked almost young enough to be Claire's older sister. "You look beautiful, Claire."

Her gaze landed on Kate and her smile faltered. Claire had tried hard to blend her family since she'd found her twin, but her mother never seemed to let go of her stiffness. She made an attempt though with a smile that didn't reach her green eyes. "You look lovely, Kate."

Kate's fake smile matched the older woman's. "Thank you, Mrs. Dellamare."

Claire's mother pressed her lips together. "I still wish your father could have gotten out of prison to give you away."

He was the last person Claire wanted to walk her down the aisle. "Grandpa is a great substitute."

Her mother inclined her head. "I'm glad you think so."

"You and Dad are talking?"

"A little." Her mother stepped forward and adjusted the veil. "I think we'd better get outside. The guests are waiting, and so is Luke."

*Luke.* The man who had swept into her life on the cusp of a wave and had changed it forever. And after today she wouldn't be a Dellamare any longer.

The door opened again and Luke's sister, Megan, poked her head in the doorway. Her brown eyes danced with merriment. "It's time. Luke is pacing the grass like he's going to make a run for it any minute. You'd better get out there and stop him." Her short, dark hair was in a cute, spiky hairdo.

"I have rope right here." Claire picked up her bouquet and went to join her soon-to-be new sister. "I'm so glad you were able to get time off for the wedding." Megan lived in Oregon and studied viruses and mutations.

"I'd have quit my job before I missed this." Megan opened the door wide and stepped out of the way. "Come on, Claire, your grandpa is waiting to walk you down to the arbor. And let me help you out, Mrs. Dellamare." She went to assist Claire's grandmother out of her chair.

They'd opted for a small wedding with just a maid of honor and a best man. Claire stepped out the back door to grasp her grandfather's arm. In spite of his age, he looked pretty good in a tux. The music wafted on the wind and she leaned into her grandfather's embrace as her grandmother, Megan, and Kate went down the steps. Her heart was nearly pounding out of her sequined bodice as the strains of the "Wedding March" grew louder.

"It's time, honey."

She straightened and rested her fingers on her grandfather's arm. Holding the skirt of her dress up, she descended the stairs from the deck and walked through the grass to where the white paper runner began. Everyone stood and looked her direction, but Claire locked her attention on Luke's face. His tender smile brightened, and he took a step toward her until his best man, Beau Callahan, put his hand on Luke's arm and said something.

Kate stepped out and began to sing "Make You Feel My Love." The lyrics enveloped Claire, but she was barely conscious of the smiles and nods sent her way as she walked to meet her destiny.

The past week had sped by, and Kate had turned over the cottage keys to Drake yesterday. She had been busy with her sister's wedding until this morning, so he'd arranged their few belongings, then taken the girls beachcombing until she started work, but today he could finally concentrate on his brother's murder.

Kate had done a fine job with the little cottage. The scent of fresh paint still lingered in the air, and most of the furniture was at least clean and semi-new, probably purchased from a secondhand store. She had a sharp touch with color and furniture arrangement, and an enjoyable summer here with the girls stretched in front of him.

The sound of Kate singing "Father Abraham" with the girls drifted in through the open window as he settled onto the overstuffed sofa. She had a beautiful voice that reminded him of Adele's. His phone rang, and he glanced at the screen before answering it. "Good morning, Lakesha. How's it going?"

"About as well as you'd expect with the boss gone." Her husky voice held an edge of impatience. "Can you come back, even just for a couple of days? Fish and Wildlife's regional director wants to meet with you personally. I don't think this deal will go forward if he can't speak with you to get a sense of how hard you think it will be to implement his changes. Did you get the documents I e-mailed?"

He'd gotten them but hadn't reviewed them yet. Could one of his competitors know about this? He made a mental note to check with his attorney again. "Hold on, let me take a look." He opened the first document and absorbed the request. "They want me to add the capability to drop supplies? That's a fairly easy fix, I think. It could be a real boon to remote areas."

"They like your drones because of the size. We need you here, Drake."

He sighed and shoved a lock of hair off his forehead. His employees depended on him, and everything in him itched to plunge into the needed modifications. His attention strayed to the box of Heath's belongings he'd been about to dig into, and he wanted to talk to people who might have known about Heath's mental state the week he died. "I just can't come back right now, Lakesha. Let's arrange a video meeting."

"I suggested that. No go." She bit the words out as if she was holding back what she really wanted to say.

"Look, I know you think trying to dig into Heath's death

is stupid, but it's something I have to do. I'm trying my hardest here. I've got a lot on my plate right now."

"I know you do, and I'm sorry to bring you more pressure. But this is important, too, Drake."

"I know. I'll think about all this and get back to you."

Her heavy sigh came over the phone. "I could try to put him off for another week."

"I don't think that will be long enough. Maybe he could come here if he's so determined to meet with me."

"Get real, Drake. The regional director isn't going to go somewhere so remote. They'll just take their business elsewhere. But I'll keep you posted." She sounded resigned.

He ended the call. He pushed the problem away for now and pulled the box to him.

The sight of it in front of him shouldn't have caused his pulse to ratchet up. It appeared innocuous enough. Just a standard twelve-by-twenty-four box, but his hands were clammy as he ripped the tape off the top. His chest squeezed when he saw his brother's baseball on top of the pile. All these things had been cleaned out of Heath's desk. Heath's pride and joy was this ball signed by Reggie Jackson. It had been owned by their dad who had caught a fly ball in Reggie's final game in '87.

Drake ran his fingers over the ball and blinked back the moisture in his eyes. This jumble of belongings had to be gone through just in case there was a clue to what had happened to Heath.

He lifted out the contents: a tweed jacket that still held Heath's scent, basketball trophies, framed educational diplomas, a desk pen and pencil set, several leadership books, and then a stack of folders. Two files, both a couple of inches thick, contained copies of every scrap of information Heath had on the Chen Wang case. There was a file of bills also, but Drake set it aside until he'd gone through the more important files.

He rubbed his eyes and opened the first file. The details of the Wang crimes made him want to slam the file shut and go play in the sunshine, but he forced himself to keep reading about murders, robberies, extortion, and beheadings. He'd need a shower by the time he was done. His eyes grew bleary as he flipped through page after page until only a couple remained in the second folder.

No doubt about it, these guys—Wang in particular—were some of the worst criminals in the world. Terror and death followed the gang's every movement. Why hadn't Heath backed away from defending Wang immediately?

Drake couldn't hear the children any longer, and he assumed Kate had taken them down to the water at the back of the property. He forced himself to reach for the next-to-last sheet of paper. It appeared to be a log of text messages. He caught his breath when he recognized the originating number on the cell phone. Why would Heath get a log of Melissa's text messages? As he scanned the messages, the pieces fell into place.

Melissa had been having an affair with Wang.

The list of times and meeting places was extensive and included expensive hotels like the Ritz-Carlton and the Mandarin Oriental. Could this be why Heath hadn't backed away after realizing what kind of man he was defending? Maybe he wanted to take down Wang instead of defend him. And it might have led to his death. Had he confronted Wang and the man decided to eliminate the problem?

But why kill Melissa too? Maybe she'd learned something

incriminating, and Wang had to silence her. Was Heath just collateral damage? Drake leaned back against the sofa and exhaled. He had to think this through and make no assumptions. Melissa could have been the target all along and not Heath.

But why would sweet Melissa have gotten involved with such an evil man? He couldn't wrap his head around the thought of her with Chen, especially after reading files detailing all the man's crimes. This put a different twist on the deaths out on that rock. And he had to find out what happened.

He glanced at the clock. He'd promised the girls he'd design a new decoding puzzle, so he grabbed some paper and wrote out the simple code they were used to, then spelled out clues for them to find some new stuffed animals he'd hidden for them. For good measure, he created two more puzzles for them to decipher when they got bored.

He rubbed his forehead when a dart of pain throbbed. He was finding it hard to balance everything he had to do.

# FOURTEEN

A familiar wave of failure welled in Kate's chest as she looked at the harvestless fields. The barren red plants broke her heart.

Emma stooped and touched a leaf on one of the plants. "Where are the blueberries?" She stopped and waved at her uncle who was picking his way through the red fields.

Kate beckoned him to join them. "Don't bother being careful. The plants are useless. You can't hurt them much."

Drake's broad shoulders cast the plants in shadows where he stood. "They look nice."

"Looks are deceiving. I didn't have the money to rent honeybee hives. I hoped there would be enough bees around to have a decent crop, but it didn't happen. There are a few berries." She knelt and moved some red leaves so Drake and the children could see the tiny blueberries. "Not enough to even harvest though."

Phoebe danced from one foot to the other. "Can we eat them?"

Before Kate could answer the little girl, Drake held out two candy bars. "I brought you each a Snickers."

Kate frowned. "It's too close to dinnertime for candy. The

blueberries are a better snack." She plucked a handful and put them in Phoebe's palm. "Go potty. We'll wait right here for you."

Phoebe popped them in her mouth, and the swipe left a blue stain around her lips. "Okay. Be right back." She ran toward the cottage.

Drake's somber expression darkened as he lowered his hand to his side. "The candy bar has nuts."

"And sugar and hydrogenated soybean oil."

"You're going to control their every bite of food?" His tone left no doubt about his opinion on that.

"Sugar is bad for them. Very bad." She shook her head as he lifted a brow her way, unwrapped a candy bar, then took a big bite. "And for you." She turned her back on him and knelt to look at the plants. "Want some blueberries, Emma? Pick all you like."

Emma brushed away the leaves and found a handful of berries for herself. "Why are they so small?"

"They're wild blueberries. We call them lowbush. They grew here by themselves. Taste them and see what you think."

Emma popped several in her mouth, and her hazel eyes widened. "They're really good. Way better than a Snickers bar. Can I have more?"

"You can have all you can find." Harvesting these few tiny berries wouldn't be worth the work, but they'd have enough to enjoy for a bit.

Emma grabbed another handful. "Why do you grow blueberries if it's so hard?"

Kate opened her mouth to reply, then closed it. Why did she? Tradition and family expectations mostly. "My mother grew up helping her parents on a barrens, and she wanted me to learn to do it too. My father bought these fields for her, and it's been my life too."

"Do you like it?" Juice dribbled down Emma's chin.

Did she? Kate flicked her gaze to Drake, and she found him watching her with a taut expression. He'd been acting funny ever since he got out here too. His shoulders were tense, and he held his mouth in a flat, hard line. She wanted to ask him what was wrong, but it wasn't appropriate with Emma there.

She knelt beside the little girl and dug around a blueberry shrub. "This is how blueberries spread. This is a rhizome, kind of like a runner. It makes a clone blueberry and spreads out to make more and more."

Emma straightened. "Uncle Drake always said I was Mommy's clone, but we didn't know what it meant. It sounded good though, and I was glad." She glanced up at her uncle.

Kate let the rich earth dribble out of her hand. If only there was some way to heal the pain in Emma's heart. "A clone means just alike. Were your mommy's eyes hazel too?"

Emma nodded. "We have Grandma's hazel eyes and cowlick." She smoothed the top of her head in a self-conscious gesture.

"No one is exactly anyone else's clone. It's just an expression." Kate brushed the dirt from her hands. "Phoebe will never be exactly like your dad, and you won't be exactly like your mom. You're you, totally unique and special just like God made you. You'll have different experiences than your dad did, and you'll want to do things that he never did."

"Then why are you doing what your mom did?"

*Out of the mouths of babes.* Kate stood and dusted the dirt from her hands. "Sometimes it takes a while to figure out your own way in the world."

"Uncle Drake says you should decorate houses. He likes the cottage."

Kate shot a glance at Drake, whose face had reddened. "I had fun doing it." She helped Emma up. "Run along to the house and get me a bowl. Maybe we can find enough blueberries to make a cobbler."

"Can I help you make it?"

"I wouldn't have it any other way." Once the little girl was out of earshot, she shaded her eyes with her hand and eyed Drake. "What's wrong? You seem ready to kick something."

He finished the last of the candy bar and wadded up the wrapper in his fist. "You're going to need to keep a close eye on the girls."

"I already am. Has something happened?" She turned and started for the house.

He fell into step beside her. "I found out Melissa was having an affair with a very evil man. I don't know if she was the target or if Heath was, but I'm not sure Wang is finished with the family. Once I start digging into this more, the danger may increase."

She stopped and stared up at him. "Then maybe you'd better let it be. You can't bring your brother back, and getting yourself killed would land the girls into foster care. They are the priority right now."

The muscles in his jaw flexed. "I intend to see justice for my brother. I just need you to do your job and take care of the girls." He stalked off ahead of her in long strides. Moments later the front door slammed.

She blinked. What had just happened?

Twilight touched the red fields with gold and purple. The darkness made it easy to blend into the fields as he lay flat among the blueberry plants. He fiddled with his binoculars until he could see clearly through the living room window.

A woman passed in front of his vision, and his fingers tightened on the binoculars. *Kate Mason.* The lighter in his pocket begged to be used. He could fire the cottage and be done with all of them. One hand fumbled for the lighter until sanity prevailed. He wanted to get back to the bright lights and bars of Boston. He missed his favorite watering hole and the comforting darkness in the alleys of the city. The vastness of this place left him unsettled.

He watched as Newham pulled the smaller of the girls onto his lap and let her eat his ice cream. He focused on the woman again. Lingering on the soft roundness of her shape, he grinned. She was a looker for sure. He'd managed to hack into the sheriff department's files, and there was little evidence on the deaths.

He swung the binoculars back to Newham. Most likely the man would have to be eliminated, if only to get him out of the way. But first he had to retrace his steps and find his journal, or he'd be in big trouble.

The kids might be collateral damage, too, but he hoped not. He didn't like the idea of hurting kids, never had. Some might call it his Achilles' heel, but he liked to think he was a pragmatic man.

The golden moonlight turned the red fields a faint orange shade as Drake walked Kate home. Immersed in watching a Disney

DVD he'd popped in after dinner, the girls hadn't wanted to come, but he'd insisted. Their lagging steps proclaimed their displeasure.

Kate had left on a porch light, but the yard was dark. He peered up the light pole. "You need to replace your yard light."

"I know. I don't have a ladder tall enough to reach it, but I'll call someone when I get a chance."

"When I get a chance" was code for when she had the money. He'd get it done tomorrow. With all the events of the past few weeks, he didn't think it was safe to ignore. He said nothing though and watched her dig in her ridiculously oversize purse for her keys. The bag was made from a quilted fabric in a bright-purple print that didn't seem her type of thing.

"Big bag you've got there."

She glanced down at it. "Hideous, isn't it? My mother bought it for my birthday a couple of years ago. I think she got it at a garage sale, and I didn't have the heart to tell her I hated it. And then I suddenly didn't hate it when I couldn't find anything else big enough. I like to be prepared, and it's hard to find something lightweight and big."

"Where does your mom live?"

She looked away and lowered her voice. "She's in prison. Kidnapping and manslaughter. She kidnapped my half sister who then died from an asthma attack. And she helped cover up a murder my uncle committed. It occurred a long time ago, back when I was five, but only came to light a few years back. My uncle's in prison too. Well, he was. He escaped last week." She grimaced. "Nice family I've got, huh?"

His gut clenched at her revelation. "Have you seen your uncle? Is he in the area?"

She shook her head. "The sheriff and his deputies are on the lookout for him." Her gaze swung toward the house. "He might have paid me a visit last week. I had an intruder who ate some pizza from my fridge, and it's unlikely to be anyone but Uncle Paul."

He eyed the dark yard again, then glanced at his nieces. "Are my girls in danger?"

"Absolutely not. He's not the type to go around killing kids. Even my half sister's death was an accident he covered up." Her blue eyes were vulnerable when she glanced back up at him. "I suppose I should have told you about this before you hired me, but I'm not anything like him or my mother."

He studied her expression, noting the pain in her eyes and the defensive slant to her mouth. She wasn't asking for sympathy. His aunt had told him she'd been sick, but Aunt Dixie hadn't mentioned the horrific skeletons in Kate's closet. And maybe she should have before he hired Kate, but he couldn't really fault her for wanting to keep it quiet. Who would want to announce something like that to a stranger?

She caught her full lower lip between her teeth. "Are you going to fire me?"

He shook himself free of his thoughts. "No, of course not. You're doing a fine job with the girls. At least when you're not lecturing me about sugar and hydrogenated oils." He grinned and touched her on the shoulder. "Is there anything else you need to tell me?"

A shadow passed over her face, and she ducked her head. "I was really sick. But I'm okay now, really. Not a trace of aplastic anemia left. The doctor is very pleased."

"My aunt told me about that. I'm glad." The thought of

her lying pale and near death in a hospital bed made his hand drop away.

He liked her spunk. In spite of everything life had thrown at her, she'd gotten back up again and pressed on. Lots of other women would have pulled the covers over their heads and refused to enter life's arena again. But not Kate. She doubled up her fists and came up punching.

She stepped past him and hugged the girls. "Remember, if you need to talk to me, even in the middle of the night, you can call. You have my number. I'll come right down, okay?"

Phoebe nodded, and Emma folded her arms across her chest and looked away. Drake had thought his older niece was warming up to Kate, but she had her guard up again.

Kate turned and went up the porch steps. "I can come over to fix breakfast at eight if you like."

"I think I can manage cereal for all of us."

She paused with the key in the lock and looked at him over her shoulder. "Cereal! Certainly not. The girls need a healthy breakfast. I'll go grocery shopping tomorrow, and I'll get some Greek yogurt and fruit. Tomorrow I'll bring ingredients to make almond-flour pancakes."

"Whoa, let's not go too far in that direction. We're all healthy and can handle a little cereal."

She jammed the key home and twisted it, then shoved open the door. "I learned the hard way that you can never take good health for granted."

Of course. She'd been near death, so it was no wonder she cared about that kind of thing. And it wouldn't hurt him and the girls to eat well for a few weeks. "Pancakes sound good. Do I have to eat them dry?"

She laughed, a musical sound that seemed to float in the air. "I'll bring homemade maple syrup and real butter. You and the girls will love them."

"I'll have to trust you on that." He waited until the door shut behind her and he saw lights come on in the living room. Her shadow flitted across the window shades, and he watched a few more moments until Emma tugged at his hand.

"Uncle Drake, can we go now?"

He tore his gaze away. "Sure, honey. I'll fix some popcorn, and we'll watch the rest of the movie. Just don't tell Kate, okay? I don't want to get in trouble."

Emma giggled. "You're the boss. You can't get in trouble."

If he told himself that enough, he just might buy it. But he had the feeling that looking into Kate's big blue eyes was dangerous.

# FIFTEEN

Their first week together had been a little rocky. Kate found the girls vacillating between obeying and trying to pit her against their uncle, but it was early and she'd win this war eventually. She'd been thrilled Drake had brought the girls to her church this morning, and she sat with them, sharing a hymnal with Phoebe and feeling a tiny bit of what it must be like to be part of a real family with children—right down to the girls' restlessness until she'd fished out pencils and a decoder puzzle from her purse that Drake had created for them. They sat happily deciphering until the service was over and several of Kate's Sunday school children had come up to hug her. Phoebe had been downright jealous.

Kate changed her clothes after church, then positioned Phoebe at the table with bowls of chopped vegetables and lettuce. She set four salad plates in front of her. "You can fix the salads for everyone. I want everything in mine. You can see what your uncle and Emma want too. I'll make some dressing, and by the time we're both done, the vegetable soup should be ready to eat." The kitchen already smelled amazing, and her stomach rumbled.

Phoebe's nose wrinkled. "I only like Campbell's. You put snap peas in yours."

"If you like Campbell's, you'll like mine better."

Emma entered the kitchen and went to the stove and picked up the ladle. "I'll stir the soup."

Kate whisked the ladle out of her hand. "How about you set the table?" She pulled out the drawer containing tableware, then lifted down soup bowls.

Emma made another grab for the big spoon. "I want to stir!"

"It's very hot, and it's a gas stove. You're not big enough to do that just yet. Maybe after we go over some safety instructions, I'll let you try to cook something. The soup is already very hot, and I don't want you burned."

Tears welled in Emma's eyes, and she whirled for the door. "Uncle Drake!"

She dashed through the opening to the living room and told Drake Kate was letting Phoebe help but wouldn't let her. Pressing her lips together, Kate ladled up soup and carried the bowls to the table. "About done with those salads, Phoebe?"

"I think they look good." Phoebe tipped her head to one side and smiled, then picked up two of the salads and carried them to the table.

"Very nice. You made faces with the tomatoes. I can't wait to eat mine. Good job!" When she turned to help Phoebe get the other two salads, Drake entered the kitchen holding Emma in his arms. A pencil drawing of a drone was in his hand.

His gaze swept the kitchen and settled on the salad plate in Phoebe's hands. "Why can't Emma help too?"

It pained her to give an explanation. When was he going to trust her? "I gave her a job to do, but she didn't want to do it. She wanted to stir the hot soup, and I didn't want her to get burned."

He frowned. "Is it that dangerous just to stir a little soup?"

*Stay cool.* She motioned for him to follow her to the stove. "Put Emma down."

He shot her a glance and set Emma down. Kate turned off the stove, then positioned the little girl in front of the burner. "Look how tall the pot is. For her to reach in to stir the soup, she'd have to stand on her toes, and she's very likely to touch the hot pot with her arm." Kate demonstrated but kept her hand on the bottom side of Emma's arm. She winced when the top of her hand touched the top of the pot. "See what I mean?"

"Yeah." Drake pressed his lips together and took Emma's hand to lead her to the table.

Kate exhaled and gave her head a tiny shake. They would have to talk this out. He had to quit questioning her every time one of the girls complained to him. Either she had charge of them or she didn't.

They ate supper in near silence except for Phoebe who kept up a steady stream of chatter about the raccoon she'd seen under the back porch. She'd already named it Vince and was planning to take it supper.

Kate started to forbid her from leaving food out for it but decided it wouldn't hurt anything, really. Raccoons all over the area were used to scrounging for human food, even though it wasn't all that good for them.

She cleaned up the table and put the girls to washing and drying the dishes at the sink, then went to find Drake in the living room. He was still going over papers he'd gotten from his brother's office. She stood for a moment and waited for him to see her. He'd gotten a nice tan in the last ten days, and it went so well with his dark, curly hair and hazel eyes. She'd never seen a handsomer male specimen.

He finally looked up and saw her standing quietly in the doorway. "I see that expression. I'm in trouble, aren't I?"

His candor caught her off guard. "You have to decide if you're going to trust me or not, Drake. I already love the girls. I wouldn't do anything to hurt them. Any decision I make seems called into question the minute one of them complains."

"So I'm just supposed to shut up and let you run the house?"

She blew out a breath. "I didn't say that! If you have a question about what I'm doing, let's talk about it. But in private, not in front of the girls. That just fuels an adversarial spirit they can sense. In fact, they play us against each other. Or haven't you noticed?"

He frowned. "We're all getting used to the new arrangements. I'm their guardian, their new dad. What kind of women they grow up to be ultimately falls on my shoulders. I want to have a say in how they're raised. I don't want them to feel picked on or shoved aside in any way."

"And I wasn't doing that with Emma."

"I realized it once you showed me, but I had no way of knowing before that."

She took a couple of steps into the room. "If you trusted me, there wouldn't be the constant questions. That's what it boils down to—you aren't sure about me. What is it that keeps you from laying down your guard with me?"

He stared up at her as if trying to figure her out, then passed a palm over his forehead. "It's not you. It's me. If I'd been more aware of what was going on with Heath, maybe he wouldn't be dead. I don't want to make a mistake with the girls. I'm living with enough regrets already."

Her chest squeezed, and she saw the situation from his point of view. "I understand, but we've got to come to an agreement to at least take our concerns to a private room."

He nodded. "I can agree to that, and I'll try to let go of my fear of failing the girls."

"You're a good dad to them, Drake. The best. We'll get them through this together."

He reached out and put his hand on her shoulder. "Thank you, Kate. I know we will."

Warmth spread from his hand down her chest and settled in her belly. This man moved her like no one else ever had.

Kate couldn't sleep. Her conversation with Drake about the girls kept her tossing and turning until after one, and she finally got up to check the locks on the doors. Maybe some warm milk would help. She heated it on the stove, then carried it out under the stars. She rubbed her burning eyes and took a sip of the warm milk at the table on her back porch.

A footfall behind her made the back of her neck prickle, and she jumped to her feet. "Who's there?" She peered through the shadows at a tall figure looming in the moonlight.

Wait a minute, she knew that floppy hat and rangy figure. He looked just as handsome as ever with his salt-and-pepper hair. "Uncle Paul?" She hurtled down the steps and flung her arms around him. "I thought you'd already headed for Canada."

His plaid shirt smelled of fresh air as she buried her nose in his chest. He hugged her back but quickly released her as if he wasn't sure her hug was genuine. "I wanted to see you before I went."

The rush of joy ebbed as reality returned. He was a convicted murderer. The things he'd done had hurt Claire and Luke tremendously. How could she claim to love her sister if she let him get away? But her phone was in the house.

He must have seen her smile fade because he crossed his arms across his chest. "I need you to do something for me."

She shook her head. "I can't help you. You're a fugitive, and you tried to kill Claire."

"I was good to you, Kate. I was the only father you knew. You can do this one little thing for me."

"And I'm grateful for all you did. I still love you, Uncle Paul. It's impossible to turn love on and off like a hot-water tap, but you need to turn yourself in. You need to pay for what you did."

He grabbed her arm and pulled her with him toward the blueberry barrens. "It will only take a minute. I'd do it myself, but I'm too big to fit."

She struggled against his tight grip, but she couldn't break free. Dew drenched her feet, and the blueberry plants tore at the skin on her soles. He dragged her toward the tree line on the other side of the fields. It did no good to fight him, so she gave up the struggle and walked with him toward the woods. Once they were in total darkness, she'd make a run for it. She never would have believed he'd manhandle her like this.

Her arm felt bruised where he gripped it. "You can let go. I'm coming with you."

His face was expressionless and he shook his head. "I know you, Kate. You think you can outrun me when we get to the trees, but that's not going to happen. Do what I tell you, and you'll be home for breakfast before the dew is gone from the grass."

She examined the dark outline of the approaching trees. She knew the area well, but her uncle was even more familiar with it. He hunted back here all the time. What could he want with her? Once he got what he wanted, he'd be out of here and halfway to Canada by the time the sheriff arrived.

The air cooled as soon as they entered the thick shade from the trees. Eastern red cedar mingled with poplar, ash, and birch in the forest as he dodged the trunks and pulled her toward a rocky hillside dotted with spruce and pine trees. Her bare feet kicked up the scent of pine from the fallen needles. She tried to remember what terrain lay this way. The small lake. Did he intend to kill her? He dragged her closer to the sound of the waterfall until they were close enough she could smell the water, and she struggled harder.

He stopped beside the lake and reached down to grab a length of rope. "I'm sorry, but I can't trust you. Besides, this way you won't be guilty of helping me. The marks on your arms will prove I forced you to help me." He yanked her arms behind her back and tied her wrists together, then attached the other end to a jack pine tree. "I'll untie you in a minute."

She twisted her wrists and hands, but he was an expert at tying knots and she couldn't budge the rope. Maybe once his back was turned she could get loose from the tree.

He bent down and pulled a small kayak from behind some shrubs, then reached inside and withdrew a flashlight. He stuffed it in the waistband of his jeans before untying her. "There's a small cave behind the waterfall. You're going to crawl in there and get a bag with a passport and money in it. It's in a Ziploc baggie on the right side of the cave about ten feet in and around the bend to the right."

Shaking her head, she backed away. "I'm not going to help you."

"You have to. I can't get in there myself."

"Then how'd you get that stuff in there?"

"An old girlfriend about your size."

"Becky?"

"Maybe." He removed the rope, then put the flashlight in her hand. "The sooner you get to it, the sooner you can get home to breakfast. I'm not letting you go until I have my stuff. If you don't go, I'll burn down Claire's house. And I'll make sure she and Rocco are in it."

For the first time she felt her chest tighten as she stared up into his expressionless face. Initially she hadn't believed he could do the things he'd done. What made her think he wouldn't do whatever he had to this time as well? For all she knew he'd pick up a rock and bash her head in too. She looked at the waterfall, silvery in the moonlight. She'd do anything for her sister.

As if to punctuate the threat, her uncle stooped and picked up a hefty rock. "I have nothing to lose anymore, Kate. Do what I ask. Now."

She looked at the boulder in his hand, then at his set face. There were probably spiders and centipedes in that cave. She suppressed a shudder and flipped on the flashlight, and then she stepped into the kayak and picked up the paddle.

# Sixteen

The side-yard light cast a wide circle of illumination into the backyard. Drake stood on the back porch as Kevin O'Connor snagged the raccoon with a noose under the cottage and transferred it to the cage. "That didn't take long."

Drake had called the game-warden service after the animal started scratching at the floorboards in the kitchen. The girls had refused to go to bed with the terrifying noise. He tried to reassure them that it was Vince, but they'd been hysterical. Phoebe had liked the raccoon when it had seemed a cuddly stuffed animal, but the noises it made now had evaporated all her warm feelings.

Kevin put the cage in the back of his pickup. "I'll relocate this big fella and everyone will be happy." He smiled at the two girls peering out the backdoor screen. "You did the right thing by having your uncle call me. This guy will be a lot happier out in the woods."

"Uncle Drake thought we were being silly," Emma said. "Are there bears out there? He said the sound couldn't be a bear."

"In this case he was right. A bear couldn't get under that small space." Kevin slammed the tailgate shut.

"In this case?" Drake glanced around but saw nothing in the dark beyond the circle of light cast by the overhead lamp.

Kevin nodded and pulled his keys from his pocket. "It's late July, and the bears are trying to fatten up as much as possible. They love any kind of berry so they've been known to come this way. Make sure you don't put any trash out unless it's in a bear-proof can." He pointed to the big rubber trash can Drake had bought in town. "That thing will just attract them. Get a metal one with a tight-fitting lid and store it in the shed out back. Or in the garage."

"I'll get another kind. Anything else?"

Kevin pointed at the apple tree at the edge of the property. "Make sure you pick up any fallen apples. Fruit like that attracts them also." He stepped to the overhang on the porch and took down the hummingbird feeder. "Bring this in at night too. And make sure you clean your barbecue grill after using it."

The entire thing sounded daunting, but Drake nodded. "Is it safe to let the girls play outside alone?"

Kevin considered the question as he looked at Phoebe and Emma staring with big eyes through the door. "If they're paying attention, they'd see any animal coming across the fields, but kids don't always look for those things, and the girls aren't used to living up here. I'd keep bear spray handy. I know Kate is looking after them, and she knows how to handle herself."

At the mention of Kate, Drake decided he wanted to talk to Kevin in private. He turned toward the cottage. "The raccoon is gone, so you girls go brush your teeth. I'll be up in a minute to read you a story."

Phoebe's lower lip came out. "I want to stay with you."

"Emma will be with you. Go on to bed. There's nothing left to be afraid of, and I'll be there to pray with you in a minute."

With a final protesting glance, the girls moved away from the door. Emma's comforting voice faded as they went up the stairs to the bathroom. Drake followed Kevin to the vehicle and leaned against the truck bed. "I wanted to ask you about Kate's situation. I just found out her uncle has escaped from prison and her mom is in jail too. Murder is a pretty ugly word, and I'm having second thoughts about hiring her."

"Kate's had a raw deal. She's nothing like her mom or her uncle. You've probably heard the story about how she and Claire are twins?" When Drake nodded, Kevin went on. "She's been the one who kept this business going even when she was sick. It belongs to her mom, a payoff for turning Claire over to Harry Dellamare to replace the dead daughter his mistress killed. I wouldn't punish Kate for the sins of her family. She was a victim as much as Claire or anyone else."

"I don't want to do that either, but I'm worried about the girls. What if her uncle shows up when she's watching them? I wouldn't want them to be in the middle of something this unpleasant." And he had his hands full with investigating his brother's death without getting tangled up in her problems too.

Kevin opened the truck door, and the light spilled out onto the grass. "Kate can handle her uncle. I don't think he's in the area anyway. All of the wardens have been on high alert looking for him, and we haven't seen any evidence that he's here."

"But until he's captured he's still a threat. And would Kate help him if he showed up at her door? He's her family. I can't see her turning him away."

"Kate has a strong streak of justice. I think she'd call me the second she could. Trust her a little. She's a good person and has a big heart. She will take good care of those girls."

Drake held Kevin's gaze. "Are you just defending her because she needs the money?"

"Nope. Her uncle isn't stupid. He knows everyone here is looking for him and would turn him in right away. If you let her go because of something she can't help, you'll just be compounding it."

Drake watched Kevin slide under the wheel and put the key in the ignition. "Thanks for your honesty. I'll hold off for now. Maybe you'll be able to track down her uncle before too long." He put his hand on the truck's roof. "I've got a chance to sell some of my drones to the Fish and Wildlife Service. They intend to use them to track poachers and to map inaccessible areas."

Kevin's eyes widened. "I wouldn't have thought of that. Guess that's why I'm not a director. Is it a good order?"

"Yeah, I'll have to hire some new workers to fulfill it. They want me to make some modifications so the drones can deliver supplies to remote areas."

"There's been a time or two I would have appreciated that."

"I need to get home, make the alterations, and see if I can wrap up the deal."

"I'll put in a good word for you. I think it sounds like a great idea."

Drake removed his hand from the truck. The tires crunched on gravel and pulled out onto the road. He still had to figure out what to do about the revelation that Melissa was involved with Wang.

The recent rain had left the woods smelling of pine and fresh mud, an appealing scent after the dry days of the past week.

He'd parked his truck well out of sight on a fire-access road, then hiked in the rest of the way through the blueberry barrens. He wore Wellington boots and a rain slicker in case the storm struck before he got out of here.

Mud squished up the sides of his boots as he made his way through the trees. Ever since Claire's wedding, he'd haunted Kate's vicinity. Claire had been gone a week now and was due back soon. He might not have as much opportunity to observe Kate with her sister back, but he could watch them both. Not a bad night's work.

He'd driven slowly past the houses on the way here and had seen the cozy scene of Kate getting the girls into her car while Newham waved at them. The domesticity of it turned his stomach, but he was sure the man meant nothing to her. He was just her boss, and there had been no sign of anything more over this past week.

Where was she going with the girls at nearly dinnertime? To the library or maybe a movie? If she knew and understood his devotion, she would have invited him to join them.

He shook off the thought and ducked under the low-hanging pine branch in his way. His haven was just ahead through the thick copse of trees. He skirted a big puddle, then stepped into the clearing by the small lake. The sound of the waterfall was loud after the rain, and he stood a moment and watched the water glisten in the moonlight.

A rock face rose twenty feet in the air on the other side of the lake, and the water poured over it into the pool below. Access was behind the waterfall. He knew of a way to get there without getting wet, but it was a tortuous climb along slippery rocks. He had no choice though if he wanted to get his trophies.

He circled the lake and began to climb the slick stones. Four feet from the ground his foot found the three-inch ledge that would take him horizontally along the rocks where he could slip behind the falls. He was panting and perspiration slicked his skin by the time he felt the cold spray of the waterfall. Then he was behind the water and in total darkness.

He reached for the flashlight hanging on his belt and shone it around. This entry to the cave was always the hardest. The opening was small, nearly too small for him, but so far he'd still been able to wriggle through. He dropped onto his hands and knees, then onto his belly, and crawled through the opening. The place always felt so welcoming. The dank smell was something that reminded him he was completely alone.

He paused when a spider raced for his left hand. He let it crawl on him a moment, then smiled as he brought his right hand down on it. He relished the way it squashed under him. That's what he was going to do to everyone who got in his way. He was too close to his goal to turn back now.

He trained his flashlight against the left wall. The rock ended and jutted back into a small pocket. It was the perfect spot for his treasure. He reached in and his fingers closed around his precious pouch. He pulled it out and put it in the pocket of his slicker.

A sound broke the silence. Someone was outside. How could it be? A flashlight beam pierced the darkness at the mouth of the cave, and he looked around for a place to hide. The cave widened near the back and split in two different directions.

He crab-crawled to the left corridor and pressed himself against the wall, then flipped off his flashlight. His pulse pounded in his ears, and he touched the reassuring hilt of his hunting knife. He would dispatch whoever got close.

The cold spray from the waterfall hit Kate's face, and its roar filled her ears. She maneuvered the kayak as close to the rocks as she could until she saw the small space between the water and the rocks behind it. Holding her breath, she paddled for that opening, but the water drenched her as she entered the falls. In the next instant she was free of the cold flow. It was totally dark back here, so she groped for the flashlight and flipped it on.

*There.* The maw of the cave was small, and she wasn't sure she would fit. Her sweep of the flashlight revealed tree roots hanging into the space. Kate tried not to look too closely in case she saw spiders and centipedes. She nearly reached for the paddle again to leave, but remembering her uncle's threat against Claire and Luke made her pause. She gritted her teeth and turned back to the cave. The light poked into the recesses, but she didn't see what she was supposed to retrieve.

She had to do this, but she didn't like it. She'd call Kevin the second her uncle left, and the place would be swarming with deputies and game wardens. She bit her lip hard and got out of the kayak onto the rock ledge, then dropped to her knees. She still couldn't fit into the opening, so she lay on her stomach and began to pull herself forward with her arms.

The dank smell of dirt and creepy-crawly things assaulted

her nose, and she nearly backed out again. The light wavered as she pushed the flashlight ahead of her, then moved along the ground to reach it. Her bare feet were fully inside the cave now, so she paused and trained the glow on the right side of the space. Something glinted and her pulse kicked. She'd grab that bag and get out of here.

Her fingers tugged at the bag, and a big wolf spider raced out from under it. She shrieked loud enough to wake the dead and smashed it with a nearby rock. Her hand shook as she yanked the baggie free. It was stuffed with hundred-dollar bills, and she caught a glimpse of a blue passport. This was what he wanted. How did she get back out without tearing the plastic up on the rocks? She shook the baggie to make sure no spiders clung to it, then stuffed it in the back of her tucked-in pajama shirt.

Her breath sounded harsh, and she felt some evil presence in the cave that made her shiver. It was just nerves. She made an effort to slow her breathing. *In and out.* She'd get out of here and forget this night.

Some small scuttling noise from the left came to her ears, and she shuddered as she imagined what might be in here. A sense of evil came in a wave again, and she backpedaled out of the cave. The cool night air brushed across her ankles. Moments later she drew in the sweetest breath she'd ever known. She quickly boarded the kayak and paddled for all she was worth through the waterfall and out onto the clear surface of the lake. After the darkness behind the waterfall, the moonlight was nearly as bright as the light of day.

She reached the shore, and her uncle yanked her out of the kayak. "Hand it over. Where is it?"

She dropped the flashlight. "I've got it." She reached behind her back and pulled out the baggie. Before he could grab it, she heaved it to his left, then turned and ran.

She leaped past him and into the blackness of the forest. He knew this area better than she did, so there was no place to hide. Her best chance was to get to the cottage across the road. He'd think she was heading for her house, but she needed help. Drake could call the sheriff and Kevin.

His feet pounded behind her, and his voice rang through the trees. "Kate, come back here! I'm not going to hurt you."

She didn't believe him for a moment. If he didn't intend to harm her, why was he chasing her instead of just slipping off to safety? She darted to the right and entered a copse of evergreens that muffled her passage. She paused and heard his steps go the other way.

He intended to leave no witnesses.

Her throat thickened, but she *would not* cry. Though he was her uncle, he didn't love her. His past actions should have made that clear. She'd just been fooling herself to believe he wouldn't hurt her.

She crept out the other side of the evergreens and ran for the road. On the other side was a line of trees she could escape into as long as he didn't see her running through the fields. She stopped at the beginning of the field and listened. To her right she saw a glimmer as a flashlight swept the blueberry plants. He must think she was lying flat in the plants. She darted across the field, but he must have seen her because he called her name.

Drake's cottage wasn't far, and she screamed his name at the top of her lungs. He would be in bed and unlikely to hear her. She should have just run to her house or stayed hidden until day-light. But moments later the front porch light came on and his wide shoulders filled the doorway. She glanced behind her and saw her uncle's back vanish into the trees.

Her knees buckled as Drake ran toward her. Her bet had paid off, but it was a close call.

# SEVENTEEN

Drake had gone over and over the papers, though he should have been in bed hours ago. He yawned and rubbed his eyes. He glanced at his watch. Nearly 2:00 a.m. Time to make himself go to bed, but he took one more look at what the Fish and Wildlife Department wanted him to do with the new drone. The modifications were a little complicated. He reached for a paper and started to sketch it out, but there was no joy in the activity that energized him most, so he rose to go to bed.

He turned out the light and started for the hall when he heard something. It almost sounded like someone shouting his name. He went to the window and peered through the darkness to see Kate running toward the cottage in the moonlight.

His pulse kicked, and he flipped open the dead bolt on the door and ran outside. He leaped down the steps and headed toward her, then put on a burst of speed as she stumbled and her knees began to buckle. "Kate!" He caught her up against his chest before she hit the ground.

She felt nearly limp in his arms, and he eased her to the damp grass. Her face was white, but her eyes were open and staring. "Are you hurt? You're soaking wet." He thought about yanking off his shirt, but it was a thin T-shirt and wouldn't do much good.

"No, no, I'm okay." She inhaled and swallowed. "M-my uncle. He was waiting outside for me." She started to get up, then sank back onto the blueberry field. "You have to call the sheriff before he gets away."

Kevin had been right—she was turning him in as soon as she saw him. Drake brushed dirt from her face, then realized she was covered in it. "Did he throw you down in the mud?"

She shuddered and shook her head. "Let's get inside in case he comes back. We have to call for help. He'll get away."

He pulled out his phone and called 911 to report it, then helped her up. "The sheriff is on his way."

She limped a little as he assisted her toward the cottage. She kept glancing back as if she expected her uncle to break out of the trees at any minute and shoot them down. The way she trembled made him hurry toward the house. The guy could be circling around to the back, and Drake wanted to make sure the girls were all right. He got her up the steps and into the house.

As soon as she crossed the threshold, Kate threw the dead bolt. "Make sure the back door is locked."

"It is. I locked it a little while ago. Let's get you warm and dry." He grabbed a throw from the back of the sofa and draped it around her. She looked like she'd been swimming in her clothes.

"Thanks." She clutched it around her.

He told her about the raccoon incident earlier in the evening. "I saw your light was on awfully late, but I didn't see you outside. What's happened? I can see you're upset."

"I couldn't sleep and warmed some milk that I took to the back porch. Uncle Paul grabbed me and made me go to the woods with him."

"Come in the kitchen, and I'll make you some toast and coffee."

She limped as she trailed after him to the small kitchen. "I'm filthy from the cave."

He paused with the coffee tin in his hands. "What cave?"

"My uncle had a fake passport and money stashed in a cave in the woods. It was too small of a space for him to get into, so he made me retrieve it. He said if I tried to run he'd torch Claire's house with Luke and her in it." She sank onto a chair at the table. "Could I have a wet paper towel?"

His mind raced as he wet a piece of paper towel. "If he wanted his passport and money, he's likely heading out of the country." He handed it to her and went back to making coffee.

She wiped the mud from her arms, then bent over to clean her feet. "No telling what path though or what name he's using. I didn't get a chance to look at the passport. As soon as I got out of the cave, I ran. I was pretty sure he'd kill me and stuff me back in that cave if I didn't get away."

He turned as her face crumpled and tears tracked down her muddy face. "I'm sorry, Kate. That must hurt since he's family. Maybe he wouldn't have hurt you."

She shook her head and mopped at her face, then grimaced when she saw the mud on the paper towel. "You didn't see his face. There was no love there, probably because I helped track him down when he took Claire."

He tore off another piece of paper towel and wet it. "Let me." He knelt in front of her and wiped the dirt from her face. This close to her, he could see a small dusting of freckles she must usually keep covered with makeup. She was even more beautiful up close. He finished the job and quickly stepped away.

"Thanks." She tucked her hair behind her ears. "I must look awful."

He wasn't about to tell her what he really thought. Backing away, he turned to pop bread into the toaster. The coffee aroma began to fill the room. "Coffee's almost done."

"I need it. I'll never sleep anyway."

"It's only two. You should try to get some rest. You can have my bed and I'll take the sofa."

She grinned. "Once Sheriff Colton gets here, he'll have me traipsing all over the crime scene while he takes notes. There will be no sleep for hours." She yawned. "But I'll still watch the girls. They will help keep my mind off it."

He shook his head. "I'll take them to my aunt tomorrow. You'll probably need to go to the sheriff's office and fill out a statement." He poured them both a cup of coffee and handed one to her. The toaster popped. "Butter, peanut butter, or jelly? Maybe all three?"

"Just butter."

Conscious of her gaze on him, he slathered the toast with butter and put it on a plate. "Here you go."

Her fingers closed around the plate. "Thanks." She continued to look up at him. "You saved my life, Drake. If you hadn't come out when you did, he would have caught me. He ran when he saw you were up. Why weren't you in bed?"

He turned to grab his coffee, then joined her at the table. "Just mulling over my brother's death and who is behind it. I have a lot of work ahead of me to figure this out."

"I'll help in any way I can."

"You have enough to worry about with your own situation." Maybe he should let her go. He could concentrate on Heath's death without getting pulled into her problems.

But the thought of seeing disappointment in those beautiful eyes made him hold his tongue.

The intruder, likely female from the scream, was finally gone. He released the handle of his knife and flipped on his flashlight as soon as the sound of the paddle faded. Leaving his hidey-hole, he crawled around the corner. The cave was empty and he exhaled. Relief nearly left him light-headed. For a moment his chest tightened as he considered the idea that he'd been followed. But surely not. It had been dark, and no one knew about this place.

At least not many could know. He crawled to the exit, then stepped out onto the ledge and made his way out from under the waterfall. A flashlight beam bobbed on the shore, and he heard a man calling a woman's name. His eyes widened.

Kate. Had *his* Kate been in here? Surely he would have sensed her presence.

He squinted in the moonlight and let his gaze sweep the shore as he clung to the rocks. A movement under a fir tree caught his attention, and he saw Kate's pale face.

She had been the one in the cave. Did she follow him? Maybe she wanted to be with him. But no. That man was chasing her. The tone of his angry voice made it clear he'd forced her. He clenched his fists and narrowed his eyes. Paul Mason was supposed to be in prison. He had no business out here terrorizing Kate.

He moved faster than ever before on the slippery ledge until he was standing on the wet grass beside the lake. Paul had to be stopped. He had time to take care of business though. No one suspected him, and he was too smart for them anyway. They'd never know what he'd done. He hurried through the barrens toward where he'd parked his truck.

Once he was safely in his vehicle, he pulled onto the road with the lights off. Newham's lights were on as the truck rolled past. Newham leaned over Kate, who sat at the kitchen table. Heat shot up his face, and he clenched the steering wheel. That man needed to be gone. This wasn't his place, and Kate wasn't his girl.

Something had to be done about Newham.

He drove to his house and parked in the drive. As he got out he stuck his hand in his Windbreaker for the pouch. His eyes widened when he felt only lint. Maybe it had fallen out in the truck. The dome light illuminated the truck's interior, but no matter how hard he looked, he found only an empty gum wrapper and a partially eaten bag of peanut M&M's. His gut clenched as he mentally retraced his steps.

It had to have fallen out on the way to his truck. He'd go back at first light and see if he could find it. It wouldn't do for anyone else to see his treasures.

# EIGHTEEN

Birds chirping in the trees beside the house added to Claire's sense of contentment. She put the key in the lock and smiled up at Luke. "Home sweet home, husband of mine." She pushed open the door and started to enter, but Luke scooped her up in his arms before she could react.

"Not so fast. My beautiful bride needs to be carried over the threshold." He smiled down at her.

She clasped her hands around his neck. "You already did this at the condo in Hawaii." Seven luxurious days enjoying the sun and life with Luke. It couldn't have been a more perfect honeymoon.

"The condo is not home." He pushed the door open a little farther with his foot, then carried her into the foyer.

His lips came down on hers in a sweet promise of forever. Her eyes fluttered shut, and she clung to him and kissed him back. How was it possible life was this wonderful after such a hard year?

She opened her eyes when he pulled away. "Put me down and I'll fix coffee. I missed our Captain Davy's Coffee Roaster coffee."

"Me too." He gently set her on her feet and steadied her. "How about steaks for dinner? I'll get some out and grill them."

"I like this married thing better and better." She cupped his cheek, then headed for the kitchen where she ground fresh beans and put the coffee on to brew in their brand-new Cuisinart, a gift from Kate.

"I'm dying to see Kate," she called to Luke, who was rummaging through the freezer in the utility room. Her smile died as he came through the door frowning. "What's wrong?"

"Someone stole everything in the freezer."

"You're kidding! We had half a cow in there." She followed him back to the utility room and peered into the big chest freezer. Nothing was inside but two freezer packs. Every package of beef, pork, and chicken was gone. She whirled around. "Let's check the house."

The back door was unlocked. She and Luke traipsed through the entire house peering in closets and checking possessions. When they came to the spare room where they'd left quite a few unopened packages, she had a sinking feeling in the pit of her stomach. When Luke pushed open the door, her fears were confirmed. Wrapping paper lay strewn around like a frenzied whirlwind had blown through the window.

She felt a breeze, too, and pointed out the open window to Luke. "He got in that way."

"And went out the back door with our things." Luke pressed his lips in a grim line. "I'll call Danny." He exited the room to get his cell phone.

Claire's eyes burned as she stared at the devastation. There was no way to even tell insurance what had been lost until she contacted all the wedding guests and found what they'd given. She stooped over and searched for discarded cards. A particularly large pile of paper lay crumpled on the guest bed. As she moved it out of the way, her hand touched something hard, and she instinctively snatched it back. Thrusting the paper out of the way, she uncovered the box that had once held the new Cuisinart coffeemaker down in the kitchen. When she lifted the box, it rattled. She frowned and opened the top to peer inside.

A crossbow bolt lay inside with a note. She started to reach for it, then snatched her hand back. "Luke!"

He was still on the phone with the sheriff, and his voice got louder as he ascended the stairs. He ended the call as he reached the doorway to the bedroom. "What's wrong? Are you all right?"

Her throat was too tight to speak, so she pointed to the box. He frowned and came closer to the bed. "What is it?"

She swallowed and found her voice. "Look inside."

He went to the side of the bed and looked into the box. "Paul." He spat the word out as if it tasted bad.

"There's a note, but we shouldn't touch this until Danny has a look at everything. He might have left a fingerprint." Her hand shook as she tucked a lock of hair behind her ear. "I don't understand why he hates me so much. I never did anything to him. I was a little girl when all this happened. He brought on his own punishment."

"I think he feels you took Kate away from him and his sister." Luke approached her and pulled her against his chest. "The sheriff will catch him. I don't think we should stay here right now. The place will be crawling with deputies. Let's go to the Tourmaline for the night. We can eat dinner there, too, and try to forget this mess."

"I don't think I'll forget it." She didn't feel safe here right now, so a bit of the darkness lifted as Luke turned her toward the door. "At least our things are all packed. I'll have to call Kate and let her know where we are."

"I wonder if she's seen Paul."

"I don't think Paul would hurt her."

"I'm not so sure." He took her hand, and they went down the steps to the door. "I'll call Danny and tell him we're leaving for now. We weren't here for any of this, so he shouldn't need us."

At the door she rotated for one final look at her beautiful home. All remodeled and perfect, yet she didn't get even one night to enjoy being Mrs. Luke Rocco in it. Her eyes burned as she turned her back and went with Luke to their SUV.

The sheriff's office buzzed with activity. Kate stood out of the way in a corner of the waiting room until Danny called her back to issue a statement. She'd been here since ten and it was already eleven. She had no idea where the sheriff was. Her eyes were dry and bleary from lack of sleep, and every muscle ached from the events of the night. All she wanted to do was get this over with and go home to relax in a hot bath. Drake had been right about her being unable to work today, but he'd been a rock for her, even taking Jackson so she didn't have to worry about the pup.

Through the big pane window, she saw Luke and Claire approaching. Claire was pale and her mouth was set. Maybe they'd heard about Paul showing up. Kate leaped for the door and met them outside the jail.

She reached for her twin sister, and Claire hugged her hard. "I'm fine, but they didn't find Paul."

Claire released her. "Paul went to your house?"

Kate frowned. "Isn't that why you're here?"

Tears flooded Claire's eyes.

"Tell me what's happened."

Luke wore a thunderous frown. "Paul broke into the house and stole everything from the freezer as well as all our wedding gifts."

Kate gasped and took a step back. "Are you sure it was Paul?" She shook her head. "Never mind, of course it was Paul. Even with all he's done, I still can't seem to see him as he really is." She told them about her confrontation with him.

Claire's blue eyes sparked, and she pressed her lips together. "What is *wrong* with that man! Why can't he leave us alone? His actions have harmed all of us so much. Hasn't he done enough?"

"I didn't realize he was so vindictive. I'm sorry."

"It's not your fault. He's my uncle, too, but neither one of us can take on any guilt because of his actions."

"No, of course not." But Claire hadn't grown up with him. She hadn't gone fishing with him like Kate had. She'd seen her uncle nearly every day of her life until he'd been arrested. Shouldn't she have been repelled by the evil in him all along? If she'd seen his true nature, maybe none of this would have happened.

Kate rubbed her forehead where pain pulsed. "Does the sheriff need to talk to you too?"

Luke nodded and pulled open the glass door. "We want to know what the note said. He left a note with a crossbow bolt in the empty Cuisinart box. We didn't touch it because we didn't want to mess up evidence. Danny should have looked it over by now."

Kate thought it through and couldn't make sense of it. "Isn't it a little weird that he would steal a freezer full of food when he's on foot and trying to escape?"

"Maybe he's not on foot," Luke said. "He could have a vehicle stashed somewhere for all we know."

Kate followed Claire into the waiting room in time to see Jonas emerge from the hallway and beckon to her.

He waited for them to join him. "You all might as well come back together. The sheriff wants to talk to you. No telling how all of this might fit together."

Kate frowned at the frustration in his voice as the three of them fell into line behind him and went to the sheriff's office. "I assume you haven't found Uncle Paul?"

Danny looked tired and had circles under his eyes. He gestured to some chairs and shut the door. "Nope. Saw that hole he made you go in though. And I called in an expert tracker to see what he could find. So far we've got diddly-squat. Paul hardly left a leaf out of place."

Jonas perched on a corner of the desk. "I've gone hunting with him a time or two over the years, and I've never figured out how he does it. The guy's a phantom."

The sheriff nodded. "I called in a dog SAR team, but they lost his scent at the road. I think maybe he's not on foot."

"And he's probably long gone." Kate waited for her sister to take a seat, then moved to the one on her left.

Danny lowered his tall form into his chair, then took an Altoids tin out of his pocket and shook a mint into his hand. "Every entry is posted."

Luke shook his head. "He wouldn't need a formal road to

get in. He could drive to an entry point, then slip in through the woods."

Danny popped the mint into his mouth and glanced at Claire. "I'm afraid he might not be done with Claire here. He seems to hold a mighty big grudge."

Kate's chest squeezed at Claire's deer-in-the-headlights expression. She sat on the edge of the chair next to Claire's. "Why are you saying that? Maybe he just took the food and gifts to scare her. There's no reason to think he'll hurt her."

But she hadn't told them what he said about burning down Claire's house with her in it. She opened her mouth to tell Danny, but he turned his computer screen around to face them.

"Here's a scanned copy of that note." His voice was grim.

The handwriting wasn't familiar. This note was a scrawl that she had to squint to make out. *Practice makes perfect, and I have all the time in the world.* Kate frowned and glanced at her sister. "What does that mean?"

Claire shook her head. "I have no idea."

Danny popped another mint. "Recognize your uncle's handwriting, Kate?"

"I've never seen him write in cursive. I'm sure he has, but I've never seen it. Can you get a copy of his signature on a legal document or something? It might be his handwriting, but I just don't know."

Danny turned the monitor back around to face him. "I'll see what I can find out. I was sure you'd recognize Paul's handwriting."

Luke leaned forward. "It has to be Paul though, doesn't it? I mean, with the crossbow bolt and all."

"You know as well as I do that there are too many bow hunters up here to count. Paul seemed the likely culprit, but since Kate doesn't recognize the handwriting, I don't think we can rule out anything. I'll keep digging."

Kate glanced at her sister. It had to be Paul, didn't it? The thought of some unknown man targeting Claire seemed even more ominous.

Jonas walked them to the door, then put his hand on Kate's arm. "You doing okay? You're a little green."

"Just a little shook up. Thanks for all you're doing to help."

"It's what friends are for. I've got a little time. Want to grab some lunch with me?"

She smiled up at him. "It's sweet of you to try to cheer me up, but I need to get back to watch the girls. Thanks, Jonas. You're a good friend."

She followed Claire out into the sunshine. "What a homecoming for you."

Claire had regained a bit of her color, and she smiled. "We got a great discount at the Tourmaline, so we're just extending our honeymoon a couple more days." She hugged Kate. "You be careful."

"You're the one who needs to be careful." Anxiety gnawed at Kate as she watched her sister get into the truck with Luke. Uncle Paul's hatred of Claire seemed to have no bounds.

# NINETEEN

The girls hadn't stopped talking about their day with Aunt Dixie until they were tucked into bed at eight. As Drake prayed with them before bed, he glanced up to see Kate in the doorway. She must have come in to get Jackson. She turned away but not before he caught sight of the tears on her cheeks. What was that about? He focused his attention back on the girls, then kissed them and turned out the light.

He found her in the living room petting the dog.

"Good boy." She rubbed his head, then looked up at Drake. She moved over so he could sit beside her. The dog lay down at her feet. "Are the girls all right?"

He went back to his seat on the sofa. "They had a great time at Dixie's. She took them to an old swimming hole and let them swim and fish. They're in bed." Her face was still a little tear-stained. "Are you okay?"

Her eyes watered again, but she smiled and nodded. "It was precious seeing you pray with the girls. Like something from a Norman Rockwell painting."

His face grew warm, and he looked away. "Your mom and uncle never prayed with you?"

"They never even went to church with me. I don't know

what they think about God. Did Heath and Melissa teach the girls too?"

"Yeah. Heath was two when his dad died, and then Mom married Dad two years later. I came along ten months after that."

"That's why your last names are different."

The memories flashed through his mind like reels of an old movie. His parents had taught them well.

"Are they still alive?"

He nodded. "They live in Costa Rica, and I don't get to see them very often." He glanced at her and saw her tears had dried up.

"I can be back to work tomorrow. Is that okay?" She clasped her hands together on her jean-clad lap. "I mean, you're not going to fire me, are you? I wouldn't blame you if you did. My family is a train wreck."

How did he answer that when he'd been trying to make up his mind all day? Looking at her anxious face, he knew he couldn't do it though. "The job is still yours."

Her eyes lit. "Thank you, Drake. You won't be sorry. I'll be ultra careful with them."

"I know you will." But what could she do if her uncle suddenly showed up? Maybe he should get her some bear spray like Kevin mentioned. "Do you carry bear spray?"

A smile tugged at her lips and she leaned over to dig in her purse before holding up a can of spray in a triumphant gesture. "Any good Mainer carries bear spray. You never know when you're going to need it. You've seen bears around?"

He shook his head. "Kevin mentioned they like the berries this time of year, so I was a little worried about the girls."

"I don't have that many berries, so I'm not sure my fields

will be much of a draw. But I'll be watching for them." Her gaze landed on the computer.

He went to the kitchen to get on the Internet. It was unlikely he'd find clues to Melissa's affair with Wang online, but he wanted to see if there were any pictures of the two of them floating around. She and Heath had gone to many fund-raisers, and Wang was known to try to launder his money that way.

He scrolled through page after page, then finally paused over a familiar face at an event to raise money for Melissa's favorite project, one for battered women. Melissa wore a black cocktail dress that showed off her model figure. Just off to the right stood a figure only partly in the frame. Though he had his head turned a bit, Drake knew it was Wang. The tenseness in the man's shoulders and head told of his interest in Melissa. And standing by the serving table about ten feet or so behind Melissa stood his brother. Heath wasn't smiling and seemed to be staring at Melissa and Wang.

Was this when Heath first became suspicious of his wife? Drake checked the date of the event. March 15, two weeks before the e-mail transcript began. Bingo.

"Research into your brother's death?"

"Yeah." He showed her the picture.

Kate studied it. "Your brother looks a little angry."

"Yeah, he probably didn't like the predatory look on Wang's face."

"How are you going to find out what was going on between them?"

He shut his computer. "I think I'll have to call a lot of hotels and restaurants and see if anyone will talk. Wang is known to frequent sushi places and high-end hotels. If I could just get enough evidence for probable cause, I'd ask the sheriff to sub-poena his credit card statements. And once the employee knows I'm investigating Wang, I probably won't find out much. People are scared of him."

She chewed on her lower lip, her blue eyes hazy with intense thought. The way her dark-blonde hair fell against her cheeks and neck as she sat there made him want to lean over and tuck it behind her ears. He wanted to get to know what she thought and felt, but it would all have to wait until he found justice for Heath.

She sat up straighter. "I have an idea. What if we look at those text messages and pick out some prime times when she was likely meeting Wang? I can pretend to be his accountant who is upset about some charges on that date. Maybe we can use the fear he generates to get answers."

He looked at her with new respect. "That's a terrific idea. A woman isn't as threatening as a man, and you can say the charges are too high for a man by himself. The employee might look at the records and report how many were eating, that kind of thing."

"And I can ask for verification on the identity because Wang is being audited." A triumphant smile lifted her lips. "I think it will work."

"Me too." He got up and held out his hand to her. "This calls for a celebratory cup of hot chocolate." She put her hand in his, and he lifted her to her feet. Her soft skin made him want to pull her closer, but he forced himself to step back. "I might even con-sent to a chick flick over popcorn. I've got Netflix."

"I vote for *Sleepless in Seattle.*"

"I was thinking more like *The Princess Bride* where at least we have some swashbuckling adventure."

The eye roll she sent his way lifted his spirits. "You can't tell me you don't like *The Princess Bride.*"

"I've only seen it about fifty times."

He took her arm. "Let's make it fifty-one."

The dog huffed as if he couldn't believe it either.

The girls squealed as they ran along the creek on her property looking for minnows, with Jackson on their heels. Kate smiled as she walked behind them. The last couple of days had gone very well between Drake and her. He finally seemed to be relaxing with her in charge of the girls. The sun blazed out of a blue sky, and the heat felt good on her face and bare arms.

Someone called her name and she turned to see Becky Oates walking across the blueberry fields toward her. A small white car was parked along the side of the road. Jackson stiffened, and a low growl rumbled from his throat.

Kate put her hand on his head. "It's okay, boy." She motioned for the girls. "Stay right here. Don't go any farther along the creek without me. Take the dog." The girls called for Jackson, but he whined plaintively before he obeyed.

Becky was huffing a bit by the time she reached Kate's side. "I was on my way to your house and saw you out here." Her purple-tipped hair was more garish in the sunlight than it had seemed in the dimly lit bar. She wore jeans so weathered they were nearly white and an orange shirt that clashed with her hair.

Kate didn't know what to make of the woman's friendly

manner. She was even smiling. "Um, okay. You probably heard I've seen Uncle Paul."

Becky nodded and tucked a lock of hair behind her ear, studded with three diamonds. "Listen, I want to apologize for how I acted the other day. I was a little stressed by everything. The sheriff had been on my case about that Peece woman, too, and I was in no mood for another interrogation."

"Apology accepted." Kate eyed her warily. "Is there something I can do for you?"

Becky's smile looked forced. "D-did Paul mention me at all? Hand you anything to give to me maybe?"

"He admitted you were the old girlfriend who had stashed the money and fake passport for him."

Becky wet her lips. "Did you tell the sheriff I was involved?"

Kate turned to check on the girls. They were picking up rocks and putting them in the pockets of their shorts. "No, it didn't seem important at the time. Should I have?"

"When I put that stuff in there for Paul, I didn't know it was a fake passport. I thought he was just stashing his valuables where they couldn't be found, kind of an unusual lockbox. And it was ages ago, a good year before he was arrested."

Kate didn't believe the woman's saccharine smile for a second. "I didn't look at the passport either, but I'm sure it was in another name. You haven't seen him or talked to him? Be honest with me. I didn't turn you in to the sheriff."

Becky hesitated. "Well, I did see him for a few minutes the other night. He showed up with some presents for me in a little trailer he was pulling behind his four-wheeler."

Kate straightened and took her hands out of her pockets. "Presents? What kind of presents?"

Becky shrugged. "Frozen meat, for one thing. And a bunch of random stuff like blankets and kitchen appliances."

Kate gaped at her. "He *did* steal the things from Claire's!"

"I don't get it. What things?"

Maybe the town gossips hadn't passed that bit of news around. "Never mind. I thought it probably was Uncle Paul, but we had no proof. Did he leave the area?"

A worried frown crouched between Becky's eyes. "I don't think so. He talked like he'd raid my freezer for meat when he needed it. He headed west through the woods."

"Did you tell the sheriff any of this?"

Becky shook her head emphatically. "I didn't want him to arrest me for aiding a felon. Until Paul showed up with that stuff, I hadn't seen him. And I was none too happy to see him then. I'm dating someone else, and I don't want to do anything to mess that up."

"Does Paul know?"

Becky hesitated, then shrugged. "He seemed different—harder and a little scary. So no, I didn't say anything. I just wanted him to leave, so I told him I had to get to work. He dumped the bags of meat in my freezer and left the boxes of stuff in the living room. What should I do with all of it?"

"Call the sheriff. He'll check it out and maybe Claire can get her belongings back."

Becky bit her lip. "Just what I didn't want to do."

"You don't have a choice. It will look better coming from you than from me." Kate heard the girls squeal. Phoebe was splashing water at her big sister. "Do you think he'll go after Claire again?"

"He seemed pretty mad when he was talking about justice. I

felt like I didn't really know him anymore. It's hard telling what he might do." Becky glanced at her phone. "I've got to get to work. I'll call the sheriff on my way there. I sure hope he's not ticked off."

"He'll be glad you're reporting it now." Kate watched her retreat to her car.

One of the girls screamed, and Kate looked to where Emma was pointing. A small black bear nosed through the blueberries, but he was a good football field away from them. "He's not going to hurt us. He's more afraid of you than you are of him. See, he's running off now." She corralled the girls and her dog, then headed for home. She had a feeling they hadn't seen the last of her uncle.

# TWENTY

T he sky was a picture-worthy sight of golds and purples as the sun sank into the horizon. The crimson leaves of the blueberries added to the beauty, and he wished Kate were there to share it with. Shaking himself from his thoughts, he looked through the plants again.

*It has to be here somewhere.* He'd been over every inch of his path from the cave to where he'd parked his truck, but his precious trophy pouch was nowhere to be found. He'd spent an hour out here at sunrise, then another hour after he'd seen Kate take the girls to the creek, but he had only blue-stained shoes to show for his efforts.

Could someone have found it? He didn't think anyone would be out here except Kate. Could it be in her house? He stared down the road. The lights were on in the cottage, so she was probably making dinner for those brats and Drake. He allowed his gaze to linger on her back door, and he set out for her house.

He'd just disarmed her security system when he saw the truck lights moving down the road. Though it was unlikely Drake could see him on the back deck, he twisted the doorknob and slipped into Kate's kitchen. It felt like home to him, and he smiled before moving around the small rooms in search of his pouch. The place was immaculate with nothing on any of the tables in the living room. He continued to the bedroom and found no sign of his trophies there either.

He retraced his steps and had just reached the kitchen when he heard footsteps on the back deck and saw Kate's form through the open window. The door to the basement was behind him, so he yanked it open and rushed into the darkness. The musty scent of the space enveloped him, and he waited for his eyes to adjust to the dim light from the basement window. Old wooden shelves containing home-canned goods lined one wall, and a rusty, dented freezer occupied part of another wall. More shelves held old paint cans and cleaning supplies.

The door at the top of the stairs creaked, and the overhead light came on. Footsteps started down the steps, and his pulse pounded in his ears as he looked around for a place to hide. *There, under the worktable.* He shoved aside the old plastic tablecloth covering it, then scrabbled under the table and pulled the plastic back into place. There was a small gap he could see through, but he doubted she'd be able to see him.

Her shapely tanned legs paraded past his vision and kept him riveted. She walked past his hiding spot to the shelves full of canned food, then put some of the jars in the box she carried. Green beans and sauerkraut. She turned toward the table, and he held his breath as she approached.

His hand went to the gun holstered at his side. He didn't want to reveal himself to her in these circumstances, but the place he'd prepared for her was ready if he had to.

She moved past him to the refrigerator and put several bags of frozen corn and peas into her box. His knees cramped and he shuffled them. Her head came up at the small sound, and she looked around.

Her blue eyes were wide, and she clutched the box to her chest. "Hello?" The word came out a bit strangled. "Uncle Paul?"

She was so close he could reach out and grab that shapely thigh if he wanted. And he very much *did* want, but he curled his fingers into his palms to stop himself. Her breath came in short, quick spurts, and it made his own chest heave with excitement. She was so close. Would she greet him if he flung back the tablecloth? Couldn't she feel his love and devotion, the power of his desire for her? They could be so happy together. He pictured them cuddling on the sofa while they watched a movie and ate popcorn.

He licked his lips. Then she suddenly whirled and sprang toward the steps. Her feet pounded up the stairs, and there was a click that plunged the basement into darkness. He immediately crawled out from under the table and mounted the stairs as fast as he dared. One creaked a bit and he stopped and waited by the basement door. The back door slammed, and he heard her on the phone telling someone she'd been spooked by a noise in the basement.

Probably Claire. He would have to do something about that unhealthy dependence she had on her sister. All in good time though, all in good time.

Drake inserted Kate's key into the back door and unlocked it. "It pays to be careful." She hadn't wanted him to search the basement, but he'd taken one look at her white face and had insisted on checking it out. There had been too many things going on for him to be comfortable with ignoring it.

Kate pulled Emma and Phoebe against her sides as Drake opened the door. Jackson pressed against her leg and whined as if he sensed her turmoil. "Please don't tell Danny. He'll say I'm crying wolf again. I'm sure it was just a mouse or something."

Drake shoved open the door and stepped inside. His gaze went to the security system. "The alarm is disarmed. Did you forget to engage it when you left?" He turned back toward the door so he could see her.

She shook her head. "It must have already been disarmed when I came for the food. I forgot all about it." She glanced around. "I left the window in the kitchen open too. I have to quit doing that."

"You're sure you turned it on before you left this morning?"

She hugged the girls closer to her. "I-I'm not sure. This dratted chemo brain. Turning it on hasn't gotten into my muscle memory yet, so maybe I forgot to do it."

And maybe the guy had figured out how to disarm it already. "I'll check with the alarm company. They'll be able to see today's history."

Her eyes went wide. "Oh! I have an app on my phone that does that." She let go of Emma and dug in her monstrosity of a purse and pulled out her phone. She swiped it on, then scrolled through the icons. "Here it is." A few moments later she gasped. "I activated it at eight o'clock when I went to your cottage. It was deactivated a few minutes later and never turned back on."

"It's possible it was a glitch, but I don't like it." The girls both looked a little scared. Unfortunately, there'd been no option but to bring them down here. "Luke and Claire should be here any minute. I'll have Luke check out the house with me. You and Claire can take the girls back to the cottage." He went back out onto the deck with her.

She slipped her phone into her pocket, then slung her purse over her shoulder and clasped hands with the girls. "I think I'll take them back to the cottage now. I've got bear spray."

He started to protest, then heard tires crunch on the gravel driveway. Luke's big truck came into view, and Claire leaped out of it before it had stopped rolling. "Looks like the cavalry has arrived."

Claire's cheeks were pink, and her hair lay unbound on her shoulders as if she'd just taken it down. Tail wagging, Jackson went to greet her and she rubbed his head, but her frown stayed in place.

Before Claire could voice her concern, Kate held up her hand. "Don't freak out, Claire. It's probably nothing, and I'm wishing I didn't even call you guys or say anything. If this gets back to Danny, he's going to ignore me the next time I call."

Drake motioned to Luke as he got out of the truck. "It appears someone might have turned off the security system after she left the house this morning. It doesn't hurt to check it out. Better safe than sorry."

Kate motioned to Jackson, then took Claire and the girls down the road to the cottage. Drake nodded for Luke to follow him back into the house. "She heard something in the basement but convinced herself it was a mouse or a coon that had gotten in. I didn't want to scare her, but I'm concerned about the alarm being disabled. I told her maybe it was a glitch, but I really doubt that."

Luke still wore his Coast Guard uniform. "Claire did a lot of research before she bought the security system. This alarm was supposed to be the best out there. I doubt it would have that serious of a glitch." He went to the basement door and opened it.

"I wasn't sure where the basement was. Glad you know." Drake peered past Luke's shoulder when the man flipped on the light. "Not finished or anything."

"No, just an old country basement." The first step creaked under Luke's feet.

Drake followed him down and grimaced at the stench of dampness and old wood. He had to duck once he reached the dirt floor. "Close down here."

"Yeah, these old basements don't have much headroom." Luke peered through the murky light. "Did she say where the sound came from?"

"South side of the steps." Drake turned to face a decrepit wooden table under a dirty window. "Not much over here."

An old plastic tablecloth hung dispiritedly on the table, its red color faded to nearly pink. Several bottles of cleaning supplies sat atop it as well as a metal painting tray and several brushes. He moved each item to see if a mouse hid underneath, though he doubted a mouse could make enough noise to frighten Kate.

"Check under it," Luke suggested.

Drake pulled the tablecloth up and piled it on the table's surface, then went down on one knee and peered under it. His gaze landed on a scuffed-up area in the dirt. Was that the indentation of knees? "Take a look at this, Luke."

Luke knelt beside him and pointed. "Look there. That might be where his shoe dug into the ground. And this looks like knee prints." He pointed out the area Drake had noticed.

Drake rose and dusted his hands off on his shorts. "There's no way of knowing if someone was just down here and made those marks or if they've been here for a while, but the chances are good someone was in here."

Drake frowned as a piece of paper caught his eye by the stairs. In two steps he was in front of it and scooped it up. "It's a receipt for a soda at the minimart. And it's dated for last night. Kate doesn't drink soda." He waved the receipt. "I think this is our proof. We need to tell the sheriff about it."

"I can drop it off to Jonas on my way home."

Drake nodded and handed it over to Luke. "Let me know what you find out." He didn't like the idea of Kate staying here by herself, but he knew her well enough by now to realize she'd insist on staying in her home.

# TWENTY-ONE

The sound of the Disney movie in the living room filtered into the kitchen where the adults gathered around the kitchen table. Kate felt like an animal at the zoo as all eyes fastened on her. She focused on her sister's face. If anyone would be on her side, it would be Claire. Jackson licked her foot as if he wanted to comfort her.

"I've got bear spray," she began.

Luke folded his arms across his chest. "And what happens if he breaks in while you're sleeping?"

The realization that someone had been in the house had hit her hard, but she was getting her equilibrium back. "I can't live my life in fear. I did that when I had aplastic anemia, and I'm tired of it. We've changed the code on the security system. I'll lock my bedroom door too."

Claire sat twirling a lock of hair around her finger and biting her lip. Her gaze met Kate's. "Come home with us, Kate, please. I won't get a wink of sleep with you there by yourself."

*So much for support from Claire.* Kate rolled the idea around in her head. "Where does it all end, Claire? I can't keep running to you when every little thing goes wrong."

"A repeating intruder isn't every little thing." Claire's voice rose. "This guy is so bold. It's as if he has total confidence in not being caught. He was in your house in the daylight."

"But not while I was home. I came back and surprised him. And it could even be Uncle Paul. Has anyone thought of that?"

Luke's expression grew more alert, and he leaned forward at the end of the table. "What makes you think it could be Paul?"

Why did she have that initial sense of her uncle's presence? Then it came to her. "I smelled that same cologne, just a faint trace, in the kitchen before I went to the basement. I didn't consciously notice it, but that's why I called out his name when I heard the noise. We aren't sure he's left the area."

Drake rose and turned to the coffeepot where he prepared decaf. "And that's not any kind of reassurance, Kate. Your uncle has already proven he's dangerous."

Kate started to protest, then remembered how he'd terrified her. Every encounter seemed to indicate he held her in the same light as he did Claire—as an enemy. All her years of loving him had blinded her to his true nature, and she didn't know what it would take for her to get the old Uncle Paul out of her head.

She tipped up her chin. "If he'd wanted to hurt me, he would have grabbed me in the basement. I think he was looking for something."

Claire gave an impatient huff. "What?"

"Mom lived in that house for a long time, and he was there a lot. Sometimes he slept in that tiny bedroom in the back. Maybe he hid something inside it."

The scent of coffee filled the kitchen, and Drake took down some mugs. "He probably knows from your last contact with him that you wouldn't help him if he asked."

She rose to help him and took the cream from the refrigerator. "No, I wouldn't. I want him caught and back in jail."

Luke stood and went to peer out the back door window. "I thought I heard something."

Kate turned as a crash sounded outside. Over Luke's shoulder she saw a shaggy black form rear up by the trash can. "It's a bear!"

They all crowded to the door and looked out. A small black bear, probably the same one she'd seen earlier, smacked around the trash can by the small shed. Jackson went into a paroxysm of barking and lunged at the door. The bear lifted its head, then went back to hitting the trash can.

Drake's hand went to the doorknob. "How'd it get the can out of the shed? I threw the crossbar on the door."

"Bears are resourceful." Luke stopped him when he started to unlock the door. "Not a good idea, buddy. It might look small, but it's way stronger than we are. Leave it be, and we'll clean up after it wanders off."

Drake stepped back and frowned. "I don't like having a bear around. It's not safe for the girls to go out."

"I'm always with them, just like I was the first time we saw it. They usually run off when they see you. And Jackson would chase them off with his barking." Kate kept a strong, cheerful tone, but she didn't like it either. She could count on both hands the times she'd seen bears back here in her entire life. And this one looked scrawny and sick, not a good combination when in the presence of humans. When bears got desperate, they tended to be unpredictable.

A little like people, including her uncle Paul.

She left the door and went to pour coffee. "It's getting late, so you'd better drink your coffee and head for home."

"Trying to get rid of us?" Claire had a teasing lilt to her voice, but there was a somber note under it. "We haven't come to a decision about what to do."

"I have, but you aren't listening." Kate laughed to take the sting out of her statement. "I'm going to be fine."

Claire slipped her arm around Kate and hugged her. "Keep your phone by the bed, okay? And barricade your door with the dresser."

"That's a really good idea. I'll sleep better too." Kate hugged her sister back.

At least they were all letting it go. For a while she'd been sure they'd pressure her so much she'd have to give in.

Life settled into an even keel for a few days, though Kate's house felt like a jail cell. Claire had the locks and the alarm password changed once again. Though Kate knew it was important to keep things locked up, it still took a conscious effort to remember to switch it on and off. The installer had set it up so Drake would be called if a window broke or someone breached the door when it was locked. Several times Jackson had awakened her with soft growls, but each time, his dismay had been over an outside animal.

She was ready to think about something else rather than her rampaging uncle. Now that the weekend was over, she would start making some calls to the hotels in Boston to see what she could find out about Melissa and Wang. Kate was a little sorry she'd volunteered because the calls felt intrusive to the dead woman's privacy, but she settled on the sofa with Jackson beside her and began to make some calls. After five dead ends, she was ready to give up, but she had time for one more.

When the receptionist answered, Kate smiled so that good energy would go through the phone. "Good morning, this is Kate Mason, and I work for Mr. Chen Wang."

"Of course, Ms. Mason. Mr. Wang is always an honored guest. How may I assist you?"

"I'm not sure if I should talk to you or someone else, but unfortunately we're having to navigate an IRS audit."

The woman made a sound of sympathy. "That's the worst!"

"Tell me about it. Anyway, the IRS is questioning the charges sent through from your hotel on April 21st of this year. Do you happen to remember that visit? Mr. Wang was there for three days. He will be so grateful if you could corroborate this visit for me along with any details you might remember. He usually keeps a journal of all his business, but the one from that month is missing, and I need to re-create it."

The woman said nothing for a moment, and Kate was afraid she had begun to be suspicious, but she must have been thinking because her voice was still light and helpful when she finally spoke. "I was on the check-in desk for eight hours every day then, and I spoke to Mr. Wang several times a day. What kind of corroboration would be useful?"

"Who he met with, how many people he bought lunch for any of those days, any guests who stayed with him and what their business might be. If we're lucky, it's something that is tax deductible." Kate gave a hearty sigh she hoped would sway the woman.

"Hmm, let me think a moment." Another pause came over the phone. "Oh yes, I remember now. My sister is a server in the restaurant, and the second night he was here, he gave an engagement ring to a woman. My sister said she'd never seen a diamond that big. Oh wait, that probably won't help prove his trip here was business, will it?"

"It might. Maybe the woman is a business partner, and that was just part of the evening." Kate's pulse blipped. Though she didn't know what to make of it, it would likely mean something to Drake. "Do you know the woman's name? Or maybe what she looked like?"

"He called her Melissa."

Kate fought to keep her tone even. "Was this Melissa there all three days too?"

"I don't think so. I saw her arrive two different mornings."

Heath would have noticed if she was gone for three days. "Thank you so much for your help."

"If it was help. I'm not so sure. We all like Mr. Wang."

She thanked the woman again and ended the call. Slinging her purse over her shoulder, she disarmed the alarm and let herself out, then armed it again. She started for the cottage with the dog on her heels. Thunderheads built in the sky, and she smelled rain and ozone in the air. A big storm was heading this way, so she'd better hurry.

She rushed through the fields toward Drake's cottage, brushing aside blueberry bushes with her feet. When she reached the edge of the road, Jackson stopped and barked. He dug under a plant, and she caught a glimpse of a bright spot of yellow. A moment later Jackson had it in his mouth and brought it to her.

"Good boy." She patted him and relieved him of his find. The small yellow pouch appeared to be the kind of thing women would use to transport jewelry. The contents were still intact, but the jumble of jewelry, watches, and hair ties didn't tell her anything new. It surely didn't belong to Uncle Paul. Who had dropped it?

She stared at the woods again. The sheriff and his deputies had been all over that area. There was no need for her to go there, too, but something compelled her to put one sneakered foot in front of the other and enter the shadows. Her heart beat fast in her throat, and she thrust her hand into her purse to close her fingers around the bear spray.

Jackson growled at her side, and she pulled out the can and held her finger on the nozzle. If Paul came out from behind a tree, she'd blast him right in the eyes with it. But she only heard the soughing of the wind in the trees and the chirping of the birds overhead.

She reached the waterfall and glanced around. The area didn't look nearly as scary in the daylight. The water pouring over the rocks was much lighter now, but with the storm moving in, it would regain its power. She was almost tempted to go into that cave again. A shudder passed over her and she took a step back. Nothing was there for her to see.

There were no answers here, only more questions.

The wind freshened, and a drop of cold rain hit her face. She retraced her steps and began to breathe easier when she and Jackson stepped clear of the shadowy forest. The wind tried to tear her hair from her head as lightning crackled overhead. An open field during a lightning storm was not the safest place to be. She broke into a run and raced for the cottage as the clouds broke open and rain lashed her. By the time she reached the porch, her hair hung in her face and her clothes were soaked.

Under the safety of the porch, she shook off along with her dog, then stepped to the door.

# TWENTY-TWO

K ate hadn't even set foot on the porch when she heard the commotion through the open door. Drake had said not to bother knocking, so she opened the screen door and dropped her purse on the entry table. Jackson raced past her to see the girls.

Emma was on the sofa with both arms crossed, and Phoebe had a pink stuffed bear in a choke hold in her right arm and a purple unicorn in the other. Both girls were red faced and staring sullenly at each other.

Dressed in denim shorts and a Celtics T-shirt, Drake stood with his back to the door. "I'll get another stuffed bear. We'll get some ice cream too."

"But it's my bear." Emma clenched her hands into fists. "I got a bear and she got a unicorn."

"You put it down." Phoebe hugged the bear tighter. "It was my turn."

"Just to go to the bathroom! I came right back." Tears rolled down Emma's cheeks. "Make her give Pinky back to me, Uncle Drake."

"You need to share," Drake said.

Kate wanted to roll her eyes, but she stepped closer so she

was in their line of vision. "Phoebe, if you want her bear for a while, give her your unicorn."

Phoebe clutched both stuffed animals closer. "No! Plum is mine."

"You don't get to have both. Give Emma her bear back."

"Uncle Drake," Phoebe whined. "She put it down."

Drake started to open his mouth, but Kate narrowed her eyes at him and gave a slight shake of her head. He pressed his lips together but said nothing. "You heard me, Phoebe. Give Emma the bear. And don't throw it. Give it to her nicely, and tell her you're sorry."

Her lips pressed in a mutinous line, Phoebe handed the bear to her sister. "Sorry." The mutter sounded insincere, but at least she'd done it.

Emma snatched the bear and hugged it to her chest. "Thank you," she muttered back at Kate's prompting.

Kate looked them over. At least they had on clean shorts and T-shirts. "We're not about to go outside with your hair looking like that. The bees will want to nest in there. Both of you go brush your hair now. Did you brush your teeth this morning?" When neither of them would look at her, she nodded. "Brush your teeth too."

Emma heaved a sigh, and Phoebe stuck out her lip, but the girls got up and went to the stairs. Jackson went with them.

As soon as they were out of earshot, Drake frowned at Kate. "The girls need to share."

"If you give in to Phoebe over every little thing, she's going to be even more of a terror. She knew Emma had just gone to the bathroom."

"Emma is old enough to share."

"So is Phoebe. She wasn't about to share her toy. She just

wanted Emma's." The man was clueless about kids, and she suppressed a sigh. "And I would have made Emma share if it were that simple. Younger kids play the parents to annoy their siblings. I see it all the time. And if you're honest, you'll admit that's exactly what Phoebe was doing. Sharing is playing together with things. Not taking another child's possessions and leaving her with nothing."

His frown darkened for a moment, then he nodded. "Okay, maybe you're right."

"And trying to placate them with more stuff and ice cream isn't helping them either. They're both old enough to learn how to behave. You need to stop it."

His eyebrows rose and his face reddened. Now she'd done it and had overstepped the bounds too far. He was trying his best, and she needed to remember that before she shot off her mouth. "Sorry. That was a little harsh."

"A little?" He shrugged. "I'm getting used to your take-no-prisoners attitude, Kate, but you might learn to soften it some."

"You're right. I've had to fight for everything all my life, and I sometimes forget we're on the same team."

"You think I'm your adversary?"

She shook her head. "That came out wrong too. I mean, training the girls is my responsibility, and I take it very seriously. I want so much for them."

"So do I, so give me a little credit."

Boy, had she botched the morning. "I'm sorry."

"So you already said."

"Could you forgive me if I tell you I found out something important from the last hotel I called? I might tell you if you ply me with fresh coffee."

"I just made some." He followed her into the kitchen and got down a cup for her. "What did you find out?"

"Wang gave Melissa an engagement ring. It was quite a rock."

He handed her a mug. "But she was already married. Are you sure it was an engagement ring?"

Kate poured coffee into the mug. "That's what I was told. She must have been planning on leaving Heath. But the bigger question is, where is the ring? Until you saw the text transcript, you had no idea she was having an affair, so I assume that means there was no ring in her belongings."

His brow creased as he poured himself some coffee. "I'm Heath's executor and I saw nothing. I'll talk to Mike."

"Mike?"

"Melissa's business partner, Mike Toucet."

"What did Melissa do? I assumed she was a stay-at-home mom."

He took a sip of coffee and gestured to the table and the almond-flour cinnamon rolls she'd made earlier. "It was a source of contention between them. Heath wanted her to stay home with the girls, but she loved being an attorney and helping the underdog. She did a lot of pro bono work along with Mike."

Kate reached for a roll and settled onto a chair. "I've always heard pro bono work can be dangerous."

"She had a guy stalking her for a while, but nothing ever came of it. It was one of the reasons Heath wanted her to quit."

The sweet, cinnamony flavor hit her tongue, and she savored it. "Maybe she stashed the ring at work. Or maybe it was stolen."

"Mike will know. I'll give him a call right now."

Drake was watching her with an intensity that made her stomach flutter, and she dropped her gaze. The spicy scent of his cologne was much more enticing than this cinnamon roll. In spite of her objections to some of his decisions, she liked the way he cared for the girls and wanted them to be happy. He was smart and focused, and she found herself drawn to that too. His short-cropped curly hair just begged to have her fingers in it. He hadn't said anything about his personal life, but she couldn't believe he didn't have a dozen other women hanging around. Maybe he was even engaged.

She'd only be around him for a few more weeks. It would be much too dangerous to let herself fall for him.

Drake liked watching Kate. Her light, quick movements were graceful, and she was a bundle of energy. He admired the way she focused so completely on any task at hand. And she was just so darned cute, beautiful really. Her big blue eyes dominated her heart-shaped face, and her dimples came and went with every expression.

He dragged his attention away from the way she licked so delicately at her cinnamon roll and reached for his cell phone. He scrolled through the names and found Mike.

Mike answered on the second ring. "Mike Toucet."

"Good morning, Mike, this is Drake Newham."

"Drake, it's good to hear from you." He sounded harried. "To say I keenly feel Melissa's loss is the biggest understatement of the year. I called Rod the other day, and he told me you'd gone to Maine. Are you having any luck figuring out what happened up there?"

"Not yet, but I'm working on it." How did he tell Mike about the affair? The man had thought a lot of Melissa, and Drake hated to destroy her good image. "Some evidence has turned up, and I wanted to run it past you and see if you'd had any inkling about it."

"I'm all ears."

"Did you ever suspect Melissa might be having an affair?" The pause before Mike answered was so long, Drake thought he might have lost the connection. "Mike?"

"I'm here." He heaved a sigh. "I never would have guessed that's what was going on. She seemed a little distracted in the couple of weeks before she died, and she left work early quite often. I thought maybe she had some personal issues she was working through, but I would have bet my life she was crazy in love with Heath. I'm shocked."

"I was afraid of that. You saw no evidence of a big ring she was wearing or hiding maybe in her office?"

"I haven't had the heart to go through her desk yet. I planned to do it this weekend though." The sound of footsteps echoed through the phone. "I'm heading to her office now. She had a locked file drawer where she kept sensitive documents. I don't know if I can get in it, but let me try."

Drake listened to his breathing and something rattling as Mike tried the drawer. Where might she have put the key? Maybe in her purse on her key ring? He didn't have Melissa's possessions, only Heath's.

"It's locked up tight. Oh wait, I think she gave me a copy of that key once. It might be in my desk." His steps sounded again, faster this time. Metal slides scraped. "Here it is. Hang on."

Drake gave Kate a thumbs-up as he listened to Mike rush

down the hall again. Metal rails screeched, and Mike gave an exultant laugh. "Holy cow, you won't believe what's in this box. An engagement ring fit for a queen." Rustling sounded before Mike spoke again. "And air tickets to China. Three sets. She's got them for the kids too. Flight date was for a week after she died."

Something squeezed in Drake's chest. "Thanks, Mike. Let me know if you find anything else of interest."

"Will do."

Drake ended the call and put down his phone. His world had just been rocked, and he wasn't sure how to deal with the doubts rising like a storm.

Kate placed her small hand on his arm. "What's wrong?"

Her touch calmed him, and he put his hand over hers. "Melissa planned to take the girls with her to China."

Kate's eyes widened. "Heath surely wouldn't have let her. With joint custody he would have to agree for them to leave the country."

"She was going to take them and leave as soon as they got back from vacation."

"Are you rethinking your belief that he'd never hurt her? That kind of betrayal might make any man do something unexpected."

Was he? The sinking sensation in his gut began to subside, and he shook his head. "While it might have pushed him into shoving her off the cliff, why would he jump himself? He'd be abandoning his kids. That's not like Heath. He adored those girls." His confidence returned and he squeezed her fingers before moving his hand.

She folded her fingers together in her lap. "Okay, so we keep digging."

COLLEEN COBLE

"We sure do." He admired the way the sunlight coming through the window lit her head in a halo. "How was everything last night? Any noises?"

"Not a sound the past couple of nights. I've still been shoving my dresser against the bedroom door though, just in case. I should call the sheriff and see if he's heard anything about Uncle Paul."

"I'll take care of it." He pulled out his phone again. "I want to ask him about that autopsy report again. He promised to get it to me, and I still don't have it." He called the sheriff's office and asked for the sheriff, but after two rings, Deputy Kissner answered. "Good morning, Deputy, this is Drake Newham. Listen, I still don't have that autopsy report on my brother and sister-in-law. I know it's been a crazy time for all of you, but could you get that e-mailed over to me?"

"I'll do it right now," the deputy said.

"And Kate is here with me. She wondered if there's been any news of her uncle."

"Not a hint of a clue, I'm sorry to say. But we're still looking."

"Thanks. Keep me posted." He ended the call and told Kate what he'd learned, which was nothing. "I'm beginning to wonder if the sheriff doesn't want me to see the autopsy. Maybe there's something in it that will strengthen my skepticism."

"Danny isn't like that."

"Maybe not." He flipped his phone over. "I dug through Melissa's cell phone records and found Olivia Maunder's number. She's Melissa's best friend and was hosting that event, the one with the picture of Melissa and Wang. I'm going to call her."

She scooted closer to him. "Good."

He punched in the number and it rang a couple of times before Olivia picked up. "Hello?"

"Olivia, it's Drake Newham."

"Drake, how good to hear from you. How are you doing?" Her voice held wells of sympathy, maybe even a hint of tears on her end.

"Surviving. I'm investigating what happened here in Maine, and I wondered if I could ask you a few questions."

"Of course. I still miss her so much." She broke off on a sob. "How can I help?"

"Did you know Melissa was leaving Heath for Wang? That she was going to China?" There was a long silence, and he thought he heard another shuddering sob escape her. "Olivia?"

"I'm here. Yes, of course I knew. Melissa told me everything since the day I first met her at a frat party when we were eighteen. I tried to talk her out of it, you know. She thought Chen was just misunderstood." Olivia made an incredulous sound. "She said his father forced him into crime and he never ordered any of the terrible things he was accused of. She was so blind."

"How did they meet?"

"It was all my fault! He'd given money to my women's shelter, and I held a dinner to thank the donors. Wang took one look at her and was smitten. He kept showing up where she was and bought her extravagant gifts. At first she wasn't interested, but she was starting to feel a little taken for granted. Heath was busy with his work, and he was extremely focused on Wang. I never understood why he took the case. He seemed to hate Wang. The next thing I knew Melissa was going to leave him for Wang."

"Did Heath talk to you at all about it?"

She went quiet for a long moment. "He showed up here one night. He was livid. It was right after he'd found out."

Drake rubbed his forehead. It wasn't what he'd wanted to hear. "You think he could have harmed Melissa?"

She gave a tiny sob. "Oh, Drake, I've agonized over this, but I think he was angry enough that if he'd had a gun, he might have shot her. The betrayal was so horrible."

His fingers were numb from gripping the phone so tightly. "I still can't believe Melissa would get close to a man like that."

"I know, but some women are drawn to that bad boy. I think Melissa thought she could help him leave his life of crime. There was talk of eventually moving to Australia and putting his crimes behind him. I'm sorry, Drake. I loved her. She was like a sister."

"Thanks for your help, Olivia. I'll be in touch." He ended the call and told Kate what he'd learned. "She thinks Heath might have been capable of hurting Melissa."

Her blue eyes held tears, and she took his hand. "Does this change anything for you?"

He gripped her fingers and shook his head. "I still don't believe it." But his words held no conviction, even to his own ears.

# Twenty-Three

K ate's steps dragged as she went home after a full day. She'd enjoyed the girls, then Drake had invited her to watch a movie again. Though the wise thing would have been to say no, she agreed. Her head was full of all the questions about the deaths on the cliffs, as well as her uncle's intentions.

It was nine by the time she entered her yard, and her steps quickened when she recognized Luke's truck in the drive. Claire and Luke sat on the porch swing in the dark. Claire wore khaki shorts and a cute orange top and was cuddled against Luke.

Jackson ran past her to leap onto their laps. "You big moose." Luke laughed and scooted over to make room.

Kate disarmed the alarm and opened the door. "Why didn't you call me? I would have come right down."

"We were enjoying the gorgeous night. A little late, aren't you?" Claire's voice held amusement.

Kate's cheeks heated as she entered the house with them on her heels. "We watched a movie after the girls went to bed."

"Hmm."

At Claire's noncommittal noise, Kate turned and shook her head. "What's that supposed to mean?"

"Nothing." A dimple came and went in Claire's cheek. "Just

glad you're enjoying yourself." She went ahead of Kate to the kitchen and headed for the coffeepot. "We came to crash in your spare room. The hotel didn't have a room tonight because of the festival, and I'm not quite ready to go back to our place." Jackson followed her. He loved her nearly as much as he loved Kate.

"Of course! But you and Luke can have my bedroom. I like the smaller bed in the spare."

"I told her you'd say that," Luke said.

Kate handed Claire the bag of coffee beans. "You should have called me."

"Well, I did, but I got your voice mail."

Kate frowned and reached for the purse she'd slung onto the back of a chair. As she dug out her phone, she saw the pouch Jackson had found and pulled it out too. The phone showed two missed calls. "I accidentally had it silenced. Sorry."

"What's that?" Luke gestured to the pouch.

"Jackson found it in the field this morning. I don't know who lost it." Turning it over in her hands, she examined it more closely.

Who would have dropped it in the middle of her blueberry field?

She opened the pouch and dumped the contents out on the table. "It seems to just be jewelry and watches. A few hair items. It's like some woman lost her travel bag, but the blueberry field seemed an odd place to be carrying it."

Luke came to her side and went through the jumble of items. "Some of this looks old. This watch looks like an antique." He showed her a delicate gold watch with a jewelry-style band.

"See if there's anything on the back." Claire flipped on the coffeepot and came to peruse the items with them.

174

Kate leaned closer to look when Luke rolled it over. "It reads *Dixie* on the back. The only Dixie I know is Drake's aunt." This was getting more and more strange. "I'll go talk to her tomorrow and see if this happens to be hers. Maybe all these things are hers. Maybe there was money inside or valuable coins. It's hard to say." A hint of blue caught her eye, and she picked up a pair of earrings. "I have some just like these."

Claire frowned. "Are you sure these aren't yours? When did you last see yours?"

Kate thought back. "I was going to wear them to church on Sunday and couldn't find them. I thought maybe I'd taken them off in the car or left them somewhere." She looked at the earrings more closely. "One of mine has a scratch on the inside of the stone." Her pulse kicked when she saw the same scratch. "I-I think these might be mine. Could someone have found them?"

"Or maybe this belongs to Paul, and he took them when he was here in the house," Luke said.

The aroma of coffee began to fill the kitchen, and Kate didn't want to think about danger any longer. For just a little while she wanted to sit with her family and forget the events of the past weeks. "I'm going to whip up some gluten-free peanut butter cookies, Luke. Your favorite."

He yawned and put down the watch. "Honestly, I just want to crash."

Claire's gaze met Kate's. "You go on up to bed, honey. I'm going to stay up and talk with Kate for a while. I haven't seen her in forever."

"Like a whole day." Luke grinned and brushed her lips with his. "You sure you don't mind if we take your bed, Kate?"

"I put clean sheets on this morning. I'm happy you're here."

She went to the cabinet and got down the peanut butter. "At least you'll have the cookies tomorrow."

As Luke headed upstairs Claire got the eggs out of the fridge, then pulled down a bowl from the cupboard. "Okay, dish. I want to know all about the hunky Drake."

"I knew that's why you were staying up!" Kate grinned at her sister. How had they spent so many years apart and yet could read each other this way? "He's not interested in me other than as a nanny. In fact, I think he was thinking about firing me when this all came out about Uncle Paul and Mom being in jail."

Claire paused in the middle of cracking an egg and stared at her. "You're kidding!"

"Nope. I told him I wouldn't blame him if he fired me, and he paused before he told me the job was still mine. I saw the indecision on his face though. He's worried about the girls. And to be honest, I am too. Paul is very unpredictable."

"I don't think he'd hurt a child."

Kate looked at her. "Right. Like he didn't hurt you at all."

Claire put her hand to her mouth. "Well, yes, there's that. But he was pushed into a corner."

"And he's not now? He's even more cornered with the cops crawling all over the place trying to send him back to prison. He's more desperate than he's ever been."

"But he doesn't need you any longer. He got what he needed."

Kate glanced at the jumble of jewelry on the table. "Unless that bag is important too. Maybe this is why he was in the basement."

"He would have had to have left it here, and you found it in a field."

Kate stirred together the peanut butter and eggs. "I guess that's true. Unless he thought he might have dropped it here."

Claire leaned on the counter and smiled at her. "So what's Drake like, really? Is he all proper and reserved?"

"Well, he likes *The Princess Bride*, so that's a mark in his favor."

"You didn't make him watch that!"

"It was his idea."

Claire took the spatula and began to mix in the flour. "I knew I liked that guy."

White clouds floated in a perfect blue sky. No storms today. Kate and Drake got the girls off Kevin's boat onto the rocky shore west of Mermaid Point, then waved him off. In Drake's backpack he had binoculars, lunch, swimsuits, and bottles of water. His flyboarding gear was in another bag. Each girl carried a sand bucket and shovel, though this area had more pebbles than sand. The dog was in his element, too, and could hardly be coaxed out of the water.

"I'll be back at two," Kevin called to them.

Drake waved to show he'd heard him before leading the girls closer to the rock face. He put his hand on Kate's shoulder, then quickly pulled it back when a wave of attraction hit him. "This was a great idea. I think we all needed a little breather from what's happened the past week. I don't think I've ever seen a puffin."

She set her backpack down and began to rummage in it.

Jackson tried to put his nose into it, and she pushed him away. "I think I was five when I saw my first one. I was entranced from the first moment. They are onshore right now to raise their chicks, but they'll be heading out to sea any day now."

"I want to play in the water," Emma said.

"And I want to play with my bucket and shovel."

"Not until we get in a little educational lesson about puffins. I want you to love them like I do." She handed each of them a pair of binoculars. "I see a bit of orange up there. Atlantic puffins are sometimes called sea parrots because of their bright colors. And some people call them the clowns of the sea because of their coloring."

Emma scratched at a mosquito bite on her knee. "I like parrots. Do they talk?"

"No, but did you know they spend the entire winter at sea? They only come ashore to raise their babies in the spring and summer. Then they're alone in the cold for months." She shivered. "Can you imagine being alone in the cold?"

A flicker of interest lit Phoebe's blue eyes. "How do they sleep if they're flying?"

"They land in the waves and sleep there."

Emma bared her teeth. "But a big shark might come up and swallow them whole!"

"They are white on their underside. That way they blend in with the waves when something is looking up. God has perfectly equipped them to rely on how he created them to survive. God is awesome that way."

Phoebe's eyes grew wide. "Wow."

Drake was impressed that she took the time to circle back to God's provision in nature.

Kate touched Emma on top of the head. "Have you ever done a belly flop in the water?"

Emma nodded and rubbed her belly. "It hurts, and my skin was red."

"Puffins are awkward flyers. They belly flop when they try to land in calm water or they crash into the waves."

The girls giggled, finally getting into the tale. Kate held up her binoculars. "Let's see if we can find some young ones up there." She helped the girls focus their binoculars and smiled when they squealed at the sight of the colorful birds. Drake took a turn and caught his breath at the bright plumage. They really did look a little like parrots.

The girls quickly lost interest, and Drake let them take their buckets and shovels to the water's edge.

"How are the plans coming for your drone modifications?"

He watched the girls shovel sand into their buckets to make a sand castle. "I'm having a little trouble with the delivery crane. I really need to work with my engineers." He raked a hand through his hair. "Lakesha is pressuring me to come back, but I know if I leave, my brother's death will be filed away and never solved."

"You have a lot on your shoulders." She waved her hand toward the children. "Making them feel safe and loved, finding how your brother and Melissa died, and now your business. I wish I could help."

He grinned at her. "I can forget about it today." He started to put on his flyboarding equipment until Kate shot him a look. "What?"

"That's crazy dangerous, Drake. You could drown, and then where would the girls be? Would your parents take them? Or Melissa's?"

He frowned. "They'd be too much for grandparents to handle."

She patted the space beside her on a large rock. "Then come sit here and talk to me."

Her pull was stronger than the tide, so he grinned and went to sit beside her.

The silence between them was the comfortable kind, and he lay back with his head propped on a rise in the rock. She had the most gorgeous eyes he'd ever seen, and he could sit and stare into those blue depths for hours. The more time he spent with Kate, the more he wanted to spend. "So tell me why you love the puffins so much. Your eyes shine and your voice gets louder when you talk about them."

Her dimples flashed, and she tucked a strand of dark-blonde hair behind her ear. "I think I felt a sort of kinship with them right from the start. They live most of their lives alone out at sea. They are only with other puffins when they come to shore to mate and raise their yearly baby."

"You felt alone as a kid?"

She stretched long, tanned legs out on the rock. "My mother was always consumed by her own troubles. Uncle Paul tried to be a dad figure, but you know how that turned out. I often felt like I battled the waves of life all by myself." She fell silent a moment. "It's better with Claire back in my life."

He saw the shadow linger in her eyes. "But now that she's married, you're afraid she won't have time for you."

She blinked and shaded her eyes with her hand. "How'd you know that?"

"I guessed by your tone. You feel alone."

She picked up several pebbles and studied them. "I don't

really have any family but Claire. My best friend, Shelley, took a job in Michigan, and I won't get to see her very often."

"I'm surprised you're not married." He inwardly shook his head at his fishing. "I mean, you're beautiful and smart. Hey, you even like guy movies like *Raiders of the Lost Ark*."

Pink flooded her cheeks. "That's nice to hear."

He told himself to shut up and escape with his dignity, but he was never one for playing it safe. "Never been engaged?"

She shook her head. "I got sick, and what guy was going to be interested in a girl who might die? I mean, what a way to take off the bloom of romance."

The thought of her lying lifeless in a casket closed his throat. "But you're okay now."

"I'm also thirty-one." She shuddered. "It's hard to even say that out loud. Most of the eligible men have been taken or moved away."

"There are always new ones coming into town." He sat up and took her hand. "Let me take you to dinner one night. I'll get Dixie to watch the girls."

Her fingers closed around his, and her blue eyes were as bright as the sun above until they dimmed as quickly as they'd glowed. She pulled her hand away. "I don't know, Drake. You might not want to yell at me if we went out. I'd never know where I stood."

"I'd make sure you knew. Think about it."

She looked down at her hands. "You're not married either."

*So she noticed.* "Nope. But I'd like to change that someday. A houseful of kids is a happy place. First school and then my career took all my attention. It seemed I had all the time in the world to date and find a life partner. But Heath's death was a wake-up call for me that I'm not getting any younger. I'm thirty-two."

"I'm hardly your type, Drake. I never even finished college, and you've got more degrees than a thermometer." She rose and brushed the debris from her white shorts. "I'd better check on the kids."

He stared after her. What had caused her smile to vanish and the frosty glaze in her eyes to appear?

# TWENTY-FOUR

K ate's face felt windburned as she mounted the steps to Claire's house with Jackson. Her sister had finally moved back home two days ago after a report that Paul had been spotted in Canada. Kate felt as upside down as a broken top. She'd been rolling Drake's invitation around in her head for a couple of days, and she wasn't sure how to respond.

Luke answered the doorbell. He wore pajama bottoms with no shirt. "Kate, is everything okay?" He opened the door wide.

"I'm fine, but I just needed to talk to Claire. Is she still up?" Her face heated. They were newlyweds, so what was she doing barging in without a call at eight o'clock at night?

"She's in the kitchen making some chamomile tea. Go on in. I won't bother the two of you. Hey, Jackson, let's go throw the Frisbee." The dog's ears went up at the word. He loved Frisbee and trotted happily outside with Luke.

That wonderful man understood. Kate kicked off her sandals and went across the polished floors in her bare feet. She caught the scent of an apple candle and the aroma of something peanut buttery. Claire stood in the kitchen with her back to the open doorway as she filled the bright-red teakettle.

"Hey, I'll take some of that."

Claire turned with a smile. She wore the pale-blue negligee Kate had gotten her for the bridal shower, and she looked so pretty with her blonde hair spilling onto her shoulders. "This is a surprise."

An easel beside the table held a partially finished painting of Drake's nieces. Kate paused and studied the likenesses. "This is wonderful, Claire."

"It's for you. I'll have it done in a few days." She eyed Kate. "Is everything okay?"

"Your husband just asked me the same thing." She went to Claire's new white kitchen table and pulled out a red chair. "Drake asked me out. I haven't had a chance to tell you, and I was trying to figure it out myself, but I can't."

Claire chuckled and grabbed two mugs from the cupboard. "And that's the reason for your woebegone expression? That's wonderful!"

"He said he wanted a houseful of kids!" Kate put her face in her hands. "I didn't have the heart to tell him that's the main reason he wouldn't want to develop feelings for me. I can't give him that."

"That doesn't mean he wouldn't understand. Any man who really loved you wouldn't let that stop him. Drake seems to be one of those guys who lets things roll off his back. And besides, he already has two girls to raise. That's a pretty good start on a houseful. It might be enough."

Kate shook her head. "I think his biological clock is ticking. The phenomenon doesn't just happen to women. His brother's death shook him up."

Claire bit her lip. "Give him a chance, Kate. Don't sell him short. It wouldn't hurt to go out with him." She picked up the mugs of tea and went to the table.

"It might hurt a lot. I'll be honest, Claire. I'm already halfway in love with him. I've gotten to know him so well from watching the girls. He's a really great guy. Kind, smart, funny. I like being around him, but I keep reminding myself he'll soon be back in his real world, and a dalliance with someone like me isn't going to last. It's already August. They'll be heading back to Boston the end of the month."

Claire stirred sweetener into her tea. "You don't see yourself clearly, Kate. You let your old illness define you, and it shouldn't. You have so much more to offer than bearing a child. You're beautiful and loyal, and you know a lot about so many subjects. Just like your precious puffins."

Kate took a sip of the tea and winced when it scalded her tongue. "Can you imagine me in Boston? As a prominent business owner, I'm sure Drake goes to all kinds of social events. I've only been to my high school prom. We're hardly on the same social level."

Claire set her tea on the table. "You could hold your own with anyone. Your mother's attitude toward you scarred you. Get it out of your head. You don't have to earn love from people, Kate. You try too hard to make people like you. It's as if you think they will only like you if you're perfect. If you say the right thing and act the right way. That's just not true."

"I'm afraid," Kate whispered. "He could really hurt me, Claire."

"He could. But I'd go after him and make him pay big-time. I'd stalk him at his big society events and he'd be sorry." She held Kate's gaze. "But if you don't risk pain, you'll never find true happiness. Remember that line in *The Princess Bride*? 'Life is pain, Highness. Anyone who says differently is selling something.'"

Kate grinned. "We watched that together last week."

"I know. That's when I knew he was right for you." She sat back and picked up her mug. "Risk it, Kate. Roll the dice. What if God brought Drake here? I mean, look at the sequence of events. He rented your house, he gave you a cushy job, and now he's asking you out. He's a good Christian man. Give him a chance."

Could Claire be right? Kate would love to believe it. And she was also right about Kate's scars. Was she going to sit back and let her mother's treatment ruin her future as well as her past?

She took another sip of tea. "I'll say yes. But pray for me, Claire. I'm scared."

"I always pray for you. I think God brought Drake in answer to my prayers in the first place. And if I'm right, you have to cook me your Cajun fettuccine. Gluten free, of course."

"It's a deal." Kate reached over and squeezed her sister's fingers. "I love you, Claire." Thank the good Lord he'd brought her sister back into her life.

Drake put the Land Rover into Park and glanced across the seat at Kate. "I hope these questions don't upset her."

The blue tank Kate wore enhanced the blue of her eyes, and he somehow managed to keep from gawking at her legs, impossibly long and tanned in those white shorts. He liked being around her way too much.

She opened her door, then grabbed the back door handle to open it for the girls. "I don't see why they would upset her."

"There were no prints on the watch and nothing to tie it to your uncle. I have to wonder if kids put it in the pouch."

He couldn't explain his reluctance to talk to Dixie about the watch. There was so much about his aunt that he didn't know, and he didn't want any old memories disrupting her mood.

Kate shut the door behind the girls, who ran toward the house calling for their aunt. Jackson ran at their heels. "They sure love her."

"Everyone does." He went to the back and grabbed the bags of take-out Mexican he'd stopped to get on the way. At least Dixie wouldn't have to cook lunch for them.

Dixie stood on the porch with the screen door held wide. She was dressed in her overalls, and her smile looked as unflappable as ever. "Took you long enough. I'm starving." She sniffed the air as he approached. "Did you get fish tacos like I told you?"

"Of course. When have I ever disobeyed you?" He brushed a kiss across her powdered cheek. She reeked of her favorite Tabu cologne.

She stepped aside to let them enter. "Lemonade and coffee are on the table in the kitchen along with plates."

"Sure thing." He went through to the kitchen, and the rest of the group followed.

The girls chattered to Dixie while they ate, then she gave them chocolate chip cookies and milk to take out to the deck along with bread to feed the ducks. Jackson went with them.

She settled her round glasses more firmly on her nose. "So, you said there was something you needed to talk to me about. Did you find out more about Heath's death?"

"No, it's not about Heath and Melissa. You heard Paul Mason had escaped from prison?"

"Oh my, yes. Everyone is on pins and needles about it. I haven't seen him though, and town gossip says he was reported up near Canada. Claire and Luke went home, so I'd guess that bit of news is accurate."

Kate pulled the pouch from her purse and placed it on the table. "I found this in the blueberries near my house. Have you ever seen it?"

Dixie shook her head. "I'm not sure why you would think of me. It's a little fancy for what little jewelry I have."

Kate opened it and dumped the items out on the scuffed wooden table. "This watch has the name Dixie engraved on the back."

"Oh my." Dixie reached for the watch and ran her fingers over the engraving. "This belonged to the grandmother I was named after. I thought I'd lost it. It was in the pouch?"

It had to have been stolen then. By Paul? Drake pushed the other items apart with his fingers. "Do you recognize anything else here?"

A frown settled between Dixie's hazel eyes. She picked up a ring. It was a gold high school class ring with the initials *AN* on it. "This is Amelia Nicholson's ring. She stayed with me about three months ago after a tiff with her parents. She was here a couple of weeks, and the ring came up missing. She couldn't figure out what had happened to it."

Drake couldn't place the name, but Kate set her water glass onto the table with a clatter. "My neighbor Amelia? The one who reported a Peeping Tom at her house a few weeks ago?"

Dixie nodded. "Poor child. She's been practically afraid to leave her house ever since. I think she's going to stay with her grandmother in Portland for a while instead of moving back to the dorm."

Drake didn't like the sound of this. He pointed to the ring.

"So that came up missing about the same time as the watch? Or do you know when you last saw the watch?"

"I showed it to her when she was here, so I know I had it at least part of her visit." She glanced at Kate. "You think Paul broke in at some point and stole the jewelry?"

"But why? And why would he be carrying it through the blueberry fields?" Kate rose and went to refill her water glass.

Drake picked up another ring, with a small pale-blue birthstone. "This stuff is hardly worth much. Why would a thief take this kind of thing and hide it? The entire stash probably isn't worth more than a hundred bucks at a pawn shop."

Kate turned from the sink to face him. Her blue eyes were somber. "I probably read too many suspense novels, but you know what keeps coming to mind? Trophies."

"You mean like a serial killer?" Drake shook his head. "You're reaching, Kate. Paul has his issues, but I don't think he's a serial killer."

Pink tinged her cheeks. "I knew it sounded silly, but we've had some issues with a Peeping Tom in the area. And there was Whitney Peece's murder. It just made me think."

He touched a bracelet. "Any of this jewelry yours other than the earrings?"

She carried her water back to the table. "Nothing I recognize."

He locked gazes with her and saw the vulnerability in her eyes. "It wouldn't hurt to mention it to the sheriff. Maybe he's had some reports of these items missing."

"Thank you. I know it's far-fetched, but I thought it was worth bringing up."

He turned the clues over in his head even as he stared at the items. He turned to Kate. "Let's go see the sheriff."

# TWENTY-FIVE

Drake and Kate found the sheriff at a table in the Oyster Bistro. Soft eighties music mingled with the tinkle of tableware and the chatter of the servers and customers.

Colton was talking to a man Drake had never seen before. "Think we should interrupt him? He looks intent. You recognize the guy with him?"

Kate nodded and headed that way. "That's Jonas Kissner, one of his deputies. You talked to him on the phone the other day. I went to school with him." She reached the booth. "Hey, guys. I hope you don't mind if we interrupt you."

Colton set his coffee cup on the table. "Just having lunch. Let me scooch over. This is Deputy Kissner."

Drake nodded to the deputy, a redheaded man in his late twenties. Kissner's pale-green eyes looked him over, and he nodded back. Drake sat beside the sheriff and Kate took the seat opposite him.

"I still haven't gotten those autopsy reports," Drake said.

The deputy frowned and the sheriff shrugged. "Maybe I typed the e-mail wrong. Give it to me again on a piece of paper."

Drake wrote out his email carefully on a notepad the sheriff handed him, then gave it back. "We have some information for you." He nodded across the table at Kate, who sat in a wash of sunlight that made her dark-blonde hair glow.

She dug in her ginormous bag and pulled out the jewelry pouch. "We have a theory about the contents in this bag." They spilled onto the table surface when she upended the pouch. "I found it in my fields."

Drake watched her animation as she explained to the sheriff and his deputy about three pieces of the jewelry they'd recognized. With color in her cheeks, she was pretty enough to snag the attention of every man in the place. But he didn't like the thought of anyone else ogling her long, shorts-clad legs.

Kate picked up Dixie's watch. "Over the past year the news has reported break-ins and instances of a man looking in windows. What if this is his trophy bag? He breaks into houses and steals things from women he's targeting."

The deputy straightened and shook his head. "Old Dixie is hardly the type to warrant a Peeping Tom's attention. I think you're jumping to conclusions."

Kate tapped the watch face. "I think the real target was Amelia Nicholson. He got Dixie's watch, too, while he was there."

Colton pursed his lips and looked over the loot. "I hope you're wrong, Kate. A man who collects these kinds of things is the type of criminal who might move on to murder." He looked up at her. "I'm going to take these into custody and have every woman who reported a break-in or a Peeping Tom have a look. If we find more correlation, this thing just got really serious." He popped a mint and sighed. "Whitney Peece reported a man in her hotel room while she was showering the day before she died. I'd better have her next of kin take a look at these items and see if anything belongs to her."

Kate hugged herself and shuddered.

"This Peeping Tom guy might have stolen something from her room that night. Many of these criminals start with peeping, then move on to rape and eventually murder." He nodded toward the bag. "If that's what we've got here, I want to nab him before he goes any further."

"Of course." Kate took the water the server brought and sipped it.

Drake watched the sheriff scoop up the items and place them back in the bag. "Those are all compromised by now, right? I mean, you can't test them for DNA or fingerprints. We've all handled them before we realized how important they might be."

Colton closed the bag. "Yeah, I'll give it a try, but it's a long shot. Any fingerprints would be smudged by now. Who all touched this?"

"Me, Drake, and Dixie. Claire too."

"I'll need DNA samples from all of you. Stop by the lab as soon as you can."

Was no one going to mention the obvious here? "What if it's related to Heath's and his wife's murders? Maybe this guy targeted Melissa first." Out of the corner of his eye, Drake saw the deputy roll his eyes, but he didn't care. His brother was murdered and he would prove it. He wasn't about to tell the sheriff about Melissa's plans with Chen. It would only reinforce his opinion that Heath killed her.

Colton paused and a frown crouched between his eyes. "They were staying at the Tourmaline. We've had some reports of a Peeping Tom out there. I suppose it's possible. But you both need to let me worry about it and quit getting so excited about everything you find. Let me find the chowderhead." He glowered at Kate. "You know better than to interfere, Kate. It shows a lack of trust in me too."

Drake ignored the sheriff's comment and stared across the table at Kate, who was looking down at her hands. "What all do you remember of that day?"

"Just what I told you. Finding the bodies."

"Back up to before that. Tell me about your morning, what you saw on the way there, what you did after you parked. All of it."

Kate's blue eyes clouded. "I don't remember a whole lot. Finding the bodies wiped out most everything else from that day. I'm sorry. That stupid chemo brain strikes again."

Maybe a hypnotist? What could he do to help jog her memory?

The sheriff cleared his throat. "I do have one suggestion, though I think this is a wicked waste of time. I've used a forensic artist by the name of Gwen Marcey before. She's been trained in helping witnesses recall things. She's holding a seminar in Ellsworth tomorrow. Let me see if she'd have time to talk to Kate."

It sounded like a long shot to Drake, but he was ready to try anything. Ellsworth was only twenty-five miles northwest from Summer Harbor. "Call her."

It was a perfect afternoon for the beach and a great way to forget about the looming interview tomorrow with the forensic artist. Kate laid out a red-and-white tablecloth onto the sand and weighted it down with rocks to keep the wind from tearing it from the shore. Jackson offered his help by plopping down on one corner. The girls squealed as cold waves hit their ankles. Sunset Cove was a great place for kids since the water deepened gradually.

She found it hard to tear her gaze away from Drake. His tanned legs were strong and muscular as he ran from the waves with the girls, and his dark thatch of curly hair glistened in the sunlight. He hadn't said much after their talk with the sheriff at lunch, and she had been glad to let the topic drop. No matter how skilled the forensic artist was, Kate was sure she wouldn't be able to remember anything important. It was just going to be more stress with no reward.

She set the basket in the middle of the tablecloth, then removed her cover-up. Though her bathing suit was a modest one-piece, she felt exposed as she went to join Drake and the girls at the water's edge. "Bunch of sissies. The water isn't *that* cold. Come on in." She bit back a gasp as the frigid water hit her ankles, but she wasn't about to show it to the girls or she'd never coax them in the water. The gentle roller coming her way was perfect, so she held her breath and dove into it as it reached her.

The shock of being immersed in the sea took her breath away, and even when her head popped out of the water, she couldn't quite catch her air. She caught a glimpse of Phoebe's shocked face and waved. "Come on in! I'll teach you to swim." Her wet hair obscured her vision, and she pushed it out of her face, then struck out for the rocks that rimmed this small cove.

When she was in the sea, she felt at one with it. Her feelings of powerlessness melted away in the water, and she didn't have to worry about what other people thought of her. She didn't have to strive to measure up but could let the water strip all those fears away.

She flipped to her back and floated in the waves, facing the warm sun. It had been weeks since she'd gotten a chance to go swimming. Gulls squawked overhead and a tern glided by on the wind.

She turned her head at the sound of a splash and saw Drake dive into a wave. The girls shrieked as he spun and splashed them. She swam closer and angled her hand to the water to throw a large spray of water over his back. The surprise on his face when he whirled around made her giggle as hard as the girls.

"Come on, girls, let's get her," he called.

The girls finally dared to run to the water and jump in. Emma brought her bucket in with her and scooped water into it. Instead of dumping it on Kate's head, she upended it onto her uncle's head.

He faced her. "Hey, you're supposed to be on my side."

"You're bigger than Miss Kate. She needs help." Emma leaped onto Drake's back as he crouched in the water.

His head went under, and Kate knew he was playing along with the little girl. She moved beside the girls. "Good job, Emma. You're so strong."

Drake's head emerged from the sea. "You're all ganging up on me. No fair." He scooped Emma up into the air, then launched her back into the water.

Her grin was wide as she hit the water and came up sputtering. "Get him, Miss Kate."

Jackson leaped from his nap and began to bark, then ran headlong into the waves to join the fun.

Kate put her hands on Drake's shoulders and shoved, but

he didn't move. "You must be stronger than me, Emma. I can't dunk him."

"We'll help you. Come on, Phoebe." Both girls leaped on top of their uncle, and his head went under the waves again.

Kate grinned at the girls. "Good job." The words were barely out of her mouth when a hand grabbed her ankle and yanked her under the water. His hand came around her waist, and a shiver raced up her spine at his touch. It took all her strength not to turn and shift closer. What was it about this man that moved her? She'd thought she was immune to attraction this overpowering. For the first time she realized how strong physical attraction could be.

She shook free of his touch and shot for the top of the waves. His head bobbed up behind her. His crooked grin told her he'd felt something in that moment too. It was pure craziness. Even if she wanted to, she'd never fit in the world where he lived. And she didn't want to try. Claire was here, and so was Kate's entire life. She didn't want to change it for anyone.

"Time for lunch." She turned and walked through the waves toward the shore.

Shivering as the wind hit her wet skin, she reached the cloth and grabbed her cover-up. The warmth of the terry cloth enveloped her, but her shaking didn't stop. It was from being so close to Drake. Maybe she should quit this job. Nothing good was going to come from an attraction this powerful.

Drake rubbed a towel over his hair and wet skin. His cell phone rang, and he glanced at the screen, then swiped it on. "Hello, Lakesha. Yes, I've been working on the modifications." He listened a moment. "Okay, let me give him a call. Text me his number." He ended the call and frowned.

"Trouble?

He shook his head. "Not really. She wants me to call the assistant director and let him know how I plan to modify the drone. I'll do it when we get home. I wish this issue hadn't come up right now. It's hard to stay focused when I want to find a killer, but my business needs attention too." He sighed. "And I want the girls to know they are a top priority for me."

"You're juggling everything, but the girls seem to be settling in well." She bent over the picnic basket and began to unload it away from Jackson's interested sniffs. Nothing made her as hungry as swimming. Lobster rolls, coleslaw, Jell-O squares for the kids, and fruit salad would fill the void in their bellies. She frowned when she felt something in the lining of the basket. Though she hadn't checked the pocket when she was packing the lunch, there shouldn't have been anything inside. She reached into the slit and touched cardboard.

The sunlight hit the candy box, and she dropped it and stepped back.

"What's wrong?" Drake frowned as he reached her side.

She stared at the brown box of DeBrand truffles. "Did you pack those?"

"I didn't pack anything." He stooped and picked up the box. "These look like premium chocolates."

"They are." Her lips felt numb. "No one knows they are my favorite. I had them once when a tourist from Indiana stopped at our blueberry market and traded them for blueberries. They're a local Indiana brand, made in Fort Wayne. You never find them here. Someone would have had to order them."

"You think your uncle put them there?"

She clutched herself and nodded. Hoping for reassurance,

she stared up into Drake's face. "It had to have been Uncle Paul. No one else would know." Jackson whined and pressed against her as if sensing she was upset.

"I think we'd better have Gwen help you figure out who else you might have told."

# TWENTY-SIX

Ellsworth Police Station, about half an hour west of Summer Harbor, was a big brick structure that sat on a small hill. Kate's stomach ached as they were guided down a tiled hallway to a small conference room. Claire was being interviewed after her, but she stayed behind in a waiting room. The room was occupied by only the sheriff and a woman dressed in a well-cut jacket and slacks. Her short blonde hair held a bit of a wave, and her only makeup was lip gloss. Sleek metal chairs upholstered in burgundy surrounded a long conference table.

The woman held Kate's gaze for a moment, then held out her hand. "Gwen Marcey. Please call me Gwen."

Kate liked her warm, confident manner and relaxed a bit. "Kate Mason. Thanks for taking time to meet with us today."

Drake extended his hand. "Drake Newham."

"Sheriff Colton explained the situation, and I am happy to help." She gestured to the table. "Have a seat and we'll get started." She sat in the chair opposite Kate, and the sheriff sat next to her. "I read the police report as well."

Kate settled onto a padded seat and forced herself to unclench her fists. There was nothing to fear from this nice woman, and maybe, just maybe, she'd be able to remember something that helped. Drake settled beside her.

"I'd like for you to share with me what happened. Please start at the beginning and don't leave anything out, even if you don't think it's important." Gwen took out a sketch pad and began to doodle on it. "Can you first tell me what you remember of that day?"

"Of course." Kate started with the first sight of the body, then the realization that there were two bodies.

"That had to have been traumatic." Gwen reached across the table and touched Kate's hand. "I'm sorry you had to go through that."

"I don't like thinking about it. I jumped into the water and tried to move to the cliff walls, but the sea is really strong right there. There's no breakwater or anything. I swallowed water, and Claire yanked me out and wouldn't let me go back in."

"I didn't know you jumped in," Drake said.

She glanced at him. "I couldn't help them though, so it really didn't matter."

Gwen frowned at him. "Please don't interrupt. It's important that we don't stop the flow of her thoughts." Her gaze landed on Kate again. "Everything matters. Even a tiny detail can lead to something else that you've forgotten. Let's back up now. What did you have for breakfast that day?"

Kate thought back to that morning. "Claire came over early to get me. We'd been so busy with wedding preparations that we wanted to spend a day doing nothing but enjoying each other's company." She saw Gwen's blank look. "She's my sister."

"Of course. Now, breakfast?"

"I had coffee on when she got there. I was going to have

yogurt and granola, but Claire said she was starving and wanted bacon and eggs, so I made those for her and had some myself." A tiny thrill went up her neck. At least she was remembering that day.

"You said you then left for a hike. What time would that have been?"

"About eight. I wanted to see the puffins coming in to feed their young." She leaned forward. "They spend all night out on the water."

Gwen smiled. "You sound passionate about puffins."

"Oh, I am!" She was really starting to relax now. This wasn't as hard as she'd imagined.

"What kind of day was it?"

"Beautiful! Sunny and warm with just a few clouds in the sky."

"Who drove to the cliff?"

"I drove my little yellow Volkswagen." Kate peered across the table at the picture Gwen was doodling. It was a sketch of her car.

"Where did you park?"

"At the top of the cliff. We hiked down so we could look up and see the puffins."

"Now close your eyes and put yourself in the car. You've just parked it. Get out of the car."

Kate obeyed and began to visualize that day. "I didn't lock the car. We started hiking down the trail."

"Were there any other cars around when you got there? Any hikers?"

She shook her head.

"What do you hear?"

Kate kept her eyes closed. "I can hear the puffins. And the sea. A truck rumbled by above us."

"Can you see the truck?"

She nodded. "It was black, I think. Covered with mud."

"How does it smell out there today?"

"I can smell the sea. And someone threw trash away. I picked it up and it smelled like stale French fries."

"How do you feel?"

Kate smiled. "Good. I'm with Claire, and we're about to find some puffins. I was really excited because no one knew puffins were nesting on those rocks."

"Mentally look around. What do you see?"

"There were just a few puffins, but it was enough to let Kevin know we had nests. And I didn't see anyone but the game warden."

"You said you didn't see anyone that day."

"Sheriff, please!" Gwen's voice was sharp. "Let me conduct this interview properly." Her voice gentled. "Now, Kate, tell me about the game warden."

Kate opened her eyes. "I forgot the game warden. We always see them when we're out, so I didn't think about it." She drummed her fingers on the table. "He didn't speak to us, and I didn't get a good look at him because he was in the shadows in the tree line."

"Do the game wardens usually speak?"

She glanced at the sheriff, who was listening intently. "Well, yes, I guess it was a little odd. They usually ask what you're doing out there and are especially protective of the puffins. I thought maybe we'd get run off, but he turned away and moved into the woods. I didn't realize until now how strange that was."

Colton scowled and gave a sharp exhale. "You should have

told me about this, Kate." He jotted something in his notebook. "I'll see who was on duty out that way."

"Sheriff, please!" Gwen flipped her sketch pad to a new sheet. "You're doing great, Kate. What was your impression of him?"

Kate tried to recall. "I didn't see him well, like I said, but with the way he moved, he seemed younger than some, maybe thirty or so. I don't know what color his hair was, but I'd guess he was close to six feet tall and thin, maybe 170. But it was just a vague impression. He was really more of a shadow."

Gwen jotted something down on the pad. "What happened next?"

"We started down the trail. There are steps partway down, then you have to be careful and climb the rest of the way."

"Did you see the game warden after you started down the trail?"

"No, I didn't. It took us nearly half an hour to safely reach the bottom." She frowned. "I just remembered something. I found a leather notebook there and picked it up. I meant to turn it in to the ranger station and forgot. It's somewhere in my car."

"Where did you find the notebook?" Drake put in. Gwen fixed him with a look that suggested he let her do the questioning. He shrugged. "Sorry."

Kate answered the question anyway. "It was just after we got out of my car and before we saw the game warden."

Gwen drew swirls on the pad. "Did he see you pick it up?"

"I don't know. Maybe. I didn't see him until we approached the steps down."

Gwen continued to ask questions and asked Kate to go through it again as if she were watching it on TV. There was nothing new to recount once she described the scene. Kate rubbed her aching neck and glanced at her watch. They'd been at this two hours. No wonder she was tired.

Gwen rose and came around the end of the table. "You did great, Kate."

"With my chemo brain, I wasn't sure I could contribute anything new. At least we know to check out the game wardens."

"You had breast cancer?" Gwen asked. "So did I."

Kate shook her head. "I had a marrow transplant to cure aplastic anemia. I'm well now."

Gwen smiled. "Lucky you. I hope I am too." She shook Kate's hand with a firm grip.

"Thanks for your help today." Kate exited the room with Drake, but the sheriff stayed behind to sit in on Claire's interview. They retraced their steps and emerged into the bright sunlight. "You don't think a game warden could have had anything to do with your brother's death, do you?"

"The timing does seem a little suspicious." When they reached his Land Rover, he put his hand on her shoulder. "Thanks for doing that today. I know it wasn't easy. I appreciate it."

The warmth of his fingers made her gulp, but she couldn't move if her life depended on it. "You're welcome." She felt a stab of disappointment when he pulled his hand back and opened her door.

The landscape of lush green trees interspersed with glimpses of blue water sped by the window of Drake's Land Rover. The clock on the dash indicated it was already six, and his stomach rumbled as another reminder. He should go home and keep searching all of Heath's files, but he was dog-tired. "The girls are spending the night with Dixie, so there's no need to rush back. How about we grab dinner? Unless you already have plans?"

He was assuming she didn't have a special man in her life, but he could be wrong. And from her reaction when they were swimming the other day, he was confident she felt the same kind of attraction he was experiencing. Unless he was kidding himself.

At first she continued to stare out the window as if she hadn't heard him, but he saw the way she tensed. She clenched and unclenched her fists as if she was thinking it through. Finally she exhaled and turned to face him. "Are you asking me on a date?"

That was his Kate, always to the point. Wait, what was he thinking? She wasn't *his* by any stretch of the imagination. At least not yet, but he was beginning to admit to himself that it was a possibility. She intrigued him with her spirited comebacks and her heart-shaped face. No woman had intrigued him the way she did.

He cleared his throat and turned the SUV into a pull-off. "Let's talk about you a little bit. Have you ever had a serious relationship?"

She shook her head and didn't avoid his gaze. "I was always busy with the barrens, and my uncle didn't like me dating."

"I think your family has made you feel like you don't deserve to be happy, to enjoy life, and to be loved by others." He knew he'd hit the mark when she dropped her gaze to her hands. "You're smart, talented, good with kids. And you're a genuinely good person, Kate. You care about other people more than yourself, and that's an amazing thing. But you have to be willing to like yourself too. What good is life if you're always turning away from a gift God wants to give you? You think he's like your real dad and will pull a bait and switch on you by offering you a blessing, then snatching it away at the last minute?"

She licked her lips and still didn't look at him. "Of course not. I know God is always giving me blessings. He brought Claire back into my life. He brought you to my door when I was at a really low point, when I wasn't sure how I would have enough money to live on until next year. I'm grateful for that."

He reached over and took one of her tightly clenched hands. "Look at me." For a long minute he thought she wouldn't meet his gaze, but she finally looked up. "Is it your past illness that makes you afraid to live? Every day is a gift, Kate. None of us knows when one day is our last. But that's all the more reason to take hold of every day we're given and live it to the fullest. That usually means risking yourself."

Her brow crinkled, and her blue eyes searched his face. "I've learned that allowing myself to really want something is a sure-fire way of making sure it's taken away. So it's better not to care." She whispered the last sentence.

He laced her cold fingers with his warm ones. "Grab life with both hands. You're well. It's okay to dream." Her fingers moved a bit under his, as though his words had impacted her. "Dinner is a great first step."

A smile curved her full lips, and light sparkled in her eyes. "What if I told you I wanted the biggest steak you could afford?"

"Steak, not lobster?"

Her smile widened. "I can eat lobster any day of the week. Steak is another matter."

"Steak it is, then. How about the Tourmaline? I've heard they fly their steaks in from New Zealand, and they're so tender they melt in your mouth."

Her fingers curled around his. "Okay. I might want dessert though. They make a crème brûlée that's to die for. I can risk a bit of sugar for one night."

"I'll buy you anything you want." He felt a ridiculous sense of accomplishment as though he'd just won the biggest contract of his life. He started the Land Rover and headed for the ferry in Summer Harbor.

# TWENTY-SEVEN

Kate glanced down at her jeans and blue ruffled top. "I think I'm a little underdressed," she whispered to Drake as the server led them through the Sea Room toward a back table. The place was all crystal and linen with tourmaline floors that were so highly polished she could see her reflection in them as she followed the server. She'd never eaten here, only at the Bistro. Floor-to-ceiling windows looked out on the moonlit water far below the cliff. It was a scene out of a movie.

Classical music poured from a baby grand piano by the window, and the pianist, Tyler Brighton, waved to her. "Kate!"

She stopped a moment to say hello. "Tyler, I didn't know you were back in town." They'd gone to school together, and he'd moved off to Boston to attend college and had never come back.

His fingers rippled over the keys, but he shot a quick grin her direction. "I wondered if you were still around. The management here is looking for a singer that I can accompany. Going to step their entertainment up a notch. I was going to give them your name if you were still around."

Heat washed up her neck to her cheeks. "I'm no professional singer, and I hate singing in public."

"You could be. You have the best voice I've ever heard. The

whole town is talking about that song you sang at Claire's wedding. You could make a living with your voice."

She laughed, but it was more of a croak, and all she wanted was to escape. "You're sweet. Listen, we'll let you get back to work. I'll talk to you later." She followed the server to their table where she was able to slide into her seat in the shadows. How embarrassing.

Drake, looking impossibly tall, dark, and handsome, smiled at her from across the table. "He's right, you know. I've heard you singing with the girls. You've got a great voice. Did you ever think about singing professionally?"

Did he have to talk about it? She swallowed and shook her head. "When I'd sing around the house, my mother always said I sounded like a frog. I was in choir, and she refused to come to any concerts because she didn't want to see me make a fool of myself."

A scowl replaced his grin, and he reached across the white linen tablecloth to take her hand. "It's a wonder you turned out so remarkable with that kind of role model. You are always encouraging the girls with whatever they are doing. I saw Phoebe's drawing of the ocean and a puffin the other day. I couldn't quite tell if it was a bird or a dog, but you told her she had a real talent for drawing."

"She has a great eye for color. She'll get better." Thank goodness the server was bringing their water now. She wanted to sink under the table so no one could see her face, which had to be as red as her blueberry fields.

He removed his hand and thanked the server, then ordered a seafood sampler appetizer. "So what would you do if there was no one to say you couldn't?"

She took a gulp of her water. "I'd love to be an interior designer. I adore playing with color and texture. I obsessively spend hours on Houzz whenever I have ten minutes."

"You did an amazing job with my cottage. Did you ever take any classes?"

She linked her fingers together and looked down. "I had a year of them before I quit to help Mom with the blueberry barrens. She just couldn't manage on her own."

"You've put everyone else first all your life, haven't you? I admire your giving spirit, but there comes a time when you should think about what makes you happy. If you could walk away from the blueberries, you'd do it, wouldn't you?"

Did he really mean all this? She dared a peek at his expression and found him staring back intently. "Mom would have a fit."

"Your mother is in jail for a well-deserved reason. She's not part of this discussion. You could walk away and leave the fields for her to worry about when she gets out of prison. It's not like the fields are going anywhere."

She blinked. "But who would harvest them? They will need to be pruned and cared for to make sure next year's harvest is good."

He went quiet while the server brought their appetizer, then dished up some of the sampler on a small plate and handed it across the table to Kate. "So what if it's not? The blueberry police aren't going to come after you if the fields are untended. It's not your responsibility."

He was right. There was nothing tying her to those fields. She could live in the house and get another job, anything she wanted. Her smile faded. "There's hardly a market for interior design skills up here. Many can't afford that kind of service."

"There are businesses. The decor in this hotel could use

refreshing. Think about your vision for the place, then go talk to the manager."

Could he be right? There were other places, too, businesses in Bar Harbor and Ellsworth as well as vacation homes. She would have a tiny nest egg after this summer. It might be enough to let her launch a design consulting business. The problem was, she had no real experience to show. But she didn't know if it would work if she didn't try. "I decorated Claire's house, and everyone has raved about how welcoming it is. I could take some pictures and show them around."

She could start small, maybe with a café or a clothing store in Bar Harbor. The ideas flashed through her head so fast she wished she had a pad to jot them down.

She studied his strong face. "Was it scary for you to start your business?"

He tipped his head to one side. "Not really scary but sobering. I put every cent I'd saved for years into it. I started building drones in my garage fifteen years ago as a hobby, and it really took off. I started a real business about ten years ago." He looked away and his face went somber.

"Something wrong?"

His gaze swung back her way. "I'm sorry. I just had an idea how to fix the design on my drone."

"Don't apologize. I know you've been struggling with it. Did you call the Fish and Game Service guy? That regional director?"

He nodded. "We had a good discussion, but the call revealed the modifications will need to be more extensive than I thought. I have an idea to try when I get home though." Drake dipped a giant shrimp into cocktail sauce and took a bite. "Eat up, honey."

*Honey.* The endearment took her by surprise and stopped her ideas dead. He admitted there were feelings developing between them, something she hadn't wanted to face. If she became wrapped up in a new career here, shouldn't he be worried there was no room for him?

She studied his strong jaw and firm lips. He was a good man who seemed to care about other people. A man like her uncle would pooh-pooh her ideas and would try to keep her chained to the past if it meant he might lose her. But Drake was different, and she was finally ready to let her guard down a little and see where it might lead.

The girls slept in the back of the Land Rover with Jackson sleeping between them even when they hit the dirt road in front of the cottages. Though the girls had been going to spend the night with Dixie, Drake was too worried about what was going on to leave them with his aunt for the entire night.

He glanced across the seat at Kate. The moonlight lit up the planes and angles of her beautiful face. If they'd been alone, he might have pulled over to the side of the road and taken her in his arms. Everything about her fascinated him, from her tiny ears to the dimples that so often flashed in her cheeks.

He slowed as he approached her house. "Hey, we need to fetch that missing notebook you remembered when you talked to Gwen today. Want to do it now?"

She hadn't said much on the ride back, but she straightened now and turned to look at him. "What about the girls?"

"They won't wake up. You can stay in the SUV with them, and I'll retrieve it. I'm curious, aren't you?"

Her dimples appeared. "I haven't thought much about it since we left. Some handsome guy has been keeping my head in a whirl."

He loved her honesty and the way she didn't try to hide her attraction to him. She wasn't coy and didn't play games. It was the sexiest thing he'd ever experienced, and he felt a powerful surge of attraction again. "I plan on doing more of that."

She caught her full lower lip in her teeth and gave a breathy chuckle. "I'm not sure I can handle much more."

He pulled into the drive behind her little yellow Bug. "Why do you have that ugly little car?"

"Ugly? That's Mildred. I bought her with money I earned myself in a summer job my first year of college. She's taken good care of me."

"College, huh? So you've had her at least ten years?"

"Twelve. She's a tough old bird."

"Rust is going to claim her one of these days."

She put a hand over her heart. "Shh, she'll hear you. I can't bear to think about losing my longtime friend."

He grinned and put the SUV in Park. "Hang tight. I'll be right back. I'm going to leave the lights on so I can see."

"It's in the trunk. I think it might be in the wheel well. I think it got shoved there when I was wrestling with the tire. Want me to help you find it?"

"I think I can find my way around an old Beetle." He grabbed a flashlight in case he needed it, then got out and released the hatch. The damaged tire was still on top of the carpet, and he walked back to the SUV. "Should I put the tire away or did you not get it fixed?"

Her cheeks went pink. "I haven't gotten it fixed." She shrugged. "I forgot."

Most likely she didn't have the money. He'd get that done right away. Returning to the car, he lifted out the tire, then moved the trunk carpet and aimed the flashlight at the tire well. Aha, there it was. The small leather notebook looked old and worn, and he hesitated. It was possible this was a clue to his brother's death. He probably shouldn't touch it.

He whipped out his phone, called the sheriff's office, and got put through to Deputy Kissner. "I found the notebook. You think you guys should retrieve it and run it for prints?"

"The notebook Kate found on her walk? It wasn't really close to the scene. I doubt it has anything to do with our investigation." Kissner sounded distracted.

Drake stared down at the book. "You're probably right, but just in case, I'll be careful with it. Come by and get it if you want it." He ended the call and jogged back to the SUV. "There should be a plastic bag under your seat. I don't want to smudge any prints, just in case. Could you hand me one?"

She reached under her seat and retrieved one, then passed it to him. "You called Danny?"

"Kissner. He doesn't think it's important, but I'm not convinced. I just want to make sure we cover our bases. We didn't think the jewelry pouch was important either." His fingers grazed hers when he took the bag, and warmth spread up his arm straight to his heart. The sooner he got this, the sooner he could get the girls to bed and spend a little more time with Kate.

He went back to the car and picked up the notebook, then

took it back to her. "I'm going to throw your tire in the back so I can get it fixed."

Her smile was his reward as he went to shut the trunk and carry the tire around to the Land Rover's trunk area. He tried to open and shut it as quietly as he could so he didn't wake the girls, but Emma's head popped up as he came around to get back in the SUV.

"Can we watch a movie when we get home?" Her voice was alert as if she'd gotten all her sleep in.

He glanced at the clock. "It's past your bedtime."

"But I'm not sleepy now. Aunt Dixie gave us a big supper, and I fell asleep before it got dark. I want to watch a Disney movie."

"Me too," Phoebe chimed in.

Drake's gaze met Kate's. "What do you say?"

Her eyes widened, and a tiny smile lifted her lips. "I think we can let them stay up this once. It's been a hectic day, and we could all use some snuggle time." She leaned over and whispered, "I took a quick look at the notebook. It all appears to be gibberish. Some kind of kid's code maybe. Nothing important, and you said Kissner didn't seem interested either."

"I was hoping for some *alone* snuggle time," he whispered as he dropped the gearstick into Drive.

# TWENTY-EIGHT

The aroma of baking cookies filled Kate's blue-and-white kitchen. Everyone loved Claire's almond-flour chocolate chip cookies, even Luke. Claire checked the cookies and decided they needed a couple more minutes. "There's nothing like that aroma. My mother always made them on Saturdays when I was little. It was the only time I was allowed to help in the kitchen. The rest of the time our cook shooed me out."

Her sister looked up with a smile. "I cooked a lot, but it usually wasn't fun things like cookies. I learned to make jerky from deer meat and how to dehydrate blueberries."

"I like your house." Emma licked cookie batter off the spoon. "I could live here forever."

"You don't like the cottage?" Kate reached for her coffee.

"I love the cottage." Phoebe ran a finger around the surface of the bowl, then licked it.

"I like the blue here." Emma carried the spoon to the sink, then washed the sticky batter from her hands. "Uncle Drake says he's going to have you come to our house in Boston and redecorate it. Can you make our kitchen look like this one? His is all dark brown and feels sad."

Claire grinned and wagged her brows at Kate. Her sister

216

seemed different today, relaxed and happier than she'd seen her since the blueberry harvest proved so bad. "Come help me with the cookies. Where's your cooling rack?"

Kate rose and grabbed the rack from the cabinet under the cooktop. "I see your grin." She turned to the girls. "You can go play in the tree house until the cookies are cool."

"Yay!" Phoebe slid off her chair and raced for the door with Emma on her heels.

Claire lifted out the sheet of cookies and grabbed the spatula. "Okay, give. I can see you're just bursting to tell me something."

"I, um, I went out with Drake last night. We went to dinner at the Sea Room."

Claire's chest could hardly contain the joy that swelled up. "It's about time! Dish! How'd it go? And how'd he talk you into it?"

"One thing I really like about him is that he's so direct and honest. He doesn't beat around the bush. He pulled off the road and told me it was silly for us to pretend we aren't drawn to each other and that we should explore where those feelings might lead."

Claire lifted a cookie from the tray to the rack. "Wow, that *is* direct. Did you shoot him down at first?"

Kate's blush deepened. "No. He was right. We went swimming with the girls the other day, and we both knew there were feelings there. He could sense it and so could I."

"Well, I think it's wonderful! How did dinner go?" She put the last cookie on the rack and laid the spatula in the sink.

"Good. We talked about what I wanted to do with my life. I actually told him the truth about loving interior design. He gave me some great ideas about starting small with local businesses. Is it okay if I take pictures of what I did in your house?"

"Of course!" Claire wanted to see Kate break free from the blueberry barrens. She had so much talent.

"And he flirted with me all evening. I wasn't sure how to even react." Kate's cell phone rang, and she went to the table to grab it. "Hello?" After a few seconds the color washed from her face. "Who is this?" She punched the phone off and tossed it back to the table. "Jerk."

"What did he say?"

"Nothing. He just breathed in my ear. It was creepy."

Claire frowned. "I don't like all this stuff, Kate. That truffle incident in the picnic basket was really creepy, and now this. I mean, even I didn't know the DeBrands were your favorite. Luke thinks it's someone you know, maybe someone you went to school with."

"I thought it was Uncle Paul, but he wouldn't call and just breathe in the phone. That's just weird. Maybe it's someone else. I have no idea."

"What if he's not? What if it's the same guy who killed Whitney Peece? She looked a little like you. Blue eyes, blonde hair."

A troubled frown lined Kate's forehead. "You're scaring me, Claire."

"I haven't heard how the investigation is going. Someone broke in and watched her shower. Maybe it wasn't the boyfriend at all. I want you on high alert."

Kate turned to the phone and grabbed it. "The caller ID reads Anonymous, so he must have blocked his information. I wonder if the sheriff could track it."

"It's worth asking." Claire listened as Kate reported the nuisance call to the sheriff's department.

Kate ended the call, then glanced out the window at the

girls. "Jonas answered, thank goodness. I was glad it was some-one who knew the situation. He took down all the information and said he'd look into it. He sounded determined."

"Everyone likes you and wants to keep you safe." Claire bit her lip and stared at her sister. "Back to Drake. Did you tell him about not being able to have kids?"

Kate looked away. "Not yet. I know I need to, but it seems a little presumptuous to think our relationship will go that far."

"It's a lot better to tell him now. Otherwise he might think you were being dishonest by not telling him."

Kate went to the sink and turned on the water. "I'll tell him as soon as I get a chance." Her tone indicated she'd rather face a snarling lion than tell Drake.

Claire touched her on the shoulder. "I just want you to be happy. If he's the man we think he is, this won't faze Drake at all."

"I hope you're right."

Drake watched Kate standing with the girls and her dog at Mount Desert Ice Cream. Bar Harbor tourists jostled past, and the festive atmosphere of the Wednesday night Seaside Cinema brought excited chatter wafting around him. The quaint seaside shops and boats dotting Frenchman Bay made for a picturesque setting. He was ready for some relaxation, especially with Kate along.

He tucked a bag of books they'd bought from Sherman's Books and Stationery under his arm. His gaze lingered on her as she exited the gray-shingled building trimmed in green. The wind blew her blonde hair around her head, and her sun-kissed face kept his attention riveted on her beautiful form. Her gaze caught his, and she smiled back at him.

She reached him with the girls in tow and handed him a cup of ice cream. "You said to surprise you, so I got Maine sea salt caramel. You can try my maple walnut though." She held up a spoonful. "This is the second time I've had sugar in a week. You're being a bad influence on me."

He slid the cold confection into his mouth. It hit his taste buds and exploded with flavor. "Wow, intense flavors! Pretty good." He offered her a bite of his.

She licked it off his spoon. "Yummy."

There was something curiously intimate about sharing food with her. The tension of the past few weeks eased away, and he wished their relationship had progressed far enough to hold her hand and stroll to a jewelry shop to buy her something. He was sure she wasn't quite ready for that.

"I got Maine maple pecan," Emma said.

"Me too." Phoebe skipped along at his side while Emma clung close to Kate's.

The girls were dressed alike today in white shorts and red-and-white tops. Kate had put their hair in ponytails with big red bows. They looked like any other typical family on vacation. He imagined a little girl with Kate's big blue eyes and a little boy with his curly hair. Crazy thought when they hadn't known each other that long, but he was tired of being alone. His career had taken everything out of him, and it was time to have a family. His house had echoed with loneliness for too long. His nieces would bring some liveliness, but it wouldn't be the same without Kate. He was getting used to seeing her tending to the girls with such sweet consideration.

They walked down the hill toward Frenchman Bay. It took a few minutes longer than usual because people kept stopping and asking to pet Jackson. His tail wagged so hard, Drake thought he might fling it right off. By the time they reached the park, people were already spreading blankets on the grass to watch the cinema even though the sun wouldn't set for several hours. He pointed to a prime spot. "Think we should grab that while we can?"

She nodded. "My feet are tired anyway. I shouldn't have worn these new sandals." She stopped and waved. "There's Jonas."

The deputy waved back and headed their way. The sun burnished his red hair to a deeper shade, and his smile widened when he reached them. Drake hadn't recognized him out of his deputy uniform. He wore jeans and a green T-shirt today.

Drake handed the basket and blanket to the girls. "You can pick out our spot and spread out the blanket. When we get done talking to the deputy, we'll play Uno with you." The girls scampered off, tossing their empty ice cream containers into a trash can as they went.

"Any word on that call I got yesterday?" Kate asked Jonas when he reached them.

The deputy shook his head. "It pinged from a spot in Ellsworth, but we couldn't trace it. I went to the spot, but it was an empty parking lot, so that was no help at all."

"What call?" Drake hadn't heard anything about it.

Kate took a bite of ice cream. "Just a prank. I wanted to make sure the sheriff knew about it just in case it was important."

Jonas put his hands in his pockets. "I'm glad I ran into you. I had a piece of information to pass along. The sheriff talked to Whitney Peece's family, and one of the bracelets was hers."

Kate's smile vanished, and she tossed the last of her ice cream with an expression of distaste. "I'm sorry to hear it. What about the boyfriend?"

Drake straightened at the term. Hadn't Claire found the woman too? Too many coincidences for his peace of mind.

Jonas shrugged. "No way to know for sure, but I've been poring over anything that might be related. The Peece woman could have even been his first victim. We haven't had anything like this in our area before. All of law enforcement is on high alert though. The sheriff wants to find this guy before it hits the newspapers and causes a panic."

Drake tossed his empty ice cream container. "Have you had any other rapes?"

"We always get a few, but the perpetrators are usually old boyfriends or people who know the victim."

"You'd better catch him fast."

"We intend to, sir. We're doing our best. We might be a rural law enforcement team, but we know our stuff." Kissner's voice turned stiff.

Kate shot Drake a warning glance. "I know you do, Jonas. Thanks for letting us know what's happening. You're off today?"

He nodded. "I have a date wandering around here somewhere." He waved up toward the top of the hill. "I'd better go. If I hear anything else, one of us will call you."

Drake took her arm, and they headed toward the blanket the girls had managed to spread out. "Why didn't you tell me about the phone call?"

"I didn't want the girls to hear about it. They were in the yard when the guy called. I'm sure it's nothing. Just a prank call."

Drake hoped she was right, but he didn't like it.

# TWENTY-NINE

The sixteen-foot screen rolled with the closing credits of the movie, and people began to pick up their things. Kate didn't want to move. Somehow she'd drifted off to sleep with her head on Drake's shoulder, and Emma curled against her other side. Phoebe slept in the circle of Drake's other arm, and Jackson lay snoring at Phoebe's side.

Kate shifted slightly onto her side. She wanted to burrow her nose into Drake's shirt and inhale the enticing aroma of his skin. A powerful wave of desire washed over her, something she'd never really felt before. If she dared, she would reach up and pull his face close enough to kiss. She needed to move—now. Instead she continued to snuggle against the strong length of his body.

Was he sleeping too? She peeked at his face and found him staring at her with the same intense longing she felt. She should look away before it was too late, but instead she moved her face close enough that his breath touched her face.

His right arm scooped her closer, and he nuzzled his face in her hair. "You smell like the beach."

"It's the coconut shampoo," she whispered. Her head screamed for her to move, but her heart refused to listen.

Did he move first or did she? She thought she was the one

who tipped her lips up in an invitation before his mouth swooped down on hers and she began to drown in such intense sensations she forgot where she was. Her right arm came up around his neck and held him tight. Her eyes fluttered shut, and she found the taste of him absolutely intoxicating. If she could, she'd stay right here in this moment forever.

When he pulled away, she felt cold. Opening her eyes, she saw his tender smile and she smiled back. "I suppose we'd better get the girls home."

"I suppose so. We're about the last ones left."

He was right. She glanced around and found the grassy field empty but for workers cleaning up the abandoned trash. She sat up and pushed her hair out of her face. "You think we can carry them?"

"I'll go get the SUV while you stay here with the girls." He started to pull his arm away, then swooped down for one last kiss. "I'll be right back."

*Is this love?* She'd never felt that dizzying combination of wanting to be close to someone and of caring what he thought of her. She watched his tall, muscular figure stride up the hill to where he'd parked the Land Rover. Did she dare let this continue? What if he didn't feel the same?

She touched her lips. He'd seemed to be as into that kiss as much as she was, but weren't men different? She'd always heard they'd take what a woman offered, and she'd been quick to make her desire known.

Heat washed up her face. What must he think of her? She wanted to groan. He was probably used to way more sophisticated women. Her leg was asleep, and she struggled to get up and stand on it. It felt like a wooden table leg, and she bent over to massage it. From the corner of her eye, she saw a large white envelope lying beside the blanket. Someone had probably left it.

She reached for it, then froze when she saw her name typed onto a sticky label on the front. Her hand shook as she picked it up and looked around. The last of the stragglers were hurrying to their cars, and she felt very alone in the open grassy field even though there were figures aboard the boats bobbing in the bay. She could easily call for help if she needed it.

Who had left this? It felt sinister after everything that had happened, and she feared opening it would change things even more. She couldn't see it anyway until she got into the Land Rover, so she stuck it in the basket with the empty food containers, then turned to watch for Drake.

The big Land Rover rolled to a stop at the curb, and he got out with a smile that faded when he looked at her. "What's wrong?"

"I'll tell you later."

She lifted Phoebe and carried her to the SUV, then buckled her into the backseat. Jackson hopped in behind her. The little girl's head lolled to the side as she slumped and fell into a deeper sleep. Emma barely stirred when Drake put her in the other side of the Land Rover. He buckled her in and shot a questioning glance at Kate before sliding under the steering wheel.

Kate stowed the basket in the back, pausing long enough to grab the envelope, then climbed into the passenger seat. "This was on the ground by our blanket. Did you see anyone put it there?"

He flipped on the overhead light and stared at her name. "No, but it would have been easy enough to miss it with the people leaving. What's in it?"

She buckled her seat belt. "I didn't open it. Go ahead."

Frowning, he tore the flap open and reached inside. "Feels

like pictures." He pulled out a handful of glossy snapshots, then turned them over to look at them.

She leaned closer to study them with him. The top picture was of the two of them at dinner the other night. It was during the time when he'd taken her hand. The expression on his face quickened her pulse. But there was also a big black X over Drake's face.

Drake laid it aside to reveal the next picture: one of her standing in the backyard with the girls. The next picture showed them walking toward the police station in Ellsworth. The last one was taken through Claire's kitchen window. It showed the two of them sitting at the table with coffee cups. "I think these were taken with a drone. See the angle from up high?"

She picked up the stack of pictures and flipped them over. There was writing on the one that had the X over Drake's face. In bold block letters it read YOU'RE MINE.

Drake shut the hotel door and threw the security bar. After talking to the sheriff, he'd decided to move the girls to a suite at the Hotel Tourmaline. He didn't like the fact they'd been in one of the pictures. The deeper he got into Heath's files, the more he worried that Heath's and Melissa's deaths had been revenge. Who knew what moved a man like Wang.

Bundled in a fluffy throw, Kate was on the sofa in the living room with Jackson at her feet. She was pale, and her eyes looked enormous. "Wow, this suite is fabulous." She offered him a smile, but it didn't reach her eyes. "Leather furniture and that carpet is so thick you sink into it. We didn't have to stay here. There's a less expensive motel in Summer Harbor."

"Don't try to make small talk." He crouched beside her. "This isn't your fault."

She rose and tossed the throw aside. "I should go home. Maybe if I face him, this will end."

He caught her arm as she neared. "You're not going any-where. I'm not about to let you confront this guy. He is a total unknown, Kate." His gaze roved over her beautiful face. Her skin would feel as soft as down if he touched it, and he could smell the scent of her hair again. All he wanted to do was kiss her until they were both breathless.

She must have seen his intention because she pulled away and shook her head. "I-I should apologize for the way I acted at the movie. I was half asleep and didn't realize what I was doing."

He gave a short bark of laughter. "You're not seriously going to try to pretend you didn't want to kiss me."

Her cheeks colored and she looked down. "I didn't mean that. It's just that . . ."

"Not another word." He grinned and cupped her face in his hands and kissed her. He'd kissed his share of women, but none of them made him feel the way Kate did. She tasted like passion and commitment. Like forever. He'd never imagined forever with a woman before, but he was in love with her and it felt great. Her lips were soft and responsive under his, and a protest rose in his throat when she finally pulled away. He could feel her heart beating as fast as a bird's against his chest.

He pulled her more tightly against his heart and rested his chin on her head. "We are right together, Kate. I think you feel it too."

"I'm afraid to read too much into it." Her voice was soft. "I don't have much experience with men. For all I know you'll break my heart, Drake Newham. I'm afraid that kind of heartbreak would leave me like Humpty Dumpty."

"I'm not going to hurt you, Kate." He wanted to kiss her again, but he was afraid of scaring her. This was moving so fast, faster than his own comfort level could handle. Was it because of the danger they were going through together?

He reached down and grabbed the fluffy white throw, then tucked it around her. "You can take the big bed, and I'll take the rollaway here in the living room."

Her big blue eyes looked into his soul. "I'm not a bit sleepy."

"I'm not either. We could cuddle on the sofa." He grinned when she colored again.

She tucked a strand of hair behind her ear. "I don't know what to make of you. You scare me, Drake."

"You scare me, Kate. I think love is supposed to feel this way." Her eyes widened at the word, and his own heart clenched when he said it, but it was what he was feeling. "You feel it, too, don't you? I love you. It's fast, I know, but I'm sure. Aren't you?"

She nodded and tears welled in her eyes. "I don't want to love you."

His fingers touched her chin, and he tipped her head up. "Why not? There's nothing wrong with falling in love."

"You don't understand." Tears began to roll down her face, and she swiped at them impatiently. "I'm doing this all wrong. I should have told you sooner. Claire told me to tell you weeks ago when she saw how attracted to you I was." Jackson whined and got up to press his head against her knee.

His gut clenched at the sadness in her voice. "Whatever it is, you can tell me. I want to wake up to your smile every morning and see your face across from me at the breakfast table. I want to grow old with you by my side and our kids all around. I think you want that too."

"That's just the point!" Her words sounded loud in the quiet room. "I can't have kids, Drake. The chemo ruined my ovaries. I'm barren now."

He blinked as the perfect dream world he'd been living in popped like an overfilled water balloon. "I see." He glanced over her shoulder into the open bedroom where his nieces slept. "We have Phoebe and Emma though. And we could adopt more children."

She backed away and shook her head. "You're just saying that now so you don't hurt me. I know how important children are to you. You've talked about it a lot."

He *had* talked about it, had made assumptions. And while the news took him aback, it didn't change how he felt about her. When he reached for her, she stepped away and ran to the other bedroom. She let Jackson in and the lock clicked on the other side.

He rattled the doorknob. "Let me in, Kate. It doesn't make any difference." When she didn't answer, he raked his hand through his hair and blew out a breath.

She was tired. He'd let her sleep and convince her in the morning.

Kate opened the door to the balcony and stepped out under the moonlight. She didn't want to hear him call her name again. She couldn't make any kind of decision about a relationship with Drake until she figured out who was trying to scare her. Her brain cried out for careful thought.

She pulled a chair and small table closer to the railing and stared out on the mesmerizing scene of waves rolling to the rocky shoreline. The lights of a distant boat went by, and the moon was huge over the water. She heard the dog shuffle behind her—his nails clicked on the concrete as he came to join her.

Such serenity should help her think. She opened the notebook she'd dug from her purse and took out a pen. She began to list all the events of the summer. The bodies she'd found, the Peeping Tom, the break-ins, her uncle's escape, the trophy bag found in her blueberry field, the chocolate in the picnic basket, the breather call, and the photographs. Staring at the list, she saw no correlation at first. Then she began to draw lines of connection between them, and the truth made her straighten and gasp.

Her uncle hadn't done all the things she'd thought.

She'd tried to believe the more serious things had been committed by her uncle, but there was no clear correlation between him and the things that had terrified her the most— like the chocolate and the photographs. The most logical link was between the Peeping Tom, the trophy bag, the chocolate, the breather call, and the photographs. This would indicate that whoever was watching women had fixated on her. No way had her uncle done them.

Then who? She looked out over the lights of Folly Shoals and thought about it. Everything seemed to center on that trophy bag of jewelry. The possessions of several young women were in that assortment.

*There's a stalker in the area.*

He wasn't just targeting her, but other women too. And he'd go on with it if no one forced him into the open. Whitney might have been his first kill, but she wouldn't be his last. The next one could be her or Claire. Or one of her friends at church. Was she just going to stand by and let the guy do whatever he wanted, or was she going to put an end to this?

Fear wasn't a condition she was okay to live with. She was going to drag that man out into the light and expose him. And the only way to do that was to be a target. In the morning she would call Danny and tell him she would be a decoy.

Drake wouldn't like it. For the first time since she came out under the stars, she let herself think about what Drake had just said. Did her inability to have children really matter so little to him, or was he trying not to hurt her feelings? She let herself linger on how he'd looked when he admitted he loved her. What if the situation were reversed, and he couldn't have children? Would she love him less?

No, she'd still love him. That realization set her world on an even keel again. Claire was right. She'd let herself be defined by what she didn't have instead of what she possessed. Kate had been through so much in her life, and she didn't need to fear the future. God had been with her through every bit of the trials she'd endured. He'd be with her no matter where her path led.

She twined her fingers into her dog's coat, then leaned forward and put her arms around his neck. Drake had helped her see in some small way that she didn't have to earn love. He loved her just because. Just like God did. Just like anyone who really mattered would love her.

She rose and inhaled one last gulp of sweet, salt-laden air, then turned and went back inside with Jackson close behind. She had to let go of the fear she'd carried for so many years. As she pulled the drapes on the door, she caught a glimpse of the moon shining down on the water. Light always shone in the darkness.

# THIRTY

Drake yawned and opened his laptop at the small table in the main area of the hotel suite. He should go to bed, but after talking with Kate, he knew he'd turn their conversation over and over in his head. It would be better to look at more of Heath's files. He checked his e-mail first, and six new messages popped up. He scanned them and saw one from Deputy Kissner. He opened the attached document titled with his brother's name and scanned it.

Seeing his brother's face on a steel table at the coroner's made him close the lid of his computer and lean back in the chair. His heart hammered in his chest, and he looked at the computer with loathing. How did he even get through looking at that autopsy? His hand shook as he reached for the laptop lid again. Maybe he should start with Melissa's autopsy report.

He made a quick jump back to his mail and opened the other document, but seeing Melissa's white face wasn't much easier. Though she'd made some poor decisions, he loved her like a sister. Moisture filled his eyes and he blinked it away, then focused on the report.

The autopsy had begun at eight thirty the morning after her death. He looked over what she was wearing: black jogging pants and a bright-yellow athletic shirt. Black-and-yellow jogging shoes. She'd clearly gone for a jog. He forced himself to change windows and look at Heath's report. His list of clothing included jeans and a T-shirt, so he hadn't been jogging with her. So what had he been doing up there? Drake flipped back to Melissa's report and scanned the toxicology report. No drugs. Nothing notable in Heath's drug report either, just some antihistamine.

Inhaling, he forced himself to look at the rest of her report. The marks on her neck indicated she'd been choked before being tossed over the cliff. If he were the sheriff, he would have assumed Heath strangled her and threw her off as well, but Drake couldn't bring himself to believe it. He scanned down to the internal exam section, then gasped.

She'd been pregnant.

The sheriff hadn't mentioned that. Had Heath known she was pregnant? There was no way he would have killed his own child. This evidence added to his certainty that his brother was being accused of someone else's crime. Who would have wanted to kill Heath and Melissa? He was going to have to keep digging. Drake had barely touched a fraction of all the cases Heath had handled. The answer had to be there somewhere.

He glanced at his watch. It was nearly ten, but maybe the sheriff was still around. He called the office and was told the sheriff was just walking out the door but to hold on. While he waited, Drake peeked in on the girls. They were sound asleep, each with a stuffed animal he'd bought in the gift shop downstairs when they checked in. He walked to the other bedroom door and put his ear against it but heard nothing. Maybe Kate had been able to sleep. He hoped so.

Finally Sheriff Colton's gravelly voice spoke into his ear. "Drake, you just caught me. Has something else happened?"

"Sorry to disturb you so late, Sheriff. I was just looking over the autopsy reports."

"Jonas told me he'd sent them. Sorry I forgot about them. It's been a crazy summer."

"You never mentioned Melissa was pregnant. I just want to say again that there is no way Heath would have killed her when she was carrying his baby. No way in the world. He was the best father you can imagine." Drake put a commanding tone into his voice. "You've got to start broadening your search. There are plenty of men who hated Heath for letting them get convicted. Maybe one of them was released from jail and is out for revenge."

The sheriff cleared his throat. "We got back some other information today, Drake. That's why I'm here so late. It pretty much shows our investigation has been on the right track all along. The baby Melissa carried wasn't Heath's."

The words crushed Drake's heart. He tried to speak and couldn't. *Not Heath's.* That knowledge could have made him snap. Had Melissa brought him to Maine to tell him the truth? Maybe she'd admitted she was taking the girls and leaving. Any man might react poorly to such devastating news.

"Drake?"

He wet his lips. "I'm here. I-I'm just stunned."

"Ayuh, I can imagine. Sorry to have to tell you such bad news. I think I told you we've got a witness who heard them arguing the night before, then with all this other evidence . . ."

"Yes, I understand. Thanks for telling me." He ended the call and pressed his fingers into his eyes. Heath appeared to have done exactly what everyone said.

Kate sat across the table from Claire in the Oyster Bistro as dawn lit the horizon with pink and gold. Only a few early risers occupied the restaurant, and they held to their coffee cups like a boat to an anchor. Claire still looked a little sleepy, and her long, blonde hair was still damp. Kate felt like death warmed over, which was no surprise after the night she'd had. She kept replaying the events of the evening over and over in her head. And heart.

This place always soothed her. The pale-green coffee cups added to the pink-and-green decor, and the booths were private and plush.

Claire examined her sister's face. "You've got dark circles under your eyes. Did you get any sleep at all?"

Kate shook her head and took a sip of coffee. The strong taste awakened her senses. "Not much. I'm not going to run from that maniac, Claire." She narrowed her eyes. "I've got bear spray and my gun. Let him just try to grab me, and I'll show him what resistance looks like. I'm done hiding out."

"Don't do anything stupid. I don't want you to be hurt—or worse."

She'd run the plan over and over in her head all night, mostly as a way to keep from thinking about Drake. "I'm not going to get hurt. I'm going to catch him."

"What are you going to do?"

Kate waited for a moment to answer as the server brought their breakfast of omelets and bacon. "I'm going to set up a decoy. I'm going to ask Danny for a wire and have the deputies surrounding the spot." She held up her hand when Claire's eyes went wide. "It will be totally safe. I'll pick a place where Danny and his deputies can hide without being seen."

"Like where?"

"I was thinking about Mermaid Point. There are plenty of places to hide in the vegetation. Plus a couple of officers could be just offshore in what appears to be a fishing boat. I think it's foolproof."

Claire folded her arms across her chest and sat back. "A million things could go wrong, Kate. I can't believe Drake would agree to this either. What did he say about this harebrained idea?"

"I didn't tell him yet. We, um, we had an interesting evening." She told her sister about the kiss and what he said in the hotel suite. When she'd called Claire last night, she hadn't mentioned anything but the note.

Claire said nothing for a long moment. Her blue eyes were shadowed with worry. "Kate, you are worthy of love. Where did you ever get the idea that your only value is in bearing children? God has a plan for your life, and he's your real security. Whether that includes children or not is immaterial. The right man will love you for you and not for anything else. And Drake told you it didn't matter, so why do you cling to your childlessness? It doesn't define you. The way you love others is your defining attribute."

Kate put her head in her hands. She kept replaying that kiss over and over in her head. But then she would remember the way he looked when he talked about children. "But if I really love Drake, wouldn't I want what was best for him? I wouldn't want to deprive him of his dream. That's not real love either." She straightened and reached for her coffee.

Claire shook her head and sighed. "Why aren't you letting Drake decide? What gives you the right to make the decision for him about what his dream really is? And who among us hasn't had to adjust a dream we thought we wanted? You thought you wanted a father who would love you for you. My life took a radical change once the truth about our families came out. But I'm happy with the change that's happened. Events alter our wants and dreams, Kate. You should know that better than anyone."

Kate studied her sister's face. Two years ago, she didn't even know her sister existed other than faint memories of a pretend friend. Two years ago she'd thought trying to please her mother was the only important thing in life. She wanted people to like her no matter what the cost to her peace of mind because she always knew she had to earn any love she got. Her life had proven it, so of course that's what she worked for. Her heart recognized the truth in Claire's words. She was unconditionally loved by real friends, by her sister, by God. Maybe even by Drake.

"It's too soon to know if what Drake and I have is love," she finally managed to say.

"Yes, it is. But you'll never know if you don't quit making assumptions."

Kate picked up her fork. "I'll try my best."

Relief lit Claire's eyes. "And tell Drake about this idea for rooting out the stalker. I have a feeling he isn't going to be in favor of it."

Kate narrowed her eyes and shook her head. "I'm going to do it anyway. That guy took pictures of us with the girls. What if he hurts them because they're in his way? I can't let anything happen to them. I love them dearly. I have to do this."

Claire held her gaze, then nodded. "Okay, I understand that. But I want Luke involved in this too. He can be in his cutter off-shore too. I'm not saying Danny and his deputies are inept, but you're my sister, and I want all the firepower around you that we can get."

Kate forked up a bite of her omelet. "I'll take that help."

# THIRTY-ONE

Drake tossed the note Kate left onto the bed and looked at the bereft dog. "You know how it feels to be left, huh?" He hadn't taken her for a coward, yet she'd skipped out this morning without a word. She was going to have to talk to him sometime though.

He peeked in on the girls, who still slept curled together on the big king bed. The bedside clock read 7:00 a.m. His stomach rumbled, and he started for the phone to call down for room service when the door opened and Kate stepped inside. Jackson immediately went to her.

Her gaze met his and she sent a tentative smile his way. "Good morning. Did you find my note? I met Claire for breakfast."

"Just read it. I thought you were avoiding me."

She looked beautiful in the slim-fitting jeans and pink top he'd bought last night in one of the hotel shops. Her hair was piled on top of her head in a loose coil that he longed to rake free from its pins.

He stuffed his hands in his pockets. "I was just about to call down for breakfast. You need more coffee or anything?"

"I'm stuffed. I need to tell you something though." She held up a finger, then stepped to the other bedroom door and peeked inside. "Good, they're sleeping."

He had a sinking feeling she was going to quit and refuse to see him. It was his own fault for rushing things last night. He'd spit out what he was feeling without thinking it through. "Okay."

She laced her fingers together in front of her. "Claire told me I had no right to make decisions for you, and she's right. So let's start over and take it one day at a time, okay?"

All she'd said was a jumble in his head right now. "Okay." What exactly did she mean? That they'd explore the possibility of his moving here? There were a million reasons that wouldn't work. His business needed him, and even now, he was itching to be back at the drawing table hunched over a design for a new drone. Working energized him. And a huge amount of work needed to be done to clear the rest of Heath's estate as well.

He freed one of her hands from its death grip on the other. "I meant what I said, Kate. Having kids of our own doesn't matter. I was just rattling off some crazy dreams that I realized aren't that important. Don't shut me out. We can work through anything if we're talking."

She stood on tiptoe and brushed her lips across his. "That sounds perfect."

Her breath mingled with his, and he caught her around the waist and pulled her closer for a real kiss, but she twisted out of his grasp. "I hear the girls." She headed for the bedroom.

He grinned and reached for the phone. As his hand touched the receiver, it rang. Who would be calling up to the room at this early hour? "Drake Newham."

"Mr. Newham, you have a visitor here in the lobby. He said to tell you his name is Mr. Wang."

*Wang?* "Are you sure that's his name?"

"Yes, sir. He asked me to tell you to meet him in the restaurant."

That was Wang all right. Imperious and dictatorial. "I'll be right down." He hung up and went to find Kate. She was getting the girls dressed. "I'm going to run down to meet someone in the restaurant. Order room service for the girls, and I'll be back as soon as I can."

She must have picked up on his tone because alarm flashed over her face. "Who are you meeting?"

He glanced at the girls and shook his head. "I'll tell you about it later." Before she could object, he quickly retraced his steps and headed for the door. Wang wouldn't try anything in a public place, but why had he come this far when he could have called? The crime lord had the resources to track down Drake's cell number.

He punched the button for the elevator and rode it down to the lobby. When he stepped out of the gleaming brass doors onto the pink marble floor, he looked in both directions in case Wang was lying in wait, but he saw no one but two older women leaving the other elevator. Hurrying to the Bistro, he spotted Wang at a corner table. The man's black hair reminded Drake of a seal's fur, all sleek and groomed. He wore a gray Armani suit and a silk tie in an understated green.

He rose when Drake reached the table and extended his hand. "Mr. Newham, thank you for meeting with me." His cultured voice held only a hint of his Chinese ancestry. "I'm sure it was a shock to hear I was down here."

Drake didn't want to shake his hand, but he forced himself to reach out and briefly touch palms. The man's dark good looks exuded power and sleek danger too—a powerful attraction to many women. "Shock is an understatement. I'm not sure we should be meeting, Mr. Wang."

Wang settled back onto his chair. "It's about Melissa."

Drake clenched his jaw and sat down. How dare the man even utter Melissa's name. It took all his strength not to leap across the table and grab him by the throat. "I see."

The man fixed calm, dark eyes on Drake. "I don't think you do. I want to help you find the killer. I don't believe Heath killed her, then took his own life. In fact, I'm sure of it."

Drake stared at the man who held his gaze with a resolute expression. "Everyone else believes it."

"I know. That's why I'm here. I have had my men investigating for weeks. Have you seen the autopsy reports?"

"I just saw them last night."

"She was strangled first by someone who was left-handed. The bruises clearly show it. And there was a large lump on Heath's forehead. It could have happened in the fall from the rocks, but I don't think so."

Drake should have looked at Heath's autopsy more carefully, but it had been too painful. He'd find the courage to do it today though. He nodded. "I thought you hired them killed because Heath found out about your affair."

Wang took a sip of his water, then set the glass back on the table. "You should understand that I loved Melissa. I intended to marry her. If I'd had to kill Heath to have her, I would have done it. But it wasn't necessary. She was also pregnant with my child."

Drake clenched his fists at the man's casual threat. "You are the father of that baby? How do you know?"

Wang took a sip of his tea. "Heath was out of town on

business when Melissa conceived, and she and Heath had been sleeping in separate bedrooms for a while."

"How long did Heath know?"

Wang's dark eyes were grave. "He found out just before they came to Maine. She'd saved the positive pregnancy test to show me, and he discovered it hidden in her dresser."

Drake winced at the thought of his brother's pain. "Yet you still believe he didn't kill her? Why?"

"He was a good man. I tried to bribe him, you know. He refused. But my outfit isn't the only organized crime working in the city. Heath was on the trail of another one he thought had set me up. I think he might have found out the truth and was killed."

"What other outfit?"

Wang pressed his lips together. "I have yet to find out which one."

"Did he know she planned to take the girls to China?"

"She wasn't going to do that. We talked it over, and she agreed to leave them behind with him."

"Her partner found the plane tickets."

Wang shrugged. "Purchased before our decision was made."

Drake knew when someone was lying, and he had the strong sense that Wang spoke the truth. "Was the target Melissa or Heath?"

"I suspect Heath was the initial target, and Melissa was collateral damage. I could be wrong. It's possible Melissa was targeted to hurt me, but I don't think so. I've been trying to get hold of Heath's external hard drive, but I can't find it. Maybe you can."

Drake ran through the possible places where he might find the hard drive.

"Do you know where it is?"

"I might." Drake reached for his cell phone and called his uncle who owned a storage company. Some of Heath's things were in storage there.

---

The waves rolled onto the rocks, then receded to the vast blue of the sea. Kate stood on a spit of land in Sunset Cove with the girls and Jackson and breathed in the tang of the salt air. Lobster boats bobbed in the distance, and she heard the hum of fishing boats. She glanced back at the pink granite steps leading to the hotel. She'd thought Drake would be back before she took the kids to the water, but he hadn't returned, so she left him a note. Her nerves hummed with her need to know the reason for his somber expression when he left to meet whoever it was down in the restaurant.

Claire and Luke were going to come over and take Kate and the girls for a ride any minute. She hoped Drake got here in time to join them. She zipped her Windbreaker. It was a good thing they'd all dressed in jeans. A chill wind rolled in off the sea, and it would be even colder out on the water. She heard her name and saw Claire wave in the distance as Luke's boat approached. It would be a few minutes before he docked.

She turned back one last time and saw Drake wave from the steps. She waved back. "Here comes your uncle."

"He would have been disappointed not to go on the boat ride." Emma pulled her hand from Kate's and went to peer into the shallow depths of a tide pool. "I see a crab!" Phoebe ran to join her, and neither girl left their entranced observation at the water's edge when Drake reached Kate's side.

His smile didn't reach his eyes. "Glad I caught you in time."

"What's wrong?"

He glanced at his nieces, then took Kate's arm and moved a few feet farther away. "Chen Wang came to see me."

"The killer?" No wonder he seemed distracted.

He shook his head. "That's the thing—he came to tell me he wanted to help me find the murderer. He claims he didn't do it, that he loved Melissa." Bending his head closer to her ear, he spoke more softly. "I got the autopsy last night. Melissa was pregnant."

Her eyes filled with tears. "Oh no!"

"Wang says she was pregnant with his child. And maybe she was. Heath was out of town a lot several months ago."

Kate put her hand on his arm. "Do you think he's telling the truth?"

"I think he might be. He's a snake, no doubt about that. But he seemed genuinely distressed by Melissa's death, and he wanted vengeance."

"What about Heath? Did he know?"

Drake let out a long sigh. "Yeah. And those plane tickets I found? They were supposedly purchased before they decided to leave the girls with Heath. I'm not sure I believe that."

"Did he have any idea who might have killed them?"

He dropped his arm around her waist and hugged her to his side. "He thinks it might have been a rival organized-crime group. There are several in Boston. He says Heath had a big knot on his head, and Melissa was choked by a left-handed man. I stopped by the room to look at the autopsies again, and he's right. I couldn't bring myself to study them very closely last night. Heath was right handed, so that's a clear sign Heath didn't do it. I need to talk to the sheriff about it."

"So we're back to square one."

He nodded. "Wang told me he feels it's related to Heath trying to find out who framed Wang for the murder charges he faces. I decided to have Heath's backup hard drive shipped to me. He'd replaced his computer at the office and put the old one in a storage shed our uncle kept. I've been looking over his new computer files and found nothing conclusive, but there might be something on the other hard drive. My uncle is shipping it out today."

She leaned her head against his chest. "Maybe we'll get to the bottom of who killed them, and you can move on." It was time to tell him her news as well, though the timing couldn't be worse when he was worried about getting to the truth.

She pulled away and stared into his face. "The more I've thought about it, the more convinced I am that whoever is watching me might be the person I saw the day Heath and Melissa died. What if he thinks I can ID him?"

"Whoa, where did this come from? You've been thinking it was your uncle who broke into your house."

She exhaled, hating to admit her desire not to face the truth. "I was up a lot last night thinking about it. Uncle Paul might have broken in, but he wouldn't have put the chocolate in the picnic basket. He wouldn't have taken the pictures or put that X on your face in the photo. He couldn't call and breathe in the phone. Someone is trying to terrorize me, and I've tried to pass it off as Uncle Paul. I don't believe it is any longer, not after last night."

His expression changed from indulgent to alert as he listened. "So you think maybe both of these cases are linked somehow?"

She shook her head. "I think it's a stalker, and I'm his current victim. He has to be stopped. I called the sheriff while you were gone."

He stared down at her with a question in his eyes. "Did the sheriff have any news?"

Her pulse throbbed in her throat at the thought of his reaction. "That's not why I called. I told him I want to be a decoy and lure the guy into the open where they can catch him."

His hands went to her shoulders, turning her to face him. "Wait a minute, that's way too dangerous, Kate. The guy's unpredictable, and I doubt he'll act like you expect him to. Let the sheriff catch him. They've got all their resources on finding him and will nab him soon."

"He was near the girls! I can't sit back and let them be in danger. If I don't do this, I'll have to quit taking care of them so they're not in the line of fire."

His eyes narrowed. "I don't want you to be his next target either."

"We will catch him. Nothing can go wrong." She told him the plan she'd devised. "Danny was hesitant at first, but I told him he could put his best deputies on it, and he'll be there himself. Luke will be just offshore with some Coast Guard buddies. Kevin will be only a few feet away and will be watching from a tree stand. I'll be surrounded by law enforcement. I'll have my pepper spray in my pocket, too, and my gun. I'm not going in there unarmed."

"What if he smells a trap?"

"I did some research on serial rapists and killers. They often fixate on a subject and imagine there is some kind of personal relationship. I think he'll be all too willing to believe I reciprocate his affection. They are highly egotistical. I think this will work." She put more confidence in her voice than she felt. In truth, her knees shook at the thought of facing him on that lonely stretch of rocks, but she couldn't see any other way of making sure this was over.

A new life awaited her, but only if she could remove the threat to the girls. And she was willing to do most anything to have a stab at what beckoned.

# Thirty-Two

Such an idyllic scene with the blue water pounding against the rocks. The vegetation along the pink-granite cliffs was thick enough to hide an elephant, and no one could see him from here. His lookout was at the top of Sunset Cove, and he focused his binoculars on the people boarding the boat. Claire, her husband, Luke, and Newham with his entourage of the children, the dog, and Kate. Everyone in one place, all nice and tidy.

His skin felt like a thousand spiders were crawling over him, and he shook himself. This place was getting to him. If he didn't get word soon, he was going to leave this place he was beginning to hate. Even the bars were few and far between out here, and forget about finding a strip joint. He itched to cut loose and have some fun, and it was beginning to feel like he was in purgatory.

He laid down the binoculars when his cell phone buzzed in his pocket. He straightened after a glance at the screen. "Yeah, Boss. You have good news for me?" His pulse ratcheted up at the thought of ending this.

"If by good news you mean do you get to go home, no. Not yet. But I'm ready to give the go-ahead. But first, intercept a package being delivered tomorrow. Destroy it, then eliminate Drake Newham, Claire Rocco, and Kate Mason. And you might as well wipe the slate clean and get rid of the kids. It's less messy that way."

He pulled the phone away from his ear a second. Did he hear that right? Frowning, he put the phone back to his ear. "The kids? I didn't think that was ever on the table."

"Well, it is now! I didn't want to have to do it either, but leaving them is just going to create more headaches than I want to deal with. Make it look like an accident. Be creative. Take them all out at once."

He wasn't too excited about figuring out a way to handle eliminating so many at once. "I never signed on to kill kids. I've never done it before, and I don't want to do it now."

"Fine. I'll hire someone else, and you won't get the rest of your money."

And he was liable to be the new guy's next target to wipe up "loose ends." He pressed his lips together and exhaled. "Fine, I'll do it. How fast does it need to be done?"

"As soon as you get that package and destroy it. By the end of the week at the latest. I'll give you a hundred-thousand-dollar bonus for making sure there is no ongoing problem."

A hundred grand more. That put a different spin on it. He wished he knew more of what was going on, but his job didn't involve knowing the motive behind the problem that needed fixing. That piece of information was liable to get him killed, too, and he'd miss out on enjoying the money coming his way.

He took another gander at the boat out on the water. "What if he gets more than one package tomorrow? How do I know which one it is?"

"Then destroy anything that comes," his boss snapped.

He lowered his binoculars again. "Okay, okay. I'll let you

know when it's over. What about my notebook? I still haven't found it. It could turn up after they're all dead. I don't want the law to come calling a year from now."

"Once they're dead, you can go through everything before it's hauled away."

"Maybe. I'll get on it."

"Fine. I don't need to know the details."

Probably because he didn't have the guts to do anything himself. He ended the call and dropped his phone into his pocket. Acid churned in his stomach, and everything in him recoiled at the thought of killing kids. What would it hurt to let them live? He could take care of the real problems, and maybe the boss would relent when the threats were gone.

He shook his head and picked up his binoculars. It would be nearly impossible to make it look like an accident and allow the kids to live. They were usually all together. While they'd left the kids with the old woman a few times, there was no guarantee that would happen in the next two days.

His gaze swept over the whitecaps, and he spied the boat with his prey aboard. Kate and Newham sat together in the stern with a kid on each side. Claire and her husband occupied the seats at the cockpit. Aboard the boat would be the ideal time to eliminate them, but this was the first time they'd all gone out together. How did he orchestrate it to happen again? He needed to figure out when they might all be together again.

He reached for his phone and called up the local newspaper. There would be a lobster fest this weekend. Most likely they'd all be there, but there wasn't a good opportunity to eliminate them there without being seen. He put his phone away. Unless an idea came to him, he'd have to arrange for an "accident" at two separate places. Even if the sheriff suspected foul play, he'd make sure he left no clues.

Something rustled down the edge of the cliff, and he grabbed his binoculars and melted back into the brush. Peering through the branches, he saw a man dressed in camo approach with binoculars around his neck. The guy fiddled with something, and a drone rose into the air and hovered over the landscape. From the angle of the drone, he suspected he was watching the Rocco boat too. Frowning, he remembered the other time he'd seen a man watching Kate's residence. Could it be the same man? What if he could use this guy to cover up Kate's death?

It would pay to follow this guy and see what he was up to.

The tension eased from Drake's shoulders as he inhaled the calming scent of the salty air. The day couldn't be more perfect for a cruise on the water. The boat rode the gentle waves with ease, and the gulls swooped low to snatch the bits of bread the girls threw to them. Kate sat close, so close he could feel the warmth emanating from her side. The girls sat on a bench with the dog between them.

He smiled down at her. "Excited?"

Her cheeks were pink from the wind, and she had the hood of her blue sweatshirt up over her blonde hair. "I haven't been out to the Petit Manan Lighthouse for ages. I used to beg my uncle to take me out on his lobster boat, and he often gave in at the end of the summer just to shut me up." Her smile faded, and she turned to look out over the sea.

He draped his arm around her shoulders. "Still no sign of your uncle?"

She shook her head and turned back toward him. "I keep waiting for him to show back up. I know Luke won't relax until he's back in custody."

"Does the sheriff think he got out of the country? Maybe he'll never be recaptured."

"The sheriff is working with the Canadian authorities, but there's been no sign of him." She rose and leaned over the side of the boat. "Look, puffins floating in the waves!"

The girls squealed and went to stand beside her. Drake followed and peered over her shoulder. A puffin, looking very much like a parrot, rode the waves and suddenly disappeared into a curl of water. It emerged a few seconds later with a fish in its beak, which it gobbled down, then began to preen itself.

"Pretty cool little guy." He shifted so he could watch her. The soft, rapt expression in her blue eyes made him smile.

She glanced up and her cheeks colored. "I'm obsessed, aren't I? Did you know they are loners at sea, then come home for months and stay with one mate? They're so hardy too. No matter what man and nature have thrown at them, they've managed to survive. They're a little awkward at takeoff and landing but are so nimble and agile in the water."

"Once they're in their natural element, they aren't the ugly ducklings they appear to be?" he suggested.

She nodded. "Maybe that's it. I'm fascinated with them."

And he was fascinated with her. He wanted to find out the reason for every smile, and he wished to be the one who brought out the dimple in her cheek and the light in her eyes. Her courage humbled him. She'd faced so much adversity but still had the energy to help others and keep on trying to overcome what life had dished out to her. He doubted he'd ever find her with the covers pulled over her head wailing for help. She liked standing on her own and solving problems. She'd been quick to want to fix his lack of discipline with the girls.

He swiveled his gaze to the girls. Her firm but loving hand with them had made a huge difference. He couldn't remember when he'd last broken up a fight between them, and just this morning he'd found Emma combing Phoebe's hair. She was taking her role of big sister seriously. And it was all due to Kate's influence. She'd been good for all of them.

Kate pushed the hood off her hair and leaned against him. "You've got a strange expression. What are you thinking?"

"About how alive I feel here. When I look back at my normal life, it feels like a dream and I've just woken up. I actually have time to feel something other than the next responsibility. I'm not working every night."

"You'll be going back soon. Another couple of weeks, and the girls will be starting school."

"Maybe I'll enroll them in Folly Shoals." The words were out before he'd realized the idea had formed in his head.

Her eyes widened, and she caught her breath. "What do you mean?"

"What if I bought a house big enough for everyone, and you kept the girls during the week? I could fly up every weekend to be with all of you." Her smile faltered and he realized how it sounded. "I'm not saying we live together. I would never suggest something like that. I care too much about you. But it would give us time to explore where this relationship is going. The girls are thriving here. I don't want to yank them out of this special place and put them in a fast-paced Boston school. I think we all belong here."

She twirled a strand of hair around her finger. "But how could that work, Drake? You'd be living one life and we'd be living another. You'd have a foot in both worlds, and I think that's an impossible way to exist. You'll never be able to fully live in the *now*."

Maybe she was right, but the thought of going back to Boston wasn't tenable.

But the thought of not working on a new drone, not following the passion he'd pursued for so many years, made him swallow hard.

He pulled her closer until her cheek rested against his chest and he could rest his chin on her head. "This is the now I am interested in exploring. It will work out, Kate. I don't know yet just how, but we'll figure it out together."

She pulled away and tipped her head back to look into his face. "And just for the record, I love the girls. If you really need me to keep them while you figure out what you want to do, I'm here for them. And for you."

Warmth settled into his abdomen at the assurance in her face. He cupped her cheek with one hand. "You're one of a kind. It's going to be okay."

# THIRTY-THREE

Kate had never had anyone actually flirt with her before, not with the intensity Drake was beginning to show. She couldn't decide if she liked it or if it terrified her. And his suggestion about her caring for the girls had given her pause. Could that even work out?

She took the empty hot chocolate mugs to the kitchen while Drake carried the girls into bed after their movie. Jackson followed her. She looked down at her dog. "He keeps my head spinning, boy." The dog woofed as if he understood.

She heard his footsteps behind her as she stood at the sink and rinsed the cups out. "Did either one of them wake up?"

"Nope." His arms slipped around her waist, and he nuzzled her neck. "You smell good."

Her pulse did a slow roll, then sped up to keep time with her breathing. What did she say? How did she handle this attraction? A deep ache built in her belly and spread up to her chest.

*Oh, to be able to have the assurance to turn and embrace him.*

She forced a light tone to her voice. "I was thinking about that notebook again. What if it's a code, and we can crack it?"

"What brought up that idea?" When his embrace dropped away, she felt cold and bereft. She curled her fingers into fists to keep her hands from reaching up around his neck as she turned to face him. "It was such a busy time the other night that I wondered if we didn't check it out well enough."

He gave her a crooked smile. "Moving too fast, huh?"

"Like a bullet train. Give me a chance to catch my breath."

His grin widened. "I'll try."

She moved past him to the counter where the notebook still lay in the bag. "Let's just take another peek."

"I've played with codes in high school. It was a great brain exercise."

"I've seen the ones you make the girls."

He pulled out the notebook, then carried it to the table. "Do we have a lined pad anywhere?"

"I have a small one in my purse."

"You carry the entire contents of the Free World in your purse."

Smiling, she went to dig out a pen and pad. The way his gaze lingered on her when she stepped back into the kitchen warmed her all the way through. "Here you go."

He took the pad and flipped it open. She laid the pen beside it, then pulled up a chair beside him. "Is there a trick to it?"

"We're going to look for the shortest words first. They are likely to be things like *a* or *I* and we'll look for patterns. The most common letter used in English is the letter *e*, followed by *t* and *a*, so that will help us too. And we'll look for double symbols that might represent things like a double *l* or other common double letters."

"That sounds easier than I expected." She looked down at the leather cover. "It looks well used."

"I noticed that too. Let's see if there are any engraved names on the back." He flipped it over and ran his hand over the worn surface. "Nothing." He turned it over and opened the front cover. "AB. Mean anything to you?"

She tried to think of anyone she knew with those initials. "Nope." She leaned past him to turn a page. The last thing she wanted right now was to look at this thing now that it appeared to be nothing more than trash. She flipped the first page and began to read through it. "It's all numbers."

He straightened. "There's a common code using numbers and letters that the Greeks devised. It's called a square cipher." He drew a grid consisting of five columns and five rows, then filled the reference along the top and bottom with the numbers one through five. In the boxes he jotted down the letters of the English alphabet starting with the letter *a* in the first box. "Each letter is represented by two numbers—the column on the left is the first number, and the row across the top is the second. So the letter *s* is represented by the numbers 43. The *i* and *j* are merged into one, and *q* is omitted as well."

"You think it's something that simple?"

"I suspect the owner of the notebook tried to muddy up the meaning enough that anyone who happened to glance in it would think it was gibberish. Let's see if this works." He grabbed the pen and began translating the words.

Her eyes widened as he wrote down words like *target* and *shot*. "We should call the sheriff. I think this belongs to the murderer."

Drake's jaw was like granite as he wordlessly flipped to the back and jotted down the translation of the final entry.

Location: Folly Shoals, Maine
Target: Heath and Melissa Emerson
Outcome: Death

Her vision blurred, and she fought tears. She turned to take Drake's hand. His eyes were wide and shocked in his white face. His hand trembled.

"I'm so sorry, Drake." She clung to his hand, trying to convey the depth of her sympathy.

His breath came in short gasps, and he pulled her onto his lap, then clung to her like a buoy in rough waters. He buried his face in her neck, and she let him.

He finally stiffened. "This proves Heath didn't do it."

The morning sun had begun to lighten the horizon when he parked in his hiding spot and walked the last quarter mile to Kate's house. The air smelled of dew, and he zipped up his jacket against the early morning breeze. He liked this time of day when no one was out and he could train his camera on her windows without fear of being seen. He found his spot and settled in, then focused on Kate's living room window. Any second now he'd be able to see her beautiful face and form.

There, the light came on and she drew open the drapes. He smiled. The white shorts she wore showed off her long legs, and the light-blue top hugged her figure. He liked it when she wore her hair up like today. He knew she'd done it just for him too. He could imagine pressing his lips against the curving sweep of her neck and up to her jawline. He quickly snapped pictures of her as she moved around the room fluffing pillows.

She was the most beautiful thing he'd ever seen. But she belonged to him. He didn't like her job being in such close proximity to a single guy. And those kids took up way too much of her attention. He'd be glad when Newham left town and went back to his own life. Just a few more weeks now, and he'd have Kate to himself. Maybe it would be time to knock on her door once he knew no one was around.

She rinsed her coffee cup, then exited the front door with her dog, pausing to drop an envelope onto the mat on the porch. Frowning, he focused on the white square. He couldn't quite make out who it was addressed to, but he intended to find out. He shrank back into the bushes as she walked along the road to the cottage. She passed near enough that he caught a whiff of the vanilla scent she wore.

Once she was inside the cottage, he stared across at the front door. The windows of the cottage were positioned so no one could see her house from inside, but there was always the chance someone might come out. He decided to risk it.

He dashed across the road and up the steps, then grabbed the envelope and ran around the side of the house just in case. Panting, he peered around the edge of the house. No movement at the cottage down the road. Perfect.

He flipped over the envelope. His breath hitched in his chest when he read the block words on the front. TO MY GIFT GIVER. Could she actually have responded to his gifts? His hands shook as he ripped the flap off and pulled out the paper inside. Handwritten. She'd sent him a *handwritten* note.

*Dear friend,*

*Thank you so much for your sweet gift of chocolates. How did you know I love DeBrand truffles? And you picked my favorite kind! I'm in awe. I also loved the pictures. Could we*

*meet? I would love to thank you in person. If your answer is yes,
keep this letter. If you don't want to meet me, leave the opened
letter back where you found it. If I don't see the envelope, I'll
meet you tonight at seven on the shore under Mermaid Point.
I hope you say yes!*

*Much affection,*
*Your Kate*

*Your Kate.* His pulse jumped at the warm greeting. He'd
hoped his gifts would win her over, but that she would reciprocate his feelings was almost too much to take in. He folded up
the note and the envelope and stuck them in his back pocket. Of
course he was going to meet her, though the thought of revealing
his identity to her terrified him. What if she didn't like his type?
Every woman had a "type," and he hadn't had much luck in the
romance department. He'd tried to get up the courage to ask
her out ever since she got well, but she'd been obsessed with her
sister. He'd have to put a stop to that.

Surely she wouldn't reject him when she'd gone to so much
trouble to reach out to him. She was lonely too. Her mom and
uncle were in jail, and all she had was her sister. She probably
looked at Claire and wished she had a happy home too. He could
give that to her. They didn't need anyone but each other. He
hadn't wanted to kill the last one, but he'd been afraid she'd seen
his face in the hotel room.

Maybe he would finally have a place to be on Thanksgiving
and Christmas. Somewhere other than at his mom's place filled
with smoke and coarse jokes. Someplace he felt wanted and welcome. He could just picture Kate bustling around the kitchen

preparing a turkey and pumpkin pie just for him. The happy thought was nearly overwhelming.

Then his smile faded. This was a little too pat, wasn't it? Could it be a trap?

He sneaked another look around the end of the house. The coast was still clear, though he longed to just walk right up the road and knock on the door. He could hold up the envelope and tell her he got her note and didn't want to wait until tonight. Then if it was a trap, he would have foiled it.

But no, he had a job to do today, and so did she. He could get the picture he took of her beside a puffin nest. Even if she was trying to trick him, he could win her over. He could frame it to match the black frames on her walls, and she'd squeal with delight. Maybe she'd throw her arms around his neck and kiss him. His face warmed at the thought until saner thoughts prevailed. He needed to be on his guard.

The sun was fully up by the time he skirted the edge of the woods and made it to his car. He stashed the note and envelope in his glove box, then turned on his car and pulled out onto the road.

Just in case this wasn't all it seemed, he needed to be prepared.

# THIRTY-FOUR

I don't like this." Ever since the envelope had been taken first thing this morning, Drake felt like he had to do something—anything—to prevent what was about to take place. But the time had come, in spite of everything he'd done to try to talk Kate out of the rendezvous.

He followed her out to her yellow Volkswagen. "At least let me come with you. Or even take Jackson with you. You could stop by Dixie's and get him."

She'd changed into slim-fitting jeans with a long-sleeved top. It was almost as if she was dressing for a date with the man, for Pete's sake. He gritted his teeth and fought down the words that wanted to burst out.

She opened the car door. "He might be watching, Drake. You can go with Jonas and hide out to watch. He's in charge of the operation anyway, and he'll know where he wants you positioned. I don't want Jackson to interrupt anything, nor do I want him to get hurt."

The tight-lipped deputy had stopped by with instructions from the sheriff two hours ago. What if it all went wrong?

She stood on her tiptoes and brushed a kiss across his mouth. "Did you check on the girls?"

"Yeah, they're fine. Dixie has them with her at the hotel room. They'll be safe there. The sheriff has a deputy in the lobby watching too."

She slid into the seat with the door still open, and he leaned on it. "I'm going to be fine, Drake. Shut my door, and let's get this over with. The sooner I get out there, the sooner he'll be in custody."

"I know." He squatted beside the car. "Be careful, Kate. Trust your instincts. If something alarms you, run. Right then. Don't wait for the sheriff or Jonas to rush in. Okay?"

Her blue eyes twinkled. "I love it when you're so protective. Did you call the UPS office to see what happened to your package?"

He shook his head. "I'll worry about it tomorrow when I know we have this guy." With reluctance he stood and shut the door.

As her car pulled away, he pulled out his cell phone to contact Jonas, but before he could call the number, he saw the deputy's truck pass Kate's.

Jonas waved at Kate, then accelerated to the driveway. He ran his window down. "Let's get going."

Drake hopped in the passenger side and fastened his seat belt. "Everything in place?"

"Yep, we're all ready." His tone was grim.

"Are you worried at all?" Drake pulled out his phone and glanced at it in case Kate had texted him, but the screen was blank.

"Nope. I've got this under control."

Drake wanted to tell him to notify his face. The deputy was strung as tight as trout line. "Everyone else in place?"

"Everything is ready." The deputy turned the truck onto a narrow road that led out to Mermaid Point.

Drake shut up and turned his face to the window. He hadn't

been out this way before, and the vegetation was thick enough to blot out the late-afternoon sun. The road was rocky and filled with potholes. This place felt very separated from the rest of Folly Shoals. He wished they'd set it up earlier. Seven o'clock felt like a long way away, though it was already six. They were going early to get things in place, and he wished he could fast-forward to when this was all over and Kate was safely beside him again. He didn't like to think about her being out there alone and waiting for a nutcase.

The truck rolled to a slow crawl, then the deputy whipped the steering wheel and turned into a tiny opening in the trees, a spot Drake would have missed. The bushes scraped the side of the truck, and the opening widened to a small clearing that would be completely hidden from the road. Tall cedar and birch trees blocked out the sun, and the grass was matted down as if other vehicles had parked here. The deputy had probably checked this out earlier today, and the thought calmed Drake.

Drake tried to see the ocean through the trees. "Are we close?"

"Yeah, the Point is just around the curve up there. I don't want my truck to be spotted. I'm going to put you where you can see the shoreline. There's also steps cut into the side of the cliff so you can get down there fast if you have to. Come on." Kissner opened his door and got out. He reached back inside and plucked an extra magazine for his gun from the floor under his seat.

"You think you'll need that?"

Kissner shrugged. "I plan to be prepared for anything." He put the magazine in his pocket.

Drake climbed out and shut his door quietly, then followed the deputy along a trail that was barely there. Bugs swarmed his face, and he swatted them away. He was perspiring by the time they fought their way through the vegetation to where it all opened up and he could see blue water.

The breeze on his face was sweet relief, and he spotted a boat in the distance. "Is that Luke's Coast Guard cutter?"

"Yeah, it should be." Kissner pointed to a spot near the edge of the cliff. "You should have a perfect view right there."

Drake walked over to the side and peered over. The water was right below him instead of the rocky beach he expected. "Where's the shore?"

"The tide is going out. You'll see it shortly."

Before Drake could answer, he felt a hard shove in his back. He tried to recover his footing, but he was too close to the edge, and he went sailing off the cliff. His arms pinwheeled and his chest squeezed. He was falling to the waves below. *Kate!*

The package looked innocuous enough, and he wondered what was in it. He'd been lucky to grab it off the porch as soon as the delivery guy left.

He drove along the island coastal road to a remote spot overlooking the water and parked in a pull-off. Once he tossed this box, it was toast. The waves would batter it against the rocks, and there would be nothing left.

He got out of his vehicle with the box in hand. It wasn't that heavy, and his curiosity got the best of him. It would be destroyed out of the box more easily. He reached back inside his car and got a pocketknife out of the glove box, then slit the tape and opened the package. A bubble-wrapped object fell into his hand, and he unwrapped it. An external hard drive plopped onto the ground.

Not surprising. Hard drives all across the world held the proof of many a crime. He'd been hoping for something more dramatic. He plucked it out of the dirt and started to fling it over the side, then paused. Why not keep it for insurance? He didn't trust his boss one iota, and he'd never know if this had been destroyed or not.

Grinning, he put the box and its packaging back inside his car, then strolled over to the edge of the cliff and looked out on the glistening water. It was going to be a beautiful night, but he wished he were back in Boston. Soon, though.

He grabbed his laptop from the backseat, then fished out a USB cord and attached the hard drive to it. In half an hour he had the answer. His boss had been taking money under the table to help skew the investigation to frame Wang. Wang was guilty as sin of a lot of crimes, but not the crime he was charged with. His eyes widened at the amount of money that had traded palms. Ten million dollars. No wonder the boss was willing to part with so much money to clear this up.

His smile faded as he considered again what he had to do. The plan he'd put into place was to send them all an invitation to a free puffin tour on a boat he'd hired. He'd planted a device at the fuel line, and it was easily detonated with the remote in his glove box. The boat owner was already instructed to call and tell them he'd drawn them to receive a free day out on the water. The plan should be foolproof. With Kate's love of puffins, Newham wouldn't deny her. The sister was sure to want to go along as well.

His troubles would be over, and he'd be on his way back to Boston a whole lot richer. He might have enough to retire down in the Caribbean in a hopping little tourist town with plenty of beautiful women. It might be enough to get rid of the bad taste in his mouth about having to kill the kids. A shudder worked its way up his spine, and acid churned in his belly again. He hated it, but there was no getting out of it.

He saw two figures across the Point as they approached the edge of the cliff. The sea foamed against the rocks below. A boat rode the waves, and he squinted to make out that it was a Coast Guard boat. Lots of activity for such a remote spot, but with any kind of luck, the Coast Guard would cruise on by. He grabbed his binoculars and turned his gaze back to the two men just in time to see one shove the other off the cliff. Was that Newham who'd just gone over? His mouth gaped as he watched the figure plummet and vanish into the pummeling waves.

Holy cow, what had just happened? He had to find out.

The cool breeze off the ocean lifted the loose strands of hair on the back of Kate's neck. She jumped at the rattle of pebbles behind her, but it was only a stray cat wandering down to take a look at her. She wished she could see Kevin's house from here. It would make her feel safer. She hadn't caught so much as a glimpse of any law enforcement, but that was the way it should be. She didn't want to scare off her stalker, but she was so ready for this to be over.

Pebbles rolled under her sandals as she paced the shore, then checked the time on her phone. He was unlikely to be here for at least forty-five minutes unless he arrived early. She thought she heard a shout in the distance and whirled, but she saw only a splash across the bay. Probably a fish or a dolphin.

She walked along the water's edge and tried to calm herself with deep breaths. Should she get out her bear spray? It was a small can that she could easily hide in her hand. She dove her hand into her purse for it and slipped it into her palm.

She saw a boat far out to sea heading for the opposite shore. Would it scare off her stalker? She wanted to wave off the vessel, but the captain would never see her from here. She turned and walked back toward the steps, but before she reached them, she heard shoes crunching on rocks behind her. Jonas was heading her way with a big grin. Her pulse responded with a happy leap.

"You've caught him?"

He nodded. "He's in jail right now. It's over. I let everyone know they could call off the surveillance. Let's get out of here."

She felt light-headed. "I'm so glad it's over!" The steep ascending steps were to her left, and she headed toward them. "Let's go have some ice cream to celebrate. I'll text Drake to bring the girls to join us. Claire and Luke too. It's a happy day."

He slid her purse off her shoulder. "I'll carry this for you."

"Thanks." She started up the steps and glanced back to make sure he was behind her.

She quickened her pace and wished she'd taken time to put away the bear spray. Not having both hands free impeded her speed in climbing the cliffside, but her spirits were as high as the sky overhead. She reached the top and glanced toward the forest. No deputies emerged from the trees to greet her, which seemed odd. Surely they hadn't all managed to return to town.

She paused to catch her breath and waited for Jonas to reach her. "I don't see Kevin's truck. Is he still hiding?"

"I don't think anyone is around." Jonas spoke in a strangely flat tone as he continued to approach her.

A tiny shudder made its way down her back. Something felt off here, and she couldn't put her finger on it. Tons of law enforcement should have been crawling all over these woods. There hadn't been time to call them all off. At least she didn't think so. And she didn't like the intent way Jonas eyed her. Unless it was her imagination, an air of menace twisted his features.

She tightened her fingers on the can of bear spray. "Where's the sheriff?"

He didn't answer, and his hand drifted to his unsnapped holster.

*Run!* The inner compulsion made her tremble. This was Jonas. Why should terror be washing up her neck like a rogue wave? To gain time, she turned and walked toward the forest.

She glanced back over her shoulder. He was just three feet behind her and was starting to pull his gun from its holster. He'd shoot her in the back if she just tried to run, so she stopped and turned. She whipped the bear spray up, then shot a full blast into his face as he drew his gun.

He screamed and dropped his gun on the ground. Profanities spewed from his mouth like vile sewage. Part of her wanted to see if he was okay, but this was her only chance to escape. She darted into the shadows of the forest and angled for the thickest part. She had hunted these woods with her uncle, but Jonas might know the area as well as she did, so she had to think about how to throw him off her trail.

She paused and listened. It was all quiet except for the rasp of her breath and the chirping of birds overhead. When she looked at the ground, she saw she'd left a clear trail. If she backtracked in her steps a few feet, she'd be able to hop along a fallen tree to an area where pine needles might cloak her footsteps. But first she had to lead him in another direction.

She ran forward fifteen feet, then marked a big tree with her feet as if she'd climbed in. Was he coming yet? She still heard nothing, so standing on tiptoes she reversed her steps by twenty feet and managed to get along the fallen log to the area she'd spied earlier. Still on her toes, she walked as lightly as she could over the needles, then grabbed a fallen tree branch and erased all trace of her passage until she reached a rocky cliffside. It would be a hard climb up, but she had to go this way if she wanted to avoid Jonas.

Where were Drake and Luke? And the sheriff? How had Jonas gotten them out of the picture?

# THIRTY-FIVE

Her chest tight, Claire peered over the side of the boat at the water churning onto the rocks. "Are you sure you saw someone fall? We need to get to town and help search for Kate." She'd alternated between crying and wanting to scream ever since Jonas had called to say the stalker had Kate. Everyone was meeting at the sheriff's office to coordinate search efforts. According to Jonas, the guy seemed to have realized what was happening. He'd forced Kate off the road on her way to the rendezvous point and vanished with her.

Claire should have done something to prevent this plan in the first place.

Luke stood at the bow with binoculars while one of the other men steered the boat. "I saw a man fall from those cliffs, honey. We can't just leave him out here to drown." His arm went up. "There! I see him. Three feet to starboard." He seized a life ring. "Oh, man." He kicked off his shoes and dove overboard with the ring in his hand.

Claire ran to the railing and searched for her husband's head. He'd nearly reached the dark shape flailing in the water. With a few more strokes he was at the man's side and had the ring around him.

Luke's arm came up. "Pull us in." Helping hold the man's head above water, he swam toward the boat.

One of the crew members began to pull on the rope holding the life ring and the hapless victim in the water. It seemed like an eternity before the two men were floating near the ladder. Claire gasped when she recognized the pale face of the rescued man. "Drake?" She backed away to allow the men to assist Drake and Luke into the boat.

Drake collapsed onto the deck. His skin was bluish, and his eyelids fluttered. Claire knelt beside him and touched his face. It was cold. Was he in shock? He'd probably been in the water about twenty minutes by the time Luke had pulled him out.

Luke dripped cold water on her as he stood behind her. "Man, that was close. Someone grab a thermal blanket. Let's get him warm. Hot coffee too." He knelt beside Claire, his body emanating cold from the water. "I jumped in when I saw he was too far gone to try to grab the ring." He tapped Drake's cheeks, and the man's eyelids fluttered again. "Wake up, Drake." One of the crewmen brought a blanket, and Luke wrapped Drake in it, then held up his head to get some hot coffee down him. "Take a sip, buddy."

Drake muttered something, then blinked and opened his eyes. He took a gulp of hot coffee, and his eyes became more alert. He struggled to sit up and Luke helped him. "K-Kissner." His lips were blue and his teeth were chattering.

Luke's expression grew grim. "We heard from him. We're heading in to try to reach Kate with Jonas and the rest of the sheriff's department." He handed the coffee to Claire.

Drake shook his head. "W-what do you mean?"

He was probably still confused. Claire offered him another sip of coffee. "Kissner is sure they'll find her."

Drake's eyes darkened. "Kissner has h-her."

"No, no. He's looking for her." Surely his thoughts would clear shortly. She gave him more coffee.

The color started coming back to his face. He pushed the coffee away and shook his head. "Kissner pushed me off the cliff. *He's* the stalker." He shook off their grips and struggled to stand, and Luke helped him up.

Claire's skin prickled with goose bumps. She looked at her husband. "What's he mean?" Kissner was a friend—and a deputy.

Drake gripped the railing to steady himself. "I mean what I just said. Kissner was supposed to be setting me up to help watch over Kate, but he lured me to the edge of the cliff, then shoved me off the side. I should have hit the rocks and been killed instantly, but a big wave rolled in as I plummeted down, and I hit the water instead. It dragged me out to sea. We have to get to shore and look for her."

A wave of dread shuddered over Claire. "How is this possible? He likes Kate."

Luke directed the boat's captain to head for the dock a little ways down the shore from where Kate was supposed to be waiting. "Stalkers often know their victims. They see them in normal circumstances and get obsessed."

Drake shivered in his blanket and looked toward land. "We've been feeding Kissner information all along. I bet he got to work this morning and heard it was all a trap, so he laid one of his own. What story did he tell the sheriff and all of you?"

Luke grabbed another blanket and draped it over his shoulders. "He told us the stalker had forced Kate off the road, and she disappeared."

"That's impossible even if he hadn't shoved me off the cliff.

He came to pick me up, and Kate left only moments before me. He passed her on the way to get me. It's the story he used to cover up what he's done. He called off everyone else with that story, but he assumed I'd be dead and there'd be no one to contradict his tale."

Luke asked one of the men to radio the sheriff and tell him what had happened. "It's only been twenty minutes since I saw you fall into the water. He couldn't have gone far with her. We were just getting into position when I saw you fall, so we never reached our viewing spot. We'll look for her tracks near the granite steps up the cliff. We'll find her. Have the sheriff call in some search dogs too."

Claire went to the railing and gripped it with cold fingers. She stared toward the approaching cliff walls. What if they found Kate dead on the shore? She'd never forgive herself for letting this crazy plan go forward.

Kate sat on a flat rock at the top of the hillside. She had no idea where she was. The woods were dark with approaching storm clouds blocking out the light. She hadn't been in this area in quite a while. The trees had gotten bigger, but she recognized the rocky hilltop she'd managed to climb. It wasn't the best place to hide. He might be able to see her from the bottom, but her muscles trembled with fatigue from the arduous climb, and she was having trouble thinking of a plan. She'd escaped him, but for how long?

She still couldn't absorb the fact that Jonas was the stalker. She'd befriended him in high school and had encouraged him as much as she knew how. Why would he want to hurt her?

If only she had her purse with her phone. She'd call the sheriff and someone would be here to rescue her. She pressed her hand to her head and willed herself to think past the "whys" and the "what ifs" and figure out how to save herself. No one would know where she was. They might think the stalker had taken her in his vehicle and may not even look for her in the forest. And they certainly wouldn't be looking for Jonas. He'd likely fed them wrong information all day.

What must he have felt when he realized the letter she'd left was a trap? Probably after he'd gotten into work and heard the plan from the sheriff. No wonder she'd felt the rage shimmering off him in waves. It was ridiculous to feel pity for a man who stalked her now like a hunter, but would he have listened to her if she tried to talk to him? Probably not.

She put her hands over her face and tried to pray, but all she could whisper was, "Please, God, please." Her breath was harsh in her ears, and she longingly remembered the bottle of water in her purse.

The muscles in her legs protested as she rose and looked around. If she remembered correctly, the east side down ended with a sharp cliff overlooking the water. No escape there. She'd come up the west flank. The north and south sides were both extremely sharp inclines, and she'd likely fall before she reached the bottom. Her best bet might be to find a place to hide up here and wait for him to be gone, but where?

Crouching over, she roamed the top of the rocky hillside. She almost gave up when she found a small indentation in the hillside, just the right size to crawl into. While not a cave, if she moved some rocks around the side of it, he might miss her if she huddled into a ball. It was worth a try.

She picked up a rock and put it into place, then another and another. By the time she was finished, her fingertips throbbed and she'd ripped her right thumbnail, but her chances might be good for escaping detection.

Shaking with exhaustion, she crawled into her hidey-hole and leaned her head against the rock to rest. Did everyone think she was dead? She prayed again for deliverance, and the tension seeped out of her body. She relaxed and began to drift to sleep when the snap of a twig brought her out of her twilight state.

She clenched her hand around the bottle of bear spray she still held. Her only weapon would be useless if he kept his distance and shot her, but she clung to the can like her last hope.

Barely daring to breathe, she waited and prayed he wouldn't find her. Footsteps crunched on rocks, and she heard heavy breathing. He was close, so close. Her heart pounded in her ears. He was going to find her.

She shrank into the smallest ball she could manage and waited. If only she'd had better cover of some kind. Her pitiful efforts weren't enough.

Then the footsteps trudged off. She lifted her head and waited. Was he leaving?

"I know where you are, Kate. That puny little hole can't hide you. I'm far enough away you can't hit me with your bear spray this time. That wasn't very nice, by the way. My eyes still hurt, but they aren't so bleary I can't shoot you. Come out of there."

What if she just stayed where she was? He'd have to get closer to haul her out, and she could hit him with another dose of her bear spray. Maybe it was all a ploy to flush her out. He might not really know where she was.

Then a sharp retort of gunfire rang out, and a bullet zipped by her head. She gulped and tried to press harder against the rock at her back.

"All I have to do is stand over you and shoot inside. This can be your coffin if you'd like." His voice was hard, and a thin layer of rage vibrated through his words.

Did that mean he didn't intend to kill her? Where there was life there was hope.

She rose on shaky legs and exited her small haven. She held out her hand toward him in a plea. "I've always liked you, Jonas. I'm really upset that you want to hurt me."

The skin around his eyes was a lurid red where she'd hit him with the bear spray. "You're the one who hurt me, Kate, in so many ways. Hitting me with the hoe should have told me what you were really like." He held the gun pointed at her chest. "You chose this way. I thought you were different. I read that letter and thought you understood me like no one else. I wanted us to spend the rest of our lives together."

"I didn't know it was you, Jonas. If you'd just given me the gifts from yourself, I wouldn't have been afraid." She wet her lips and attempted a smile. "Can we start over? I remember how nice you were to me after Claire was rescued. Then after my stem-cell transplant, you brought me flowers. I saw your kindness, but I never knew you were interested in more."

His scowl faltered, and he lowered the gun a few inches. "How could you not know it was me?"

"Think about it! How could I know? Please, let me make it up to you. You frightened me when I saw you pull your gun. I wouldn't have hurt you otherwise."

His mouth worked and he blinked rapidly. "I have our marriage license in my pocket. I'd thought we'd go to Bangor and get married tonight."

If she could get to a courthouse, she'd have help. "I think that's a fine idea. Let's go now." She held her hand out to him.

The gun came back up. "Prove you mean it and throw the bear spray away."

She managed to keep her smile pinned in place as she tossed the can onto the ground. "There, see? I trust you."

He lowered the gun again, and a smile finally lifted his lips. "Let's go."

# THIRTY-SIX

Gulls squawked overhead, and the wind had nearly dried Drake's clothes. The storm would be here any minute. Claire and Luke kept pace with him as they rushed down the length of the rocky beach toward the place where Kate had planned to meet her stalker. As long as he lived he'd never forget that moment he'd gone sailing toward what he'd thought was certain death in the choppy waves below. God had other plans, and he prayed God was keeping Kate safe until he could find her.

Luke reached the steps cut into the rocks and knelt to examine the thin sand. "Looks like a man's footsteps here." He rose and began to climb the granite stairs. Drake hurried after him.

Claire started up with them. "Does Jonas have a boat? He might have taken her off that way."

Luke's voice floated down as he continued the climb. "The sheriff says he has no boat. Danny is on his way here now. It hasn't been that long, so Kissner is probably still on Folly Shoals somewhere. The only way off is by ferry, and they've shut it down."

Drake shook his head. "I don't buy it. Kissner has thought this all through. He's not going to get trapped here on the island. He could have chartered a boat or borrowed one. We have to think of every possible escape route."

But what if his intentions weren't to escape? Maybe Kissner planned to kill Kate, then slip off by himself. Drake curled his hands into fists. They had to find her first—they had to. It had been an hour since he'd plummeted into the ocean. They could be anywhere by now.

"You have a point." Luke paused on the steps and pulled out his phone, then shot off a quick text. "I'm having my crew check for boats docked offshore. We'll get more Coast Guard cutters around here. He won't get away."

The first drops of rain began to fall when Drake stepped onto the cliff top. The forest began twenty feet away on the other side of a dirt road that circled up to Mermaid Point. He stared at the marks in the dirt. The rain would soon wash away any footprints. Tires crunched in the rocky dirt, and he looked up to see a truck sporting a Maine Warden Service emblem roll to a stop.

Kevin O'Connor got out and jogged toward them. "Any sign of her?" He wiped rain from his face. "Man, I bought his story hook, line, and sinker. He found me settled into my hiding place and told me he'd found her car abandoned with her gone from it. We all believed him. Drake, if you'd died, he wouldn't even be suspected right now. We'd all be looking for some unknown attacker without a clue. He probably still doesn't know we're on to him."

"I bet he got Kate to go with him willingly. She wouldn't have any idea he was the man who'd been stalking her." Drake pointed at the footprints. "You're good at following a trail?"

"Yep." Kevin knelt in the rain and looked over the disturbed ground. "Two people came this way. One big set of shoe prints and a smaller set wearing sandals. And it looks like the guy was on his knees at some point."

"Kate and Kissner."

"Most likely." Kevin rose and headed for the trees.

Claire pulled the hood up on her Windbreaker and followed with Luke. Drake gave another quick look around. "Could he have parked his truck somewhere close and maybe he's circling back around to it?"

Kevin paused by a large sycamore tree. "It's likely. He's got to have a getaway, but the tracks lead here. It looks to me like Kate was running. She may have disabled him temporarily and gotten away."

"She's resourceful, and she had a pistol and bear spray," Claire said. "We're wasting time. He's tracking her right now. We have to find them before he hurts her."

Drake jogged over to join them. "Lead the way, Kevin. You're the tracker."

The warden nodded and walked slowly through the trees. In the shadow of the forest it was harder to see, so he paused often and shone his flashlight at the moss and grass. "Looks like she tricked him for a while. She backtracked, then climbed the rocks here. He went that way"—he pointed to his right—"then came back and went up here after her."

The rain continued to fall in a gentle patter, soaking his skin, but Drake was already chilled from his dunk in the ocean, so it made him shiver even harder. She might just be up this hillside. He could only pray they found her alive.

With Kevin leading the way, they clambered up the steep incline. Shale slid away under Drake's feet, and he fell onto his knees several times. He wanted to rush past Kevin, who moved at a steady pace, but he knew the warden was stopping often to make sure they stayed on the right trail.

Her expression set, Claire trudged along and shook off Luke's help. Drake thought some of the moisture on her face was tears, not rain, but he said nothing to comfort her. Any words of reassurance would ring false. None of them knew what Kissner planned, and it was clear he'd laid a macabre net that they'd all fallen into. They'd trusted him completely, and he fooled them.

What did he want with Kate? Rape, murder? When he'd pushed Drake off the cliff, he'd proven he was willing to do anything to get to her. And they'd been friends in school.

Now her friend planned something for her that didn't bear thinking about.

He stood hidden in the thick foliage and watched the scene in front of him through binoculars. A deputy held Kate captive. He still couldn't believe the scheme he'd watched play out ever since the guy shoved Newham over the edge. One dead that he didn't even have to take care of.

Knowing how close the sisters were, he was sure Claire would be along to look for Kate soon. This could all play out to his advantage. If the deputy killed Kate and Claire, he'd be off scot-free and would just have to take care of the kids in a realistic accident. The situation couldn't be better. Good thing he'd disabled the deputy's vehicle so there was no danger of the pair escaping the forest until Claire arrived. Or the perfect plan could all fall apart.

Dry in his slicker, the rain didn't bother him as he waited for Kissner to bring Kate down to where he'd parked his truck.

Last time he'd seen Kissner, Kate's purse still dangled from his shoulder. If Claire didn't show up soon, he'd text her from Kate's phone and end this.

He felt almost jovial as he swiped the moisture off his face. The heft of his gun in his holster reassured him of his plan. Kissner wouldn't be expecting such a rude interruption of his plans.

Muffled by the rain, the sound of voices to his left was faint. He recognized Kate's and grinned. The game was about to get interesting. He melted into the hazy fog of rain behind a large tree and waited for them to appear out of the mist. His hand settled on the butt of his gun, and he went ahead and pulled it. Holding it casually at his side under the rain slicker, he squinted toward the trail to the clearing.

Kate appeared first. Her hair hung in wet strings around her face, and she was pale. Kissner was right behind her. He was smiling as if he'd gotten everything he ever wanted in life, but he was about to be in for a rude awakening. They half slid and half walked the rest of the way down the hillside, then stepped from under the gloom of the trees into the small clearing where Kissner had left his truck.

Kissner took Kate's arm and led her to the vehicle. He opened the door and helped her inside. "Don't try to run, Kate."

She flashed a smile up at him. "I'm not going anywhere, Jonas. We're finally together, and it's what I want."

*Smart, very smart.* Play along until the right time. Unfortunately for Kate, there would be no right time. Kissner went around to the other side and climbed under the wheel. The engine ground as Kissner tried to start it and failed.

Grinning, he stepped out from behind the tree and opened the truck door, then aimed his gun at Kissner. "You might as well give it up. I disabled it. Hand me your gun." He gestured with his Glock. "I'm going to let you stay in there out of the rain until Claire gets here."

Kissner's jaw flexed, but he handed over the gun. "Who are you?"

He ignored the deputy and tucked the man's handgun into his belt.

Kate stared at him. "Claire? She's not here."

"But she's coming. I'm sorry to say neither of you will leave this clearing, and I have the perfect patsy to take the fall for your deaths. Lover boy here took care of Drake for me, so I just have a few strings to tidy up."

Her blue eyes widened, and she stared at Kissner. "What about Drake?"

Kissner looked back at her with an almost bored expression. "I tossed him over the cliff a little ways down from Mermaid Point. He's dead."

Her eyes flooded with tears, and she put her hand over her mouth. She closed her eyes and took several deep breaths, then opened them again and dropped her hand back into her lap. "Listen, I'll do whatever you want. Just don't hurt Claire. She's been through so much already. Just take me and let her go."

He shook his head. "Sorry, that's not the way I get paid."

She stared at him. "You killed Drake's brother and sister-in-law? You're AB, aren't you? You've killed a lot of people. But why?"

His gut clenched. Good thing he'd already laid the plans for her death. She'd figured out the notebook. "Money. Lots of money."

"Who paid you to kill Heath and Melissa? And why?"

"You wouldn't know him. And I need my notebook back before I kill you."

Her chin came up and she held his gaze. "I have no incentive to give it to you. Let Claire live, and I'll get it for you."

He grinned at her. "Tell me where it is, and I'll make sure her death isn't painful. If not, I've got a knife here in my belt, and I can make her scream."

Kate shuddered, and her gaze fell to her hands. "Please, you don't have to do this." The words were a defeated whisper.

"Sorry, but that's not true." He leaned against the hood of the truck and tipped his head. "I think I hear voices. Claire and her husband are about to join us. Unfortunately, Luke will be a casualty as well."

Before he could react, Kate leaned over and pressed hard on the horn. The sound made him jump, and he brought the gun around. "Stop it!"

But she pressed the horn again. "Claire, run!"

Her words sounded loud as she threw open the door and screamed, but the rain would muffle them. "The horn will just bring them quicker. Go ahead and blare it. You're just making sure she gets here faster."

Kate's hand fell away from the horn, and she looked past his shoulder. He turned to see what she was looking at, because the voices hadn't come from that direction. Seconds later the car door squealed, and he flipped back around to see her leap from the passenger side. She stumbled on a tree limb and went down on one knee.

It slowed her just enough for him to dash around the front of the truck and grab her by the arm. As she opened her mouth to scream, he hit her in the head with the butt of his gun, and she collapsed onto the wet ground.

He turned to face the approaching sound of voices. Let the fun begin.

# THIRTY-SEVEN

The drizzly rain continued to fall, and mud covered Drake's boots as he moved through the misty forest with the others. Kevin had found where Kate had hidden until she'd been discovered. The sets of prints had come this way, but the rain was quickly washing away the imprints of their shoes.

Kevin paused and looked toward the tree line. Rain dripped off the edges of his hat. "They can't be far ahead of us."

"At least she's still alive, right?" Claire voiced the question Drake contemplated.

"Looks like it. There's a woman with him, anyway."

"Anyone hear from the sheriff?" Luke moved a branch out of the way of Claire's head. "It was bad luck he believed Kissner had left Folly Shoals."

"I got a text from him," Kevin said. "The ferry is down for engine repair. He's rounding up a boat to get out here on his own, but it'll be at least an hour before he reaches us."

"That's good though," Drake said. "That the ferry isn't running. Kissner can't get her off Folly Shoals that way."

Luke nodded. "I heard from my team. They found a boat Kissner chartered and have it under surveillance."

"So they're still on the island somewhere." Kevin started forward again. "There's a clearing ahead where hunters often park. Kissner might be heading for it."

Drake stopped and listened. "I thought I heard someone yell Claire's name. Did you hear it?"

"I thought I heard a car horn too," Claire said. "Was it Kate calling for me?" Her voice was tight, and she leaped forward until Luke grabbed her arm.

"I couldn't tell." Drake trotted after Kevin, who had picked up the pace.

"She needs me!" Claire tried to twist out of Luke's grasp.

"Honey, calm down. We've got to be smart about this if we want to make sure no one is hurt."

At his gentle voice, she stopped struggling and nodded, but tears tracked down her cheeks.

Kevin halted and held up his hand. "There's a truck in the clearing." His words were a whisper. "Luke, circle around the other way. Drake, go west and come up on the road side."

Drake nodded and moved in what felt like the wrong direction. Every instinct told him to rush for the clearing and make sure Kate was all right. He reached the road, then circled back. He crouched under bushes lining the clearing and peeked over the tops. His blood roared in his ears.

Kate lay on the ground with blood covering her forehead.

A rag in his mouth, Kissner sat beside her with his hands bound behind him. A man in his thirties crouched next to Kate with a gun in his hand. He snugged his baseball cap over sandy-brown hair. His tall and lanky frame was outfitted in camouflage hunting gear.

The man rose and coughed weakly. "I know people are out

there in all directions. I can hear you. I need help or she's going to die. Please, I'm shot too. I managed to subdue this guy, but we are both wounded."

The hunter must have heard Kate scream and saved her. Drake ran toward the clearing.

Claire shot out of the trees and dashed for her sister. She fell to her knees and touched Kate's head. "Oh, Kate, look at me. Open your eyes." Luke jogged out to join his wife. He pulled his cell phone out to call for help.

Drake was moments behind Claire and dropped to Kate's other side. He touched her hand and examined her head. She seemed to be bleeding from a scalp wound. "What happened to her?"

The man coughed again. He looked vaguely familiar to Drake now that he was closer, but he couldn't put his finger on where he'd seen the guy. "Head wound. That deputy smashed her in the noggin with a rock. We need to get to the hospital. I don't think you can get a signal in here. I never can."

Luke shook his head. "No signal. I'll have to hike out to get one."

Kevin appeared from the tree line. "I'll call the sheriff. I know a shortcut to get out. Luke, see what you can do for their injuries. I'll be right back." He jogged past them and pushed through the scrub to the road, then disappeared around the bend in the dirt track.

*Open your eyes, honey.* Drake would give anything to see those big, beautiful eyes smile up at him. The blood pouring out of her head wound terrified him. Her skin was pasty gray and she felt so cold. He wanted to cradle her in his arms, but he was afraid to move her.

He looked over at Claire. "See if there's a blanket or something in the truck. She's freezing cold."

Claire nodded and moved with reluctance away from her sister. She paused by the hunter. "We're lucky you were in the area. Where are you shot?"

"It was luckier than you think." The man's voice was stronger, and his arm circled Claire's throat. He put the gun in his hand to her head. "All of you, drop your weapons."

Drake gaped at him, then his gaze traveled to the gun. It was a Glock 22. Efficient for a shot to the head. What was going on? He couldn't figure it out, but he hovered over Kate in case he needed to be a human shield.

When Luke hesitated, the guy pressed the gun barrel against Claire's forehead hard enough to make her yelp. "Do it or she's dead."

Drake glanced at Luke, whose face had lost all color. Luke pulled his gun out and tossed it to the ground. Drake held his hands out. "I don't have a gun."

"I saw you go over the cliff," the man said. "Kissner here would be upset if it weren't for the fact that you'll be dead soon enough."

"Look, let me tend to Kate," Luke said. "You can tell us what you want while I take care of her bleeding."

"Patch her up so I can kill her?" The man laughed. He dragged Claire back with him closer to the pickup parked in the clearing.

Kate stirred a bit, and Drake touched her cheek. "Kate?"

Her lids fluttered and opened. Her gaze was unfocused at first, then sharpened when he spoke her name again. "Drake?" Her hand reached for his face. "He said he killed you. Am I dead too?"

"No, honey." He pulled a handkerchief out of his pocket and pressed it to the wound on her head.

"She's going to be. It would have been kinder not to make her live through all this."

In that instant Drake recognized the man. "I've seen you in Rod Sisson's office. You're his maintenance guy or something. Austin Buckler?"

"I think it's the 'or something' you need to worry about. I clean up Rod's messes."

"You killed Heath and Melissa." He clenched his fists and started to rise, but Buckler aimed the gun at Drake's head and he stopped. "Why would Rod want them dead?"

"I'd wondered the same until I took a look at the hard drive I stole this morning. Ol' Rod was taking money under the table to help send Wang away."

Drake got it then. Rod was helping Wang's rival. "All that sympathy was phony. No wonder he gave me the name of an incompetent private investigator. He wanted me to focus on Wang too. It would be just one more nail in the guy's coffin."

"And it's going to get me even more money." Buckler narrowed his eyes at Drake. "Which one is going to die first? Maybe this one right here?" He dug the gun into Claire's forehead hard enough that she cried out again.

"No!" Kate sat up and reached for her sister. "Don't hurt my sister, please. You still don't have your notebook back."

Buckler dragged Claire back a few feet.

"Please, please, don't hurt her." Tears clogged Kate's voice.

The guy had no choice but to kill everyone who'd seen his face. Drake still couldn't accept the fact that Heath's partner was behind this.

COLLEEN COBLE

An arrow whistled by his head, and he dove to the ground to cover Kate. "Get down!"

***

Drake's warm breath on Kate's neck gave her a sense of security even though bullets zipped by their heads like hailstones. She turned her head and looked around to see Claire on the ground with Luke atop her. His face pale, Jonas lay on the ground with his eyes closed. A crossbow arrow had pierced the right side of his chest, and blood stained his shirt. He looked dead.

Her brain still felt fuzzy—it was hard to think through what was happening. Who was shooting from the trees? Kevin? He might have turned around before he called and seen what was happening. But no, he wouldn't be using a crossbow.

"Are you hurt?" Drake's low voice spoke in her ear.

"My head hurts." It was thumping like someone was repeatedly hitting her with a hammer. "Are you hit?"

"No, I'm fine. I've got to get the gun away from him."

She clenched her hands in his shirt. "Jonas said he killed you."

"He tried."

Claire was only three feet away, and Kate reached out her hand toward her sister. "Claire, are you all right?" She spoke as softly as she could.

Bullets zinged into the trees about ten feet away, and she winced at the sound. Buckler was trying to hit the bowman.

Claire's pale face turned toward her. "I'm okay. Is it Paul out there?"

"Maybe. Or a hunter."

Luke jerked his head a bit to the right. "We've got to try to crawl into the woods. Let's try rolling that way." He eased off his wife. "You roll that way a few feet, honey. I'm right behind you."

Before Claire had a chance to implement his plan, Buckler leaped toward them. His boot connected with Drake's side, and the impact shoved him off Kate. Buckler grabbed her by the arm and hauled her to her feet.

He turned her to face the woods. "I've got Kate. Throw down your weapon, or I'll put a bullet in her head." He pressed the gun against her temple.

The cold metal cut into Kate's skin, but she was too numb to flinch. Her head pounded with every heartbeat, and nausea roiled in her belly. Spots danced in her vision—she knew she was about to pass out. Her legs sagged under her, and her head lolled to the side no matter how hard she tried to keep it steady.

Buckler managed to hang on to her. "Stand up!"

She tried to comply and managed to force a bit of strength into her trembling legs. She stared through the thick foliage blowing in the wind. Lightning flashed with a loud crackle and shook the ground as it hit a tree in the forest. In the brief illumination, she caught a glimpse of Uncle Paul's face before he ducked down. More thunder rolled in. Had Buckler seen her uncle? And what was Paul planning?

She fought against the blackness hazing her vision and struggled to stay conscious. There had to be some way to distract this guy. Maybe if she made it harder for him to hold her up, she'd throw him off balance. She let her eyes flutter shut and sagged into a deadweight.

He cursed and struggled to hold on to her. The gun swayed a bit away from her head, and she saw something flash by her eyes at the same time a fresh lightning bolt lit up the sky. Buckler's hand fell away, but a gunshot nearly deafened her right ear.

Kate screamed when the gun when off. "Claire! Drake!" Her lungs compressed, and she wasn't sure where she should run.

With Buckler on the ground, Luke snatched up his gun, then ran toward the motionless man.

Claire sat up. "I'm all right." She scrambled over to Kate. "You're still bleeding."

She also felt like she might throw up. Her vision doubled and wavered, and she swallowed. "Do Drake and Luke have him pinned yet?"

Claire's face wavered again in Kate's vision. "Kate, do you need to throw up? You look green."

"Maybe." She swallowed the sour taste in her mouth, then lay back on the ground. The rain fell on her face, but it helped sharpen her thoughts.

Moments later Drake was at her side. "I'll need to go get Kevin and see where the sheriff is." He glanced over at Buckler and Jonas. "Do you know the full story of all this? I don't get how these two are connected." He leaned close to inspect the cut on her forehead. "And how did you get this?" His jaw clenched and his eyes narrowed.

"Buckler hit me with the butt of his gun." She shook her head and pushed his chest when he started to lift her. "Just let me lie here for now. I get dizzy when I stand up, and I want to tell you what happened." She launched into an explanation of everything that had occurred from the point when Jonas found her on the beach. "I'd convinced him I was going with him willingly. He planned to take the boat he'd rented to the mainland, and we'd go to Bangor to get married. Once we were in Bangor I was sure

I could get help. We had just gotten in the truck when Buckler showed up." She swallowed and reached for her sister's hand.

Kate's head pounded like rough surf on the shore, and all she wanted to do was close her eyes and sleep, but Drake had to know the rest. "Buckler intended to kill us, then go after the girls. It would look like Jonas killed us all."

He straightened. "The girls?" He started to rise. "I'd better check on them."

She caught his hand. "He didn't get to them yet, so they're safe. Who is this Rod Sisson you mentioned?"

"Heath's partner. Rod was taking money from that rival crime organization Wang told me about. He knew someone had framed him for the murder charges he was facing. Heath must have figured it out."

His voice was fading in her ears. She was cold clear through, and the thought of a hot bath and her soft bed was enticing. How soon could she get out of this rain? She glanced toward the trees. "What about Uncle Paul? It was him with the crossbow. I saw him. He saved us all."

"He hasn't come out of the trees yet, but he's here on the island somewhere. I doubt he'll get away, not with so many officers crawling all over it. I still can't believe Kissner was the stalker or that Sisson was behind Heath and Melissa's deaths."

Her chest hitched, and she closed her eyes. "I felt sorry for Jonas. He had a rough home life. His dad left when he was in grade school, third grade I think. The few times his mom showed up at school, she was drunk and loud. I was glad when he got a job as a deputy. I thought it would help him gain some self-respect."

Drake slipped his arm under her neck and legs. "I'm going to carry you to the car. We need to get you out of the rain. I think you might have a concussion, honey."

Her vision wavered again. "You might be right. I-I think I'm going to be sick." He rolled her over to her side, and she vomited into the wet grass.

He pulled out the tail of his shirt and wiped her mouth. Worry hovered in the grooves in his forehead. "I'm taking you straight to the Folly Shoals clinic." He shrugged out of his slicker and snugged it around her. "I'll be right back." Worry creased his forehead as he jogged off in the rain.

Claire dug in her purse and produced a bottle of water that she uncapped and offered to Kate. "Take a sip." Her gaze lingered on Kate's forehead. "At the very least, you're going to need stitches."

The cool water washed down Kate's throat in a blessed stream. "I was so afraid I was going to lose everything today—Drake, you, the girls." She choked on her tight throat, then swallowed another gulp of water.

All she wanted to do now was get warm and find out the rest of the story. She closed her eyes as Claire calling her name faded into the distance.

The aroma of corn chowder filled the Bistro, but even the delicious scent didn't tempt Kate's appetite much. She stared out the big windows toward the forest at the edge of the property. Every muscle in her body ached, and she wanted to crawl back into the lush bed upstairs.

Drake sat close beside her. He'd hovered close to her side ever since they'd gotten back from the clinic. She had a concussion and had been told to rest. Pain pills and antinausea meds had made her feel half human. She'd wanted to go home, but it was late by the time things wrapped up, and they hadn't wanted to disrupt the girls. After a night's sleep she'd managed to get warm, but the shock from the past twenty-four hours hadn't really worn off.

She took a bite, then set down her spoon and looked at the sheriff. "What did you find out?"

The dark circles under Danny's eyes and his wrinkled uniform told of a long work night. He scooped the last of his lobster bisque from the bowl, then sighed. "Ayuh, that hit the spot. The last time I ate was noon yesterday."

She reached across the table and patted his big, freckled hand. "Sorry I'm being so impatient, Danny. Eat up. I appreciate all you've done."

His smile didn't reach his eyes. "It was a close call. I thought I'd lost you, Katie girl. My old ticker couldn't have taken it." His gaze swiveled toward Drake. "Boston PD arrested Rod Sisson this morning. Buckler spilled his guts all night long, and we also found the evidence on that hard drive in his car. He intercepted the shipment from your uncle. Heath found out his own partner was working with the Brogan group and demanded Sisson turn himself in. Sisson had taken over two million dollars from the group, and he'd helped plant information about Wang. Sisson wasn't about to go to jail, so he decided to kill Heath and Melissa instead. That only cost him a couple hundred thousand."

"Heath thought a lot of him." Drake's words came out hard and choked. "Even though he had to hate Wang, he always put justice first. Wang has done plenty over the years, but he didn't commit the murder he was charged with."

Kate's chest squeezed and her eyes blurred. "Those poor girls are orphaned just because of greed. It's horrible." She leaned her head against Drake's shoulder, and he hugged her, then brushed a kiss across her forehead. "What about Kissner?"

Danny gave a heavy sigh. "I thought a lot of that boy. He was my star deputy. I saw him taking my place someday. To my mind, he was my career son. It's pretty painful to realize I was such a poor judge of character. When he came in yesterday morning and I told him what we were planning, he got real quiet. I thought he was just focused on protecting you. I was wrong. I'm really sorry, Katie girl." He gave her an awkward hug.

"It's not your fault, Danny. I trusted him completely. I'm sorry this happened, that he felt so rejected that he did this."

Beside her, Drake tensed. "Let's not forget the man tried to kill me. All this feeling sorry for him is a little out of line."

"Ayuh, and we're looking for evidence in the Peece murder at Jonas's place. I'm sure we'll find it."

She raised her head. "He's an evil man." She brushed a kiss across Drake's chin. "You could be dead right now. I'm so thankful you're not." Her voice broke, and she swallowed down the lump forming.

Those long minutes when she'd thought Drake was dead had been the worst of her life. They still hadn't talked about the future, and she was waiting to hear him say he was going back to Boston with the girls. What if he asked her to go with him? Could she leave this place of safety and strike out in a new life that held so much that was unknown? Could she leave her sister?

She'd rather have Drake decide to stay here in Maine, but

was that even fair to him? He had a successful business. He thrived on challenge. There would be a lot of opportunity for the girls in Boston too. How could she be selfish enough to want it all her way?

There wasn't a good answer, and she knew she would have to talk this all out with Claire. Her sister always helped bring clarity to her life. How could she bear to move away from that?

# THIRTY-EIGHT

Claire sat on the closed toilet lid and stared at the faint line on the pink stick. *Pregnant.* Part of her wanted to dance, and the other part wondered how she'd break the news to Kate. While she knew her sister would be thrilled for her, that joy would be bittersweet when Kate so desperately wanted children. And after the events of yesterday, this news might be another blow.

She washed her hands and opened the bathroom door. Luke whistled in the kitchen as he made coffee, and a smile curved her lips as she headed that direction. He'd be thrilled at the news.

Her heart always gave a kick when she saw him. Dressed in his uniform, he was a handsome sight in their beautiful new kitchen. The odor of coffee filled the air, unappealing this morning, and he flipped pancakes on the stove.

His smile emerged when he saw her. "I was giving you five more minutes, then I was going to come pull you out of bed. I have some news we need to talk about."

"So do I." She wasn't about to let him upstage this momentous occasion. Nothing he had to say would be as big as this. She held out the pregnancy test. "See what you think."

His brow furrowed and he blinked. "What is it?"

Of course, he likely had no idea what this even was. "It's a

302

pregnancy test, silly. We're going to be parents!" She flung her arms around his neck.

He went still, then whooped and picked her up, spinning her around the kitchen until she was laughing and breathless. When he set her on her feet, the room was still whirling around her, and she grabbed hold of his shirt to steady herself.

He pressed a kiss on her lips. "A baby. I can't believe it. When?"

"I'm only about two weeks late. With everything going on, I hadn't even noticed until this morning." She pressed her hand to her tummy. "I felt a little queasy and suddenly thought of it."

"So a spring baby." His expression sobered a bit. "Um, like I said, I have some news too. I wasn't sure how to tell you."

Her stomach roiled, and she went to sit down. "Could you get me a cracker first?"

With a worried glance her way, he reached into the cupboard and pulled out a sleeve of soda crackers. "Want some peanut butter with them?"

Did she? She examined the way she felt and shook her head. "Just crackers for now." She bit off a piece of the cracker he handed her and waited for the salty flavor to quell the nausea. "So what's up?" She wasn't too worried. It wasn't like he was about to get fired or anything. Then something in his expression made her stop and inhale. "Is it bad?"

"I think it's good, but I wanted to see what you thought." He pulled out a chair and sat across the table from her. "We've got an offer for the cranberry farm. A good offer. Dad wants to take it."

It seemed a clear decision to her. "Then take it. It will relieve you of the burden of it all. I know it's been in your family for a long time, but your heart is really with the Coast Guard. And with the baby coming, not having that extra work will give you more time to spend with me and our new little ensign."

His grin spread across his face. "A baby. I'm still shocked."

"Me too." She couldn't wait to go shopping. And to tell her mom. Kate would get drafted into helping her pick out a layette and fix the nursery once she got over the shock. She realized Luke's grin had faded. "What is it? You don't seem all that excited. You don't want to sell?"

"It's not that." He chewed on his bottom lip, then reached across the table to take her hand. "I know we just finished this house, but I've been asked to transfer to Washington State. When I first heard about it, I planned to ask for an extension of my duty station here because of the farm, but, well, now that it won't be a concern, I'd be free to take it. If you're willing to move, that is. And maybe the baby changes everything."

She opened her mouth, then closed it again. The baby would be far from Kate, who would make a terrific second mother to the little one. Her mom lived in Boston, close enough for frequent visits with her new grandbaby. And there was Luke's dad as well. On the surface the right answer should have been no, she wanted him to try to get out of the assignment. But looking into his earnest brown eyes, she didn't have the heart to throw water on his enthusiasm. He loved the Coast Guard. This could be a great opportunity for him. Her mother had enough money to fly to Washington whenever she pleased, plus Claire had her plane and could always make frequent flights back.

She took another bite of cracker. "I'll go if that's what you want. I can be happy wherever you are."

His eyes lit up. "You're the best wife ever." He squeezed her fingers. "When can we tell people about the baby?"

"Not for a little while. We want to make sure everyone is okay. I'll tell Kate, of course."

"Of course. I hope she'll be happy."

"She will be." But Claire dreaded the telling, just a little.

"Out enjoying this gorgeous day?" Kate mounted the wide steps leading up to Claire's porch. Jackson bounded up after her and went to lay his head on Claire's lap. The afternoon sun was hot on Kate's bare arms, and she dropped into the swing beside her sister out of the glare. A plate of soda crackers and cheese sat on the table beside the swing, and Claire's skin looked a little green. "Are you feeling okay? Yesterday was pretty traumatic. I feel like I've been through a war."

"A little tummy upset." Claire reached over and grabbed the plate. "Want one?"

"Okay." Kate took a cracker and a slice of cheese and munched on it. "I needed to bounce some things off my Yoda today. You're like the wise older sister."

Claire gave her a slight punch in the ribs. "Say that with a smile." She fed a cracker to the dog, who settled on the floor to eat it.

Kate grinned. Every problem felt surmountable today. Nothing could mar her mood after yesterday's frightful events. Drake was alive. Claire was alive. *She* was alive. It all could have gone very differently.

Claire dusted the crumbs from her fingers. "So what's on your mind?"

"The summer is nearly over. Drake will be going back to Boston."

Claire's finely shaped brows rose. "I thought he was thinking about traveling back and forth for a while with the idea of eventually living here permanently."

Kate gave a kick to get the swing moving. "Let's be realistic. That's not going to work. The girls need him every day, not just on the occasional weekend. And I love him. I want to be with him every moment I can. A long-distance relationship like that will never last for long."

Claire stopped the movement of the swing with her foot. "So what do you want to do?"

"What if I went with him? I don't think he'll ask me because he knows I love my home here. He'll try to make the sacrifice for me, but I don't think that's right. The girls will have a lot of opportunity in Boston. I've seen him sketching out drone ideas on scrap paper. It's part of who he is, not just what he does. He'd never be happy for long if he gave it up. He'd say he would, but I don't think it would last."

Something like relief lit Claire's blue eyes. "You always said you'd never leave here. I think it's about time you spread your wings and flew off to an adventure. You know what this means? You're finally beginning to see people can love you for yourself. You don't have to cling to the old life for fear of not fitting into the new one. You've discovered confidence in who you are and what you can offer to those you love." Claire grabbed her in a tight, fierce hug. "I'm proud of you."

Kate hugged her back and inhaled the aroma of her expensive cologne. They were so different yet so alike. Her eyes stung, and she blinked against the tears. Losing Claire was her biggest fear, but they could stay close with video calls and visits. Claire was a pilot. She could fly to Boston every week if she wanted to. And she would want to. Kate knew Claire loved her just as fiercely back.

She pulled away and dabbed at her eyes. "Look what you've made me do. You'll come see me all the time, right? It's nothing for you to fly to Boston."

Claire hesitated and a bit of color crept up her neck. "I have some news of my own to tell you. Two bits actually. Let me tell you the most important first. I'm pregnant." Her gaze locked with Kate's and held a bit of fear.

A slight pang struck Kate, but joy quickly washed it away. "I'm going to be an aunt!" She grabbed her sister again and hugged her. "I'm so happy." She released her and studied her reserved expression. "That's why you seemed a little scared to tell me. You thought I'd change my mind about going. I admit it gave me pause, but I can still see the baby all the time. You'll fly to Boston to see your mom and me. I'll get to babysit." She realized Claire's smile hadn't returned. "What is it?"

"There's more." Claire wet her lips and twisted her hands in her lap. "All that talk about being ready to fly to a new adventure? That was a pep talk for me too. Luke is getting transferred to Washington State."

Kate gasped and her arms fell away from her sister. "No." She shook her head. "No, no! I can't lose you, Claire! You'll be all the way across the country. I'll go too. You can get a house with a nanny suite, and I'll help you take care of the baby." Tears sprang to her eyes and spilled down her cheeks. She felt as though she couldn't catch her breath. It was one thing to be a few hours from Claire, but it was something else altogether to be clear across the country from her. Not now when they'd just found each other after all these years.

Claire took her by the shoulders and gave her a slight shake. "You love Drake. You're ready for this, Kate. *We're* ready for it. Families survive separation like this all the time. Nothing can tear apart the bond we have. You'll always be part of me, and I'll be part of you. Can't you sense God's plan in this? We were getting too dependent on one another and weren't listening for what God wanted us to do. This is healthy."

Kate's tears fell faster. "You're right. I know you're right. But it hurts." She embraced her sister again and their tears mingled. She jumped to her feet. "I-I have to go right now."

Claire bolted to her feet as Kate ran for her yellow Bug. "Wait, let's talk about this."

"I'll call you later." She needed to process this. Jackson leaped into the car with her and she drove off, not daring to look behind her.

# THIRTY-NINE

By the time Kate reached the turnoff onto Highway 1, the tears had stopped flowing. A sense of rightness settled over her. She was leaving Downeast Maine herself, so how could she expect Claire's life to stop and never change? Change was good. Last week's sermon about how adversity helps people grow was a good example. God would go with them both.

She slowed the car when she reached Machias. A crowd was gathered around the sheriff's office and jail, and she slowed even more, then slammed on her brakes when she recognized her uncle standing in cuffs beside the sheriff.

She parked at the curb, ran the windows down partway, and leaped out. "Stay," she told her dog.

Using her elbows and determination, she fought her way through the throng crowding the steps to the brick building. "Danny!"

The sheriff turned and saw her, then motioned for his deputies to part the crowd to let her through. "I was going to call you as soon as I had him in a cell."

Her gaze went past him to Uncle Paul, who looked older and more shrunken than the last time she'd seen him. Had he been eating? Defiance was in the slant of his mouth and the depths of his eyes.

She looked back to the sheriff. "Can I talk to him for a minute?"

"Ayuh, but only for a few minutes. I want to get him processed."

"Where'd you find him?"

"A Coast Guard cutter hauled him aboard. He was trying to swim from Folly Shoals to the peninsula."

She gasped. "That's three miles in the cold water."

"Only Paul would be so cocky." He told one of the deputies to put Paul into the backseat of the sheriff's car, then let Kate slide into the front seat where she could talk to him in private through the bars.

She closed the door behind her and turned to face her uncle. For a long moment they stared at one another as if waiting for the other to speak. She finally cleared her throat. "Everyone thought you were out of the country."

He still wore camo clothing, but it looked stained and ragged, as if he hadn't changed it in the weeks since she'd seen him. Though he was only in his midforties, he looked older somehow.

He held her gaze. "I saw that guy watching you. I couldn't leave once I knew he was up to no good." His lip curled. "A deputy ought to uphold the law. I knew something bad was coming down, and you were walking around with your head in the clouds, oblivious to everything around you, the way you always do."

Her cheeks heated. "You risked being captured for me?"

"You're my blood. Your mama would want me to take care of you."

"Is that why you killed Jonas first?"

He shrugged. "I didn't want to risk him getting away and coming after you later."

"Have you talked to Mother?" He and her mom were in separate prisons.

He shook his head. "Tried to call her once, but she was in detention." He yawned. "Looks like I'm going back to the clink. At least I'll get three squares and have a bed to sleep in. Been hunkering down in the woods all this time."

"Why did you steal from Claire?" The question had been burning in her mind ever since she'd found out what he'd done.

His eyes went flat. "I didn't want her to ever get to feeling safe."

"She's your niece too. Part of me, Uncle Paul. She did nothing wrong."

He settled against the seat back. "She'll try to keep me from being paroled when the time comes. I wanted to put a little fear into her so maybe she'd think twice about testifying against me."

"Claire's a really good person. She never meant to hurt anyone. And she's going to have a baby. You'll be a great-uncle."

His expression didn't change. "Not my blood. She belongs to Dellamare and always will. She's not like you, Kate. You grew up here. You belong to the woods and ocean. This is your place and always will be."

"I'm leaving," she blurted out. "I'm going to go with Drake."

He nodded as if he'd expected it. "But you'll be back. This place never lets you leave, not permanently."

Maybe he was right, but she was finally ready for a great adventure. "Thank you for saving me, Uncle Paul. You saved all of us—Drake, Luke, Claire, the baby. And even Drake's nieces.

COLLEEN COBLE

That terrible man intended to kill them too. If you hadn't shown up, we'd all be dead."

His gaze darted away, and he cleared his throat before he glanced back at her. "I wouldn't let anyone hurt you, Kate. Not ever. You tell your man that he'll have to answer to me if I ever hear he made you cry."

Her eyes welled with tears as so many memories flashed through her mind. He'd been a great uncle to her. She reached for the door handle. "I'll tell him, Uncle Paul." Blindly, she thrust open the door and stumbled out. Conflicting emotions tore at her chest. Love, grief, guilt, anger. Everyone had good and bad in them. She prayed someday Uncle Paul would find his life and worth in God.

The sun was low in the sky, highlighting the cliffs in gold and red, as Drake walked along the edge of the water with Kate and the girls. The children skipped ahead with Jackson to gather sea glass in their buckets. He was going to talk to Kate about the future. It wasn't going to be as rosy as he'd tried to make it out. He didn't want to lose Kate, but he dreaded telling her about his phone call this afternoon.

She stopped and smiled up at him. "You're very pensive all of a sudden. Still reacting to everything that's happened? I know it's hard to accept such evil in the world. I was in the same place when I realized what my family had done to Claire and to Luke's mother." She tucked her arm into his. "We'll get through it together."

"I know we will." He tried to put confidence in his voice.

He loved the shape of her face, all sweet curves and gentle planes. He hated to spill the words trembling on his tongue, but he straightened and held her gaze. "I'm going to have to go back to Boston sooner than I expected. We just got a big order for my new drone from one of the biggest electronics stores in the country. I've finally figured out the modifications on the one for the Fish and Wildlife Service, too, and Lakesha is about to have a heart attack over being left to deal with all this alone."

"How wonderful!" Her smile faltered only a little before resuming at full wattage. "When do you have to leave?"

"Immediately."

"Just like that?" She pulled her arm out of his.

He took her hand. "Can we talk about my initial idea of leaving the kids with you while I travel back and forth on the weekends?"

Her blue eyes grew luminous. Tears? She was taking this all wrong. His fingers tightened on hers. "I want to marry you. A marriage shouldn't be spent mostly apart. Forget I ever mentioned that idea."

Her lips parted, and her eyes crinkled in a broader smile. "I think that's the most prosaic proposal I've ever heard of. What, no bended knee, no declaration of everlasting love?"

He grinned and took her by the shoulders, then turned her to face him. "I love you now and forever. I think you already know that. I'm not good with flowery words. But I'll always be by your side, Kate. You'll never have to worry about being someone you aren't. I love you just the way you are. I love the way you try to take care of people. I love the fierce loyalty you show to family. You're smart, funny, and beautiful inside and out. But I mostly love the inside beauty you show. You're tenacious and strong. The girls will be too."

She blinked and several tears rolled down her cheeks. "I think you're pretty darn good with flowery words. I love you more than I ever thought I could love someone. I love you enough to leave Maine and go with you wherever you want me to."

He was so busy trying to figure out how to tell her he wanted her to think about going to Boston that it took a second for her words to register. The breath whooshed out of his lungs. "What? Boston? Are you sure?" *Idiot.* He shouldn't be trying to talk her out of it.

"I'm positive. Claire says it's time for me to fly, and I think she's right. I might be a little awkward like the puffins when they try to take off, but I'll keep at it until I'm airborne. I'm not saying you won't come home sometimes to find me crying, but I'll be all right. This is what we need to do for us and for the girls." Her grin slanted up at him again. "I take it that's a marriage proposal too?"

Still stunned, he blinked and nodded, then grabbed her and swung her around. The feel of her in his arms was as right as the ocean foaming on the rocks. He was never going to let her go. He set her down and pulled her into a kiss. Her soft lips under his were warm and pliant, giving and taking as she wrapped her arms around his neck and kissed him back.

He pulled away and looked down into her face. "Soon?"

"As soon as I can get a wedding dress and plans pulled together. Don't think I'm going to a justice of the peace, mister." She wagged her finger at him. "I want a wedding with all the trimmings. It doesn't have to be expensive, but I want us to get married in the blueberry barrens where I grew up with my sister standing up for me."

"I wouldn't have it any other way. How long?"

"Late October? I want us to savor our engagement. I'll have to find a place to live."

"There's a house for rent in my neighborhood. I'll snag it for you." His chest felt as though it might explode from the bubble of joy expanding in it. He gave a whoop and lifted her in his arms again.

The girls looked up, then came running to them. Jackson barked and ran in circles around them.

"What's wrong, Uncle Drake?" Emma's hazel eyes were round.

"Kate's going to marry me. She's going back with us to Boston." Drake set her on the ground.

Phoebe slipped her hand into Kate's and looked up at her. "Are you going to be our new mommy?"

Kate knelt beside the little girl and drew her into a hug. "I wouldn't want to replace your real mommy, and we'll make sure we always talk about her and go to see your grandparents. No one can really replace your mommy and daddy. But I love you very much, and I'm going to take care of you the very best way I can." She held out her other hand for Emma, who leaped into her embrace and put her arms around Kate's neck.

Drake dropped to his knees, too, and embraced the three of them. "I know it's going to take us a while, but we're going to be a family." The best kind of family—one that was held together by love.

# FORTY

Kate peeked out the window of her bedroom toward the backyard. The autumn winds had stripped the color from the trees, but they'd subsided into blue skies and unseasonably warm weather for late October. It was over sixty today. The blueberry barrens stretched to the east and west in a carpet of red and gold. Her gaze lingered on the arch Claire had decorated for the wedding. Sprigs of red blueberry leaves contrasted with the white gauzy material. Guests already milled about the lawn, and she caught a glimpse of the girls with their flower baskets.

She turned from the window as the door opened, and her sister came into the room. "It looks so beautiful. Thank you for doing it. Are you feeling okay?"

Claire wore a blue dress that skimmed her curves and flared out at her calves. She was glowing. "Just fine. I'm way too excited to have any morning sickness today. Everything is about to start. Are you ready?"

Kate pressed her hand against her stomach. "I think I've got morning sickness for you. My tummy is flipping like a fish on the shore." Was she doing the right thing? She shot a glance over her shoulder at the red fields. Could she really leave this place where she'd grown up?

Claire's fingers bit into Kate's shoulders, and she gave her a little shake. "Stop it right now. I see you second-guessing yourself. Change is hard, but you're ready, Kate. Drake is wonderful, and you're going to have a great life in Boston."

"I already love it there." Kate blinked and forced back the moisture in her eyes. "When God decided to bring in the right man for me, he chose a special one."

"And a ready-made family. God went all out." Claire messed with Kate's hair, affixing a pin in a different place. "You look beautiful. Drake may pass out when he sees you."

"Let's hope not." She moved toward the door.

Sheriff Colton met her outside the bedroom door. His shirt and tie looked like they were about to choke him, but he was smiling. "I wouldn't dress like this for anyone but you, Katie girl." He offered her his arm, and she took it.

She'd been feeling a little low about not having anyone to give her away. Luke had offered, of course, but in the planning for the wedding, she'd keenly missed having a dad around. Both her real dad and her uncle were in jail. But Danny had shown up at her cottage one day, hat in hand, to ask if he might give her away. She'd thrown her arms around his neck and kissed him on the cheek until his face was as red as her fields.

The music started up outside. Claire waved at her, then took Luke's arm and went out the kitchen door. Kate saw them move past the window toward the blueberry field where Drake and the minister waited at the arbor. Her pulse tried to jump out of her chest, and she took a deep, calming breath.

Dixie opened the kitchen door. "Let's get this party started, sugar." She twirled in the doorway. "I clean up pretty nice, don't I?" She wore a lavender dress that showed she wasn't as shapeless as the overalls usually made her seem.

The flutters in Kate's stomach intensified as she went out the door with Danny. Her gaze went straight over the heads of the waiting guests to the group standing in the arbor. Pastor Jerry stood tall and distinguished in his black suit, and Drake stood beside him in a gray tux. Her heart squeezed at the sight of him, and a wave of love crashed over her. He was her man in all ways. True, honest, loving, and compassionate. He always tried to do the right thing, and she knew he'd never leave her side while he lived. Luke was beside him and Claire waited on the other side with the girls, who were trying to keep Jackson still beside them.

The music rose in a crescendo, and Danny tugged her forward, across the yard to the blueberry fields, and down the aisle in the middle of the guests. She spotted the O'Connors with their girls and smiled at Mallory as she passed. Other faces passed in a blur: church friends; Claire's mother, Lisa; Luke's sister, Megan; and his dad, Walker.

Then her gaze landed on Shelley, and she stopped in her tracks long enough to hug her best friend. "I can't believe you're here!"

"I wouldn't miss this for anything." Shelley's red hair was in a smart updo, and she looked bright and happy. She gave Kate a little shove. "Go get married. We'll talk later."

Kate finally dared to lock her gaze with Drake's, and the love in his eyes nearly buckled her knees. His smile was crooked and tender, and he mouthed *I love you* as she walked on trembling legs toward him. She reached him, and Danny put her hand on Drake's. She couldn't look away from his beloved face and the devotion in his eyes.

Pastor Jerry began to speak, and Kate tried to focus on his words about love and marriage, but a giggle built in her chest as she remembered the priest from *The Princess Bride*. It was sitting beside Drake that evening watching that movie that she'd felt the first stirrings of what she later came to recognize as love.

He squeezed her hand, and seeing the laughter in his eyes, she knew he was remembering too. She swallowed down the giggle and repeated her vows to the only man who had ever held her heart. Her new life was starting as twilight deepened the colors on the blueberry barrens, and it was just as it should be, with her hand and heart safe in Drake's embrace.

# DEAR READER,

Shew, we made it through another book together! It was great fun for me to go back to Maine in this story. Have you ever been there? It's like stepping back in time, and I love that beautiful wild coastline.

I wanted to explore how often we try to earn the love of everyone around us. We get so focused on making sure people like us that we never relax and be ourselves. We often even apply that mindset to God and try to earn his love as well. Kate had a lot of growing to do in that area. She had to learn to spread her wings and dream a little.

I love hearing from you! I read and answer all my own e-mail, so let me know your thoughts anytime.

Much love,
Colleen

*colleencoble.com*

P.S. If you'd like to try Kate's okra brownies, here is the recipe:

4 ounces Lily's chocolate chips
$3/4$ cup butter ($1^1/_2$ sticks)
$3/4$ cup frozen okra
3 large eggs
$1/_2$ cup xylitol
1 teaspoon vanilla extract
2 pinches mineral salt
$1/_4$ cup coconut flour
$1/_2$ cup coarsely chopped black walnuts (or pecans)

Melt chocolate with butter on low heat. Meanwhile, put partially thawed okra in blender or food processer with eggs and blend until smooth. Add xylitol, vanilla, salt, and flour to chocolate mixture, then add okra/egg mixture and nuts. Stir together and put in greased 8 x 8-inch pan. Bake at 350 degrees for 30 to 35 minutes.

# DISCUSSION QUESTIONS

1. Have you ever had a serious illness? Did it change your priorities?
2. What is your view on discipline? Did you identify with Kate or Drake?
3. Kate always felt she needed to prove her worth because of the way she was raised. Is there anything in your uprbringing that has impacted how you relate to people?
4. Drake had a lot of things to juggle in his life. Do you think he had his priorities in the right order?
5. Trying to please other people seems to be a common trait with women. Is that good or bad?
6. Many of us have lost a loved one. What do you think is the most important thing to do to heal?
7. God gives all of us gifts and sometimes we don't notice. Is there any gift of yours that you're not using? If so, what's holding you back?
8. Have you ever been faced with leaving people you love behind in a move? How did you handle it?

# ACKNOWLEDGMENTS

I'm so blessed to belong to the amazing Thomas Nelson dream team! I've been with my great fiction publishing house for fourteen years, and it's been such an inspiring time as I've learned more and more about the writing process from my terrific team. I'm blessed to work closely with my editor, Amanda Bostic, and publisher, Daisy Hutton. They are both dear to my heart and have taught me so much!

Marketing director Paul Fisher is my go-to guy for marketing ideas and has such a great grasp of how to get my books in front of new readers. Kristen Golden (Goldie) took over helping me with promotion and has fabulous ideas. Plus I just love her eidetic memory. ☺ Fabulous cover guru Kristen Ingebretson works hard to create the perfect cover—and does. You rock, Kristen! And, of course, I can't forget the other friends in my amazing fiction family: Becky Monds, Jodi Hughes, Karli Jackson, Samantha Buck, Stephen Tindal, and Becky Philpott. You are all such a big part of my life. I wish I could name all the great folks at Thomas Nelson who work on selling my books through different venues. I'm truly blessed!

Julee Schwarzburg is a dream editor to work with. She totally gets romantic suspense, and our partnership is pure joy.

She brought some terrific ideas to the table with this book—as always!

My agent, Karen Solem, has helped shape my career in many ways, and that includes kicking an idea to the curb when necessary. And my critique partner, Denise Hunter, is the best sounding board ever. Thanks, friends!

I'm so grateful for my husband, Dave, who carts me around from city to city, washes towels, and chases down dinner without complaint. My kids, Dave and Kara (and now Donna and Mark), and my grandsons, James and Jorden Packer, love and support me in every way possible, and my little Alexa makes every day a joy. She's talking like a grown-up now, and having her spend the night is more fun than I can tell you. And you know how I love coffee! My son-in-law, Mark, has a coffee-roasting business now, CaptainDavysCoffeeRoaster.com, and he sends me the most fabulous IR roasted coffee. You'll notice my characters drink it! ☺

Most important, I give my thanks to God, who has opened such amazing doors for me and makes the journey a golden one.

# ABOUT THE AUTHOR

Photo by Clik Chick Photography

Colleen Coble is a *USA Today* bestselling author and RITA finalist best known for her romantic suspense novels, including *Tidewater Inn, Rosemary Cottage,* and the Mercy Falls, Lonestar, and Rock Harbor series.

*Visit her website at www.colleencoble.com*
*Twitter: @colleencoble*
*Facebook: colleencoblebooks*

# THE SUNSET COVE

*series*

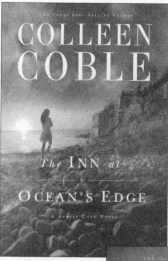

AVAILABLE IN PRINT,
E-BOOK, AND AUDIO

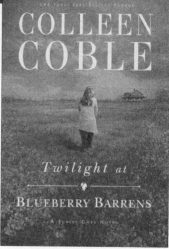

AVAILABLE IN PRINT,
E-BOOK, AND AUDIO

AVAILABLE IN PRINT, E-BOOK,
AND AUDIO SEPTEMBER 2016

# COLLEEN LOVES TO HEAR FROM HER READERS!

Be sure to sign up for Colleen's newsletter for insider information on deals and appearances.

Visit her website at www.colleencoble.com
Twitter: @colleencoble
Facebook: colleencoblebooks

THOMAS NELSON
*Since 1798*

ENJOY AN EXCERPT FROM
CARRIE STUART PARKS'
*WHEN DEATH DRAWS NEAR*

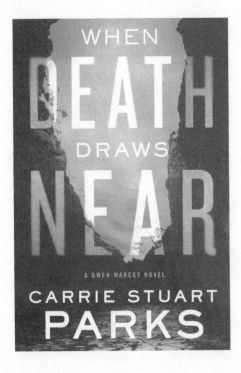

# PROLOGUE

M iriam knew, she *knew* tonight would be the night the Holy Spirit would anoint her. The tingling filled her chest and ran down her arms. "Shananamamascaca," she whispered in prayer language, spinning to the pounding, driving music.

The Spirit was powerful in the church tonight. Around her, the congregation, led by Pastor Grady Maynard, danced, twirled, and praised the Lord in tongues. The bare lightbulbs hanging from the ceiling cast a harsh yellow light on the worshipers. The odor of candles, sweat, and musty carpet rose like incense. Arms were raised, voices lifted, eyes closed.

The burning power of the Holy Spirit rushed through Miriam's body. An indescribable sense of joy and peace filled her to overflowing. Time was meaningless. The music faded, singing muffled, shouts muted. Her lips moved in a prayer she could barely hear. "Shaaaanaamaascaca." Tears slid down her face, pooling on her chin.

Pastor Maynard placed his microphone on the pulpit and reached under the pew in the front of the church. Sweat soaked his green dress shirt and streamed down his face.

Several men moved closer, arms raised and waving or hands clapping.

Pulling out a wooden box with a Plexiglas lid, Maynard reached inside. Louder shouts of praise erupted around him. Tambourines and cymbals joined the cacophony of sound.

Miriam took her place in the circle surrounding Maynard.

From the box came a slow *chchch* speeding to a continuous *cheeeeeheeeee*.

The pastor drew the giant timber rattler from the serpent box. The snake twisted and coiled in his hand, its flat, gray-black head darting from side to side. He draped the serpent around his neck and reached for more from the box.

Miriam moved closer.

Pastor Maynard raised several serpents overhead before handing them to the next man. Keeping the timber rattler around his neck, he lifted his voice in jubilant tongues.

The snakes passed around the circle. Worshipers would drape the snakes on their heads or cuddle them in their arms while spinning or dancing.

Miriam moved out of the circle and slipped next to Maynard. This would be the serpent she would handle. She reached for the rattler.

Pastor Maynard slipped the snake from his neck and into her hands. She lifted it over her head and closed her eyes. The Spirit's power over the serpent charged up her arm. She stomped her feet and whirled, the serpent held high. The Holy Spirit claimed overwhelming victory.

She lowered the serpent.

The snake whipped around and struck her wrist, sinking its fangs deep into her flesh.

Pain like a million bee stings coursed up her arm. Someone

snatched the serpent from her hands as she doubled over in agony and dropped to her knees.

The drumming music stopped. A chorus of voices rose, then faded.

Miriam gasped. Blackness lapped around her mind. The world retreated into velvet nothingness.

# CHAPTER ONE

M a'am. Sheriff Reed told me to come and get you. He said he was sorry you had to wait so long. The body's here. I mean, it was here before . . . downstairs. In the morgue."

I craned my head backward to see the young, lean-faced deputy standing over me. He had to be six foot four or taller, very slender, with wispy brown hair. His eyes were blue with heavy lids and his mouth red, probably from chewing his lips. Sure enough, his cheeks flushed at my studying him and he started gnawing his lower lip.

Sitting outside the Pikeville Community Hospital, I'd been enjoying the late-October sunshine and waiting for someone to remember I was here. I picked up my forensic art kit and followed the officer through a set of doors to an elevator next to the nurses' station. "I'm sorry. I didn't catch your name."

"Junior Reed." He nodded at his answer. "Sheriff Reed is my father."

I did a double take. He didn't look anything like Clayton Reed, the sheriff of Pike County, Kentucky, who'd picked me up from the Lexington airport yesterday. "Nice to meet you, Junior." I stuck out my hand. "I'm Gwen Marcey."

He hesitated for a moment, staring at my hand, then awkwardly shook it. His hand was wet.

The elevator door opened. As we entered, I surreptitiously wiped my hand on my slacks. The elevator seemed to think about moving, then quietly closed and slipped to the floor below, taking much longer than simply running down the stairs. The elevator finally opened. The smell hit me immediately.

I swallowed hard and took a firmer grip on my kit.

Several deputies had gathered in the middle of the hall, talking softly. They turned and stared at us. I couldn't quite decipher the expressions on their faces. They parted as we approached, revealing a closed door inscribed with the word *Morgue*.

Junior entered the room and moved to the body bag resting on a stainless steel table. Sheriff Clayton Reed—a large man with a thick chest, buzz-cut hair, and gray-blond mustache, stood next to a man in navy blue scrubs. I nodded at the man. "Hello. I'm Gwen Marcey, the forensic artist."

"Ma'am. I'm Dr. Billy Graham." He noted my raised eyebrows and grinned. "My parents had high hopes for a particular career direction."

I grinned back, then slowed as I approached the table. I'd seen bodies before. Too many times before, but I still had a moment of hesitation when I knew what was coming. This was once someone's son or daughter, parent or friend. And no one knew of the death. Then the analytical part of my brain would take over, and I could concentrate on drawing the face of the unknown remains.

I just had to get past the *ick* moment.

"Here you go," Sheriff Clay Reed said in a deep Appalachian accent. My brain was still trying to translate his comments for my western Montana ears. "So far, no one has recognized . . . what was left." He unzipped the body bag. Several flies made an angry exit. The odor was like a solid wall.

Junior spun and made it to a bucket near the door before losing his lunch.

I fought the urge to join him.

The sheriff frowned at Junior, then caught my gaze. "He never had much of a stomach for smells."

I could relate to that. "What . . . um . . . what can you tell me about the body?"

"According to the doc here"—Clay nodded at the man— "he's been dead for at least a month, but hard to say exactly at this time . . . critters and all . . . in his late teens or early twenties. Slender. Teeth in pretty good shape, but obviously never been to a dentist. No help there."

Pulling out a small sketchbook and pencil, I jotted down the sheriff's information. "No one reported him missing?"

The sheriff shook his head. "But that's not surprising. A lot of folks around here steer clear of the law."

"Cause of death?"

"Can't be sure just yet," the doctor said. "But I'd guess . . . snakebite."

I stopped writing and looked up. "I thought, I mean, didn't you say he was murdered?"

"In a sense, he was." Clay nodded toward a counter beside him. "We found those with the body."

A white cotton bag, badly stained; a golf club with a bend at the end; a long clamping tool; a revolver; and a moldy Bible all lay spread out.

"Okay. What does that tell you?" I asked.

"I'd say he was snake hunting," the sheriff said.

"I still don't understand."

"The golf club with the metal hook on the end is a home-made snake hook. They cut the club off the end, then bend a piece of metal to form a U."

"Can't you just buy one?"

"That can cost a bit. But folks are always throwing away golf clubs." Clay chuckled. "I've tossed more than my fair share after a bad round of golf."

He stopped chuckling at my expression. "Well then, those are snake tongs, and the bag is to put the snake into. The revolver is loaded with snake-shot ammunition."

"But that doesn't mean—"

He unzipped the body bag farther. Lying across the man's stomach was what was left of a very dead snake.

I dropped my pencil and paper. "Ohmigosh!"

"That's a big 'un." Junior had stopped throwing up and had moved next to me. He wiped his mouth with the back of his hand, then started twiddling his fingers as if playing a trumpet.

Resisting the urge to bolt from the room, I bent down and snatched up my materials, then reached into my forensic kit and tugged out my digital camera. I stayed bent over until I felt some blood returning to my face. "What kind of snake is that?"

"I put in a call to Jason Morrow with animal control to identify—"

"Rattler," Junior said. "*Crotalus horridus*, also known as a canebrake or timber rattler—"

"That's enough, Junior," Clay said.

When I heard the zipper close on the body bag, I stood. Only the man's ravaged face was now exposed.

"Now, Sheriff," Dr. Graham said, "we don't know for sure yet that he died of snakebite. I only said he *may* have—"

"Come on, Billy," Clay said. "The snake's head was full of bird shot from that pistol. Obviously he got bit while trying to catch a snake. He didn't even try to go for help."

I felt at a loss as to what the men were talking about. Snakes in general gave me the creeps, and a stinky body with a snake on top really was pushing my heebie-jeebies meter. "Gentlemen, my knowledge and experience with snakes is very limited." I resisted the urge to add, *Thank the Lord.* "I still don't get why you consider this a murder."

"Oh, not an out-and-out murder," the sheriff said. "I mentioned he didn't even try to go for help. He shot the snake, then sat down, read his Bible, and prayed."

Before I could say anything, the sheriff held up a finger. "I'm not done. That Bible falls open to Mark 16. I think he was catching snakes to handle in church."

"Church?" My creeped-out meter ratcheted up a notch. "Uh, regardless of how he died, you did still want me to draw him for identification, right? Or are you just planning to go to his church and ask around?"

All the men exchanged glances. "Not that simple," the sheriff finally said. "We'll need that drawing."

I took a deep breath, instantly regretting it as the stench of the body filled my lungs. "Here's how this works. I'm going to photograph him from all angles with this evidence scale." I held up what looked like a small ruler. "I'll be ready to work on this drawing when I return to my hotel. You said the rape victim is upstairs, so I'll interview her—"

"Well now, Miz Marcey." Clay rubbed his chin. "Seems you

have a lot to do with this here sketch. You can maybe meet with Shelby Lee tomorrow—"

"Why not now?"

"There's just no sense in overloading you with work."

I blinked at him. "I'm hardly overloaded. I'm here. Although I'm glad to help you with the unknown remains." I nodded at the body bag. "You did fly me out all the way from Montana to work on your serial rapist cases."

"Well now . . ."

"Is something wrong, Sheriff?" I asked.

"No. No. No. Nothing. Nothing's wrong." He shook his head, then turned and headed for the door. "Follow me."

I stared at his retreating back. *He's lying.*

---

The story continues in Carrie Stuart Parks' *When Death Draws Near* . . .